THE SILKIE

Also by Gill Edmonds

The Common
The Album

THE SILKIE

GILL EDMONDS

MULLER BLOND & WHITE

First published in Great Britain in 1986 by
Muller, Blond & White,
55 Great Ormond Street,
LONDON, WC1N 3HZ,

British Library Cataloguing in Publication Data

Edmonds, Gill
    The silkie.
    I. Title
    823'.914   PR6055.D6/

ISBN 0-584-31174-5

Printed and bound in Great Britain by Billings & Sons Ltd, Worcester

Contents.

The Silkie

An earthly nurse sits and sings,
And, "Aye" she sings, "by lily wean,
And little ken I my bairn's father,
Far less the land where he dwells in."

For he came one night to her bed feet,
And a grumbly guest, I'm sure was he,
Saying "Here am I, thy bairn's father,
Although I be not comely."

"I am a man upon the land,
I am a silkie on the sea,
And when I'm far and far frae land,
My home it is in Sule Skerrie."

And he had ta'en a purse of gold
And he had placed it upon her knee,
Saying, "Give to me my little young son,
And take thee up thy nurse's fee."

"And it shall come to pass on a summer's day,
When the sun shines bright on every stane,
I'll come and fetch my little young son,
And teach him how to swim the faem."

A Hebridean Folk Song
from *Child Ballads*

Prologue

The room had seemed full an hour before, yet still another and another crowded in to sit upon the long bench under the window, or perch awkwardly on the side of a neighbour's straight chair at the table. The men, in their tight jackets and heavy boots, shuffled and laughed among themselves, while the women with a sort of bustling ease made tea. A brown enamel pot brewed on the hearth fire. Another, two handles to lift it by, stood on the table. Women who had brought their cups with them passed them around. The fire was stoked again and broken driftwood piled upon the glowing peats. As the heat grew one or two women unbuttoned their coats, but the men, sweat shining along their cheeks, kept muffled in their scarves and jumpers. A squat dark bottle came from a pocket and made the rounds by the window; pipes jutted, evil smelling; smoke drifted up to the dark rafters. Talk was quite and shy, the singing still to come.

Life is scraped lean for the people of the Western Isles, and yet for centuries men have lived there, forcing a living from the sparse landhold, pulling its gifts from the sea. The islands are lonely, bent up out of the roaring waves of the North Atlantic to provide a fingered shelf for home. In long days of rain and gale a man might never see his neighbours. But calm weather brings them together and in the times before the roads were laid, before the first whispers of wireless could reach into their lives the local gathering, the ceilidh, was all their entertainment. So they sat, with their knees to the fire, and drew close to gossip of old friends or,

1

eyes distant with wonder, wove the stories which filled their world with sprigs of mystery, bringing light and colour into its sturdy fabric.

One young man, Angus Macrae, who had recently bought his own boat, was being teased now to think of marriage. It was an old joke but he could only shake his head.

"Did ye never hear, Angus, of the man who would not marry a girl of the islands then?"

Young Angus only grinned and muttered to his boots in the Gaelic, his face an embarrassment to him.

"Well he did marry a girl from the sea instead. That was how it was."

The young man shook his head again at the murmur of laughter.

"He never had any luck after." An old man in the corner held out his pipe solemnly before them all, then he said no more.

Angus looked up from under an awkward frown: "Is it one of the seal people you mean? The selchies?"

"Yes it is, then. The people of the sea." And, his pipe still held before him, the old man prepared himself to tell a story:

"There was this women, and a Norway woman she was. A Norway woman of the north isles. And this woman was married for her father's land and she had no love for the man that took her. But her father was proud to make the match, and she with her pride would say nothing against the man, though she had no love for him. And though the time passed and she a married woman, she would have no knowledge of her husband, so that he should have no child by her. She was saddened however in her heart that she should have no bairns in her house, and one day she took her sadness secretly to the shore. She sat down upon the rocks and she shed three tears into the sea. Then she looked up, and there before her was a great seal. As she watched, the seal also wept three tears into the water—for they can cry you know, and are like ourselves in many ways."

2

The old man paused, and into the quiet of the room, as if prompted by his tale, came the song of the seals from the rocks below the house. The crofters looked about them, startled, though all had heard the wild crying many times before. But the seal people seemed closer, and in tune with themselves for a moment.

"Aye they're listening below. Finish your piece now, Iain."

"So the seal wept with her, and in the night she woke in her lone room to see a stranger stand at her bed foot. But as she looked, by his eyes she knew him. It was the selchie she had seen upon the rocks, but walking now in his earthly guise. He lay with her then, and a fine boy she had of him. And that boy became a gunner and sailed with the Navy, for the King!"

This was a new twist and all eyes turned to a quiet girl who stood back in the shadow behind the door.

"There, Mary!" the women cried smiling to encourage her, "in the Navy like your very own man!" And they all laughed and nodded together.

From his place by the fire Malcolm Macrae, brother of Angus, riffled the notes of his mouth organ for the first time, and whispered with it the melancholy little air that came to everybody's mind with the mention of the seal people. As he began to play, the girl Mary, shy at their pleasure in her, so out of place, slipped out of the house door and walked the path that led down towards the sea. In the soft light of the long summer dusk she watched the seals, silent now on their rocks below her. Shivering after the solid heat of the house she clasped her arms together and sang quietly with the music that rippled from the harmonica:

"I am a man upon the land,
    I am a silkie on the sea,
    And when I'm far and far frae land,
    My home it is in Sule Skerrie."

Where is Sule Skerry, she wondered, the home of the Great Silkie? If he knew my loneliness, like that Norway woman's, would he come here, to me? But no, I cannot

3

weep any more. And she smiled sadly at her own fantasy, and sang again:

"And it shall come to pass on a summer's day,
When the sun shines bright on every stane,
I'll come and fetch my little young son,
And teach him how to swim the faem."

She shook her head, braved up her face and turned back to the house. But as she walked the path over the headland later that night, going home to her own croft in its lonely bay, she seemed to hear the seals again, calling and calling, as if in greeting. For many days after she found herself watching out over the water.

PART I

Chapter One
The Silkie

The majestic clouds that had swept across the sky all day were hurrying toward the edge of the world, and with misty fingers outstretched were catching the last of the Day Star's light in wild hues of red and orange. The sea was gilded and the low streaming light made of every wave a sea in miniature, its stately sides faceted by the ripple and flow of etched wavelets shining and alive. Between the glittering tops the dents and vales were dark, all colour gone, lightless as the deep trenches of the sea bottom. Resting on the sliding wave sides the wet head and gleaming eyes of a lone swimmer were seen only by the sea-birds as they flew upward, calling their last sad farewells to the falling Star.

Over the northern waters day fades slowly and the swimmer was still bathed in light when he found firm bedrock beneath his feet and stood, bracing himself against the insistent nudge of the waves. He raised his arms to shoulder height and, stretching, he leaned back against the slow-moving water as a man might lean against a faithful horse who has carried him far, or against the sun-warmed wall that held his land. A tight smile bared his small teeth, and with the last of the light streaming across the sea behind him he looked out at the land.

The shore rocks rippled with hanging weed as the waves swept by. Where they trod the land the waves teetered and fell in a white foam of confusion, tearing

5

and rattling at sand and pebbles as they slid back defeated from the beach. Sieglid, the swimmer, crept unsteadily forward through the sea wreck, pebbles jarring and bouncing against his soft feet. At last he reached the quiet of the waves' highest reach, and there he stood, watching and waiting.

He could hear her before ever he saw her, her crooning gentle song calling to him as it had done night after night across the water. He bared his teeth again with the longing that swelled within him and he swayed with her music, his arms clasped over his chest where the pain grew with the bounding of his heart and flooded through him, making the palms of his hands vibrate until he pressed them into his trembling loins. The music held him and called him and he knew he must go forward; but he was afraid. Hesitantly he crept up the beach, through the dust-dry weed and whitened wood of the sea's winter cast, down the lee of the storm drift and up to the path between the banks of heather. There he stopped and, falling to his knees, he grasped the woody stems of the plants where they stood in the earth. His fear dragged at him so that he seemed washed over by storm waves, first toward the house, where he longed to be, then back into the sea which he dared not leave.

Crouched there by the bank he sniffed at the path. She had walked there during the day, her warm feet bare on the hard earth. He smelled her, and identified the dripping-tangle weed she carried. Gazing up at her lonely croft he stretched out and, daring, he laid his hand where her feet had passed. Then, turning, he ran stumbling but silent to fall sobbing into the shallows once more. He lay for a long swing of time, his hands buried deep in shingle and sand until, in the grey dusk, her lamp shone out. He stood then, his face turned toward the glowing gold, motionless. His own long sigh of self-disgust spoiled the timeless moment and he turned toward the curving waves and fell forward into the dark water. Far off from the treacherous land his gleaming head broke the surface once more, but there

6

were no eyes to see where he went.

In the quiet cottage Mary moved back and forth singing and dreaming. She covered the fire, her custom at the end of every day, drew water from the barrel at the house-end for the morning and spoke quietly to her little cow who had come down from the hillside for the night. Then she closed the door for the last time, slapped down the bolt and turned to her bed.

There was a sleeping room beyond, but with only herself to please Mary chose the shelf bed beside the chimneypiece where she had slept since she was a child. In the winter she could close its shutters and keep warmth to herself all night long from the stones of the chimney. But during the short summer night she loved to lie in her blankets and watch the half-light of the northern dusk and the moon that silvered the heather. She drifted into sleep with the sigh of the sea in her ears and her dreams took her far out over the waves.

The Day Star was lifting again over the far side of the world before Seiglid turned toward his home. All through the hours of darkness he had swum, forcing his body to exhaustion, cruising beneath the swell of the waves, ten feet down, and rising to the surface only to fill his great lungs with sweet air before burying himself again into starless dark. When he saw that the purpled sky was softening to the grey of early dawn he took a final bearing from the fading stars. Behind him Arcturus was sinking to the horizon, the one whom the Sea Folk call Vernan, the Head. As the short summer night paled rapidly, Seiglid lifted himself upright on the wave tops searching for the Twins who would bring him home.

For generations, through all the long memory of the silkie folk, their home had been on the narrow, sparsely turfed rocks that lay above the sea beyond Sgeir. There he returned in the broadening light and, rolling, lay on his back to watch the still shore. A few of the little ones played in the last low waves of the small beach. Behind them the sand was settling into solid ripples of the sea's form; with every ebb new wrinkles lay there like a fresh hand print. One old nan, an eye to the young ones, crept along the sand, searching for shellfish or sand worms. As Seiglid watched, a little maid left her fellows in the sea-swirl and with tottering skips of pleasure joined her nan to learn from her the signs in the sand which showed that there was food for the folk below. With every tide the generous sea brought in fresh wealth of food and the women of the folk hurried to gather for the families. No-one of the Sea Folk went hungry at home.

Old Marthy, with the little girl-child at her side, looked for the sandy casts which the worms left. Beside each worm-shaped heap she pointed out to the child the little round depression which showed where the worm was now digging down below. With speed her calloused hands dug into the damp sand; the little granddaughter squealed with delight as the morsel of worm was flung out onto the surface. She fell on it grabbing with tiny fingers to capture it and put it safe into the bowl. All the women of the folk, the old nans from whom all the families were born and the mothers with new babies at their knees, owned a bowl for the gathering of food, their daily task. This bowl was for most families made of solid wood worn and scoured by smooth stone and sea-sand, but the old woman who searched this early morning beach carried a metal bowl of great antiquity, fetched up from the bottom of the sea many generations ago. By its dull gleam Seiglid knew her and a warm joy held him. He almost cried out to her, and would have run up the sand as the little one had done to press close to her side. But doubt held him back. Would she want him near her? It seemed to him lately that all the folk turned from him, that everywhere a gentle pressure told him that he was no longer one of them.

With a cry he flung himself away, deep into the waves, to surface again below the shelf of rock where he and his born companions rested the days away. His cry would have gone unnoticed but the disturbance of the water caught the old woman's eye; she had known he was there since it was to watch for his return that she was out so early on the sea-clean beach. Where did he go night after night? What was the pain that she felt in him, resonant in his mind, a pain of which he could not speak? She ached for him, this strange one, whom so short a time before she had held in her arms, lulling him to sleep in the slowly rocking waves when his parents were gone.

"Seiglid" she murmured softly, "Seiglid, stay with the folk."

He sprang up onto the rock, his face ready to smile, to be accepted. He was tense with his effort to be an easy figure in their world, but no-one noticed his return. They were playing a game with stones, intricate in its rules and quite without meaning. As Seiglid approached, laughter ran bouncing among them. It was hard to forget the clean emptiness of the dawn water from which he had just risen and to feel part of their warm company. Wanting to seem pleased with them all, he could only appear aloof. Their love reached out to him shyly, afraid of his harsh eyes and taut face. Still too young to work well with words they were also too old for the easy contact they had known when long ago and little they had rolled about together like pebbles under a wave's outstretched hand.

"Perrid! Why do I play with you, you're quicker than cold." Idranil swept the silly stones into the water with a bark of laughter and leapt up.

On the instant Perrid, his face alight, twisted in one supple movement into the sea, to reappear some way off carried on a wave-top with his fingers rudely against his face. With a roar Idranil and the other two were after him and without thought Seiglid followed. Under the waves they rolled and grappled, lines of bubbles tumbling past them as they played. It was a game they all knew well, a game that hardened their muscles and improved their reactions for the great ventures ahead. When the proving time came these youngsters of the silkie folk would have to be ready to outswim any danger, to chase for their food in the wild ocean, to be alert for days and nights alone on the open seas. Their games were taught them from the moment they first floated on the quiet waves of home. On their skills their lives and the future lives of their folk would depend.

Wearying at last of the antics, of the rough thrusts and grabs, Seiglid kicked his way slowly to the surface. Head back, he watched the glittering, swaying sunlight above him and with a wide practised curve of his arms held himself at the last moment from breaking through into the air. He hung there for a heartbeat then lifted slowly to search the wave troughs before he let himself be seen. So near to home this waiting caution was unnecessary, but it was good to have control, to know that every part of his body would respond, whatever demands he might make. If only the mind could be held back in the same way. In a flood his longing ripped through him, crippling him so that he clung panting to the rock.

"Why me?" His mind, caged within his aching head, beat one more time on this thought. "Why am I caught in this current of despair? I did not ask to be like this, marked different and alien from my folk. I love her, I love a woman who is not of the folk. I want only to be near her, to see her, to watch her, to touch her."

At this last panic thought he smashed the heel of his hand into the shell-crusted rock and the sharp pain helped him to find calm.

"Why could I not love here, with the maidens who live on my beach? What drives me, me alone, to this idiot fancy? If I am not the master of myself, who owns me? I long to move in unison but no, the timing will not fit. As well ask me to breathe the deep."

The moment passed and, sighing, Seiglid lay on the rock. He should sleep or eat, allow his body to rest, but he could not. He was aware of every heartbeat, every breath, every breathing pore of his skin.

Perrid found him and laid a hand gently on his troubled friend, in the deliberate way of the folk when

10

they want to give comfort and show care. The tide was rising once more and water lapped around and under the rock with a glutinous, tonguing sound which murmured to Seiglid of sensual, forbidden things so that the warm touch on his shoulder was a sudden threat to his peace. Pretending sleep he rolled wearily away, breathed open-mouthed and widened his ears for whispers.

Sorrowed, young Perrid turned away, whistled on his teeth then began softly to sing:

"All waters of the sea together flow
But I, alone, am here with none beside
To watch with me the ebbing of the tide
Nor hear the seabird's mournful cry ....."

"A song for Seiglid!" cried Idranil, as he leapt from the water. "Come, you wretch. Wake up and join us, we must eat." He shook his dripping body, causing the flying drops to spatter Seiglid where he lay. "My nan has a bowl full to the brim and she's distressed that we don't eat it all. Move, you stone, you solid lump."

His well-aimed toe shifted Seiglid, who jumped up to find with relief that tension was gone and he could laugh and roar with the rest. They ran awkwardly down the rock, wide feet sliding, arms held out for balance.

Feeding is a random thing for the folk but usually follows the tide's ebb, when the beach has been gleaned and the bowls are full. First the little ones are fed, their elders popping the choicest morsels into their groping mouths. Then the oldest grandsires hold out their cupped hands to be filled. The women of the folk eat as best they can, always on the move, with a special care for young mothers with babes still at their breasts. The sires, the fathers of the Sea Folk, rarely join this communal feast. They find their food alone, out in the wild waters, although sometimes one would step forward proudly to take the good things offered by his womenfolk. The youngsters, unproven useless boys, had to take their chances. When there was plenty it was lavished upon them with yearning love for their

11

vulnerable youth, but if there was little to spare they were beaten off and forced to forage for themselves, so they could learn to survive when the testing time of venture came.

Led by Idranil they edged around the group, grinning, a cupped hand held out in hope, and sure enough the bowls were laden and they could have their fill. The afternoon sun warmed the sheltered beach and the folk rested and talked. Young maidens spread out their hair with combs of white bone, little maids at their sides waiting to be groomed too. Babies were rocked in old nans' arms or were crooned over by loving sisters as they lay sleeping in warm nests in the sand. The lazy youths stretched their limbs and their eyes slid often to their heroes.

As the shadows lengthened the tide emptied out of the cove once more and women wandered away to search the glistening rocks. Idranil, with Gladrid, lay in the water's ripple and sway, playing with little ones who rolled and dived into the curling waves at their feet. One old nan lay on the swell, a babe in her arms, pinching his nose shut whenever the waves broke over them both, laughing at his sneezing splutter, echoing with him the broken wave sounds.

"Tsh-tsh then, tsh-tshsh, my little one." And she sang one of the many lullabies of the folk, her voice warm with love. Babies on the beach were held and surrounded constantly with love; comfy arms cuddled them, gentle fingers stroked them, there were no harsh words: the sea would be their master soon enough.

After a second mealtime, in the long level light of evening, the folk began to settle to sleep. Scratching and yawning, shuffling out familiar sleeping troughs in the soft sand, they muttered the warnings, the old safeguards to keep death, the longest shadow, away.

"Morning bright to my sight come in flight, end this night."

Seiglid rattled the words away as he always did, shifting and stretching in the comfort of the cave, tumbled among his companions. Ever since they had

12

left their mothers' sides they had slept like this, limbs tangled together, drawing warmth. But sleep was hard to find: an elusive scent of the woman's passing brushed his face and the forefront of his mind, unstilling him. In the heavy dark he felt a fellow move away, heard, could not see, the maid who started up under the searching hands. Shadows against the shell-tint of the sky, they slipped away. Seiglid too knew the rhythms that pelted them, but there was no-one here to please his need.

Impatient, he left the cave, longing flooding over him once more, pressing him down. He was being drawn toward that distant beach as the geese are drawn across the sky when they fly at the end of summer. Unable to speak, he brushed comfort aside and turned toward the bending waves. A cold wind blew in his face, but the tears were already there.

Self-pity drained Seiglid as he swam away on the tide. He felt more forced away from his home than drawn toward the fey island as he swam the long waves all that grey day. The clouds swelled down from the sky but no rain came. There was a sense that everything waited. He saw no birds.

The wind tore the tops from the waves, throwing heavy drops against his face as he reached for air, cross currents confused him and, once, his arms and legs were smothered in slipping weed which, mouthing, tried to hold him. The long night of sleeplessness had drawn out his emotions until only a thin thread was left, rubbed by an irritable weariness. Determined, he swam on, his heavy limbs forcing a passage through the delaying water, his body obedient to his need.

The sun had cut a hurt red gash on the western horizon when at last he surfaced within sight again of the stone hut on the land's bank. The smell of wet leaves and earth told him that rain had fallen here and he searched the air for her traced passing. There was nothing, she had not left the shelter of the roof all day and the rain had erased memory.

He crossed the sea litter of the beach rapidly on hands and feet, arms swinging in an ungainly arc, but at the walked-smooth path he stood boldly, drawing trembling breaths as he tested for her presence, every sense alert. He heard her step within the house, quick on the hard earth floor, and caught a sighing breath of sound. A metal latch cracked and the door was open. She stood only yards from him and the exact perfection of the instant filled him with gratitude.

Mary McBride stepped out of her croft in the last of the day's light, to go for blankets she had left wrenched out in the burn. Black against the fiery sky she saw a man straddle the path. Her mind wide with singing innocence she went out to him crying in the Gaelic tongue to ask what his need might be.

They met on the path, he reaching out to touch her bare arm with his cold hand, she staring at his strange nakedness beneath his hair.

The warmth of her skin drew him, the incredible softness of her washed cotton frock. He pressed closer. His feet, stumbling against hers, were unsure and tumbled them both to the ground. Shocked and breathless she lay beneath him, his face against her breast. Now the full tide drove against the sea wall forcing its way through, now the first wave raced up the avenue, now with probing fingers another found the threshold, now the breach was made and now there was a way. Now there was freedom, rhythm and singing, now there was thrusting and finding and joy. Flood gates forced open, waves flowing, rebounding: now was the height of it, now was the master wave, now the flood. Now. And the ebb came and Seiglid had lain with a woman.

Rain fell rattling in the bracken. Mary lay racked on her own house path, each breath a long shudder of awe as she knew him, the silkie, king of the seal folk, the swimmer. Her body was bruised, a stone lay embedded in her back and the rain flattened her frock. Sopped cotton licked her skin and she wept. Seiglid, all the gentleness of the folk filling him as the passion ebbed

14

away, wiped her eyes with his thumb, leaned over her and stroked his cheek against hers. Water ran from his hair tickling her to sneeze with surprise. He laughed at her, pinching her nose together like a babe's and her frightened eyes opened, searched and were lost in the warm dark love of his look. Shyly she reached up to wipe the rain from his heavy brows above her and the water ran through her fingers and fell on her lips. Her tongue slid out and nervously licked it away. On a sobbing breath she smiled.

"*He fooar*," she said. But he shook his head at her, unable to understand.

"I know you," he told her. "All this moontime I've watched you and wanted you. You've never seen me, but I've been here, night upon night, lying in the waves afraid to come near." She gazed at him fascinated, her glance flickering from his eyes to his lips as she tried to follow his unknown lilting speech.

"I don't know why I hid or what I was afraid of. I was a child then, yesterday. Now I am a man!"

He laughed and again pressed his face against her wet perfumed hair. The clean smell of soap was an unfamiliar delight to his senses. Timidly she moved and sat up, speaking and turning her face toward her home. She was shivering and Seiglid tried to rub her shoulders, holding her against him, but the wet cloth rumpled under his hand and the grit of the path pricked him. She shook her head against his shoulder and pointed again. This time he understood and lifting her he carried her to her door.

But this was everything that he feared and he could not step inside. She waited, recognising his fear, then wriggled from him, but left one hand to lie on his shoulder and with calm gentling words eased him into the room. A fire of dull red peat glowed in the fire-basket hearth and the smell of burning was acrid in his nostrils. A moment's hesitation and then he stepped toward the chimneypiece, crouched down and reached out inquisitive fingers. Thinking that he too was cold, the woman slipped away out of sight, removed her own

15

wet dress and, wrapping herself in the coloured quilt
from her bed, snatched up a blanket to lay about his
shoulders. He barely noticed what she had done as he
gazed so intently into the fire. He was distracted when
she moved the blackened kettle, swan-necked, from the
side into the centre of the heat, but delighted when it
began to sing. Matching his voice to the note he
hummed mournfully. She knelt beside him watching
his face closely and, still humming, he lifted the quilt
from her shoulder with one sly finger. It fell from her
and, rising, he took her again on the floor at her hearth.
The kettle sang, Seiglid was humming softly and, all her
limbs at peace, she slipped into sleep. Shadows
gathered in the room and drifted silent through the short
night.

Seiglid's eyes glittered alert, watching the pale square
window in the dark wall. Green dawn stood in the sky
and he left the dying hearth. A throb of fear was in him;
he could not smell the sea. Never in his life had he been
without that comforting breath. In the shadowed room
he was unable to see the door. His hands stumbled along
the wall, fell on the latch and the wood swung toward
him. Without a glance back into the tired air of the room
he stepped out into the clean day, ran down the path
and gladly slid back into his own world once more. So
few hours, but he had worn lifetimes.
    He was afraid but did not know what he feared, why
he could not return. The woman had given him delight,
even in his fear. And she would, he knew, carry his
child. But just as he could find no peace among his own
people, so he knew now that there could never be any
quiet with the woman, who lived without the secret of
the sea. Could he, he wondered, find another answer?
Find far away in the wide waters another family of the
folk? Such a thing was never spoken of. In all the tales
the old grandsires told they spoke only of their own
lives, of their ventures and of those who went before. If

there were others they were a world's turn away. No travellers from the home beach had ever returned with news of them. For so many months unsure, Seiglid now turned with purpose to his own time of venture. He would search for a people, for a place and as he searched find his own peace, if the old tales were true.

All that long summer he swam alone, often for many days without sight of land. He watched for signs that would warn him of his folk, for patterns of their passing in the long waves. He followed the sea paths of the North Atlantic. Fishermen saw him from time to time but he dived deep before they knew him. He suffered in storms, sick and cold. He knew hunger and fear. And he began to know himself.

He travelled south until he reached the seas where flying fish were seen and delighted with them in their freedom, following their excited journeys. He learned to explode like them through the water's surface, though he could never shake himself entirely free but fell back, gasping, his thick legs still held by the waves.

He hoped to meet others of his kind, cousins, but though he searched he never found them, could not know their place, though he became steadily more certain that they lived. He travelled north again at last, on warm-water currents, and one morning beyond the rollicking wave tops saw the massive rock stacks where sea-birds congregate.

Guillemot and tern, black-back and herring gull lifted on the air above him or, dipping a wing, slid down the wind. He admired their skill and lay watching them for hours. They had such fine control that they seemed to command the very element in which they lived, bending it to achieve their freedom. But as he watched them he learned that they were not marshalling the wind but simply by their skill were proving themselves free.

All through his youth among the Sea Folk Seiglid had been trammelled by the silkie traditions and customs which smelled stale to him. Against his training he had left the water and forced his way into a woman of the land: had taken her and pressed her into the earth. Sadly he had found no freedom but its reverse, and fled back to the sea for safety. Through these long summer days he had yielded to the commands of the waves and had won for himself here in the wide emptiness of ocean the freedom of his own life. He could leap and swing in his own world and that world had become a wonder to him. His anger had passed and he had found peace. He was himself. He was free from self-doubt and on a crescendo of major music he sang his praise to the light above him. He was himself!

As the nights lengthened and dawn came later and later to the eastern sky, Seiglid left the bird sanctuary and began slowly to go home. He lay quietly on the sides of the sea swell, letting the ocean drift bring him back where he belonged.

Swimming under the pale pearl belly of an autumn mist Seiglid returned to his beach. The folk clustered round and made much of him. Perrid was there before him, fat from the plenty of southern waters. Idranil and Callidray came later. Of Gladrid there was no sign. In the winter caves they talked about their ventures, moving among menfolk at last. They talked of ice mountains and coral reefs, the still sea of weeds and the gale force of storms. Little ones stood at their knees to listen wide-eyed young maids came close to gaze and old nans touched them with caressing hands. Seiglid opened his heart to his folk as never before, welcoming and belonging, but he felt in Idranil a constant pulse of frustration. With the spring his friend would be away again to pit himself once more against the bitter north. Idranil could not rest.

"And you, Seiglid, what will you do when the weather makes us free of the seas once more? Do you come with me to seek the Snow People? Shall we find a walrus herd? The world is ours now to search in, Seiglid! Where shall we go? What new legends and memories shall we make?" He laughed his eager barking laugh. He wanted to take his world by the shoulders and shake it.

18

"No I shall not come with you, Idranil." Seiglid's slow smile was known and loved by the folk. "I have a duty now. I have to bring home my son."

Chapter Two
Seachild

The storm had been built in the troughs of the North Atlantic, had swelled and raged there for days, its anger growing. Now with a shrieking cry it threw itself to battle across the whipped grasses and the twisting heather to tear the land and trample it. Only the rocks stood firm: on cliff sides tenuous roots were ripped away and the shattered fistfuls of earth washed back to be devoured in the clamouring waves. Outraged, the mountains shredded cloud and were deluged in reply, torrents grappling their crags, forcing boulders from the teeming face. Stone-built, the tiny crofts cringed and clenched against the gale which howled defiance. Keening past the windows' frames, the wind screamed its challenge into the crannies of the roof.

The old door of ship's timbers thudded wearily, was allowed no rest, its random hammering a judder in the easy beat of the woman's will as she sat crouched at her hearth, feeling that the rise of the storm echoed the cramps that strained her. With a grim satisfaction Mary recognised that in this crescendo of noise her time was come, her body too was stretching to its climax.

As well that it should be now, she thought, when no-one can be by. She felt no fear of what was to come any more than she feared the gale outside. Both would tear and destroy during their moment, but the peace that followed would be sweet. Her preparations were all made and now in the storm's centre she gave in, let herself be swept flat, trampled by the force of the birth.

Soon, when it was over, the old women would come across the hillside, and if the bairn was wholesome she would give them it for bathing, for tying the body bands. But if her seal-child, silkie and mis-begotten, were too strange in her own sight — well then, in first light she would take it out, undetected, and give it back to the sea from which it had come.

She felt no guilt at her getting of the child. The silkie's attack — was it anything other than that, however gently he had roused her — was like a tumbling in the waves, the onslaught of a searching tide. These too could break into her private ways: not for her to understand them. As she swelled with the child she let her neighbours believe that it came of her sailor husband's stay when last he had shore leave. How should they know that in three years of marriage his six nights with her had left her virgin still? No, the bairn would be his if he came home again. If the silkie let him be.

In spite of her calm, her confidence, the birth was a struggle and when at last she held the infant, trying to test its figure against others newborn, a fresh pitch of terror gripped her and threw her back, gasping on her mat. The arching pain was not done yet: there was to be a second wean.

After two days the storm gathered up its last rags of cloud and stalked away leaving the islands washed to a bitter calm. Three women, their black shawls wound over their coats, men's boots on their feet for the slurry of the path, came over the headland and down to the isolated croft, where Mary had lived all her life, alone even before her parents died, alone in spite of her married state. The women whispered together in the Gaelic, distressed at the stubbornness of her that she wouldn't come round to their more settled homes, to the place where the road reached over from the east coast and the world of the mainland. Here where she was Mary would never see the motor cars such as the

21

tourists were bringing with them. Certain she had never heard the radio waves, though they reached now to the post office at Lochboisdale even. Of course none of the women had heard the radio themselves. But they knew of it, enough.

Mary met them at her house door. She was pale yet, they agreed, but not sickly. Neat, contained as always, her hair braided and wound in heavy coils at her ears, her sensible woollens wrapped under a sleeveless overall, she kept her arms folded at her chest and nodded a tight-lipped greeting to her neighbours. She let them pry but gave nothing away, showed them her child when they asked, then tucked him firmly back again, in the shelf bed beside the fire. She gave them all a cuppie of dark sweet tea, but refused their company with stillness, so that in the end, frustrated again by her withdrawal, they wound their way over the track and were none the wiser.

Once they were gone Mary closed up the shutters and hung a blanket at the door. Now more than ever before she needed to shut out the sound of the sea where it called among the cliffs and the weed fringes of the rocky cove. If she could she would stop it, keep it from beckoning her boy.

While winter held the seas, stripping the wave tops and winding the deep water currents tighter in its fist, the silkies sheltered in their sleeping cave. After the long journey of the summer the men of the folk were happy to rest, sleeping for long hours of darkness, feeding when their women brought them morsels. The spirit of the folk was strengthened in these times. They drew a force from their numbers gathered together, dandled the new babes with pride and told over again stories of the great ventures to renew their courage for another testing time.

Idranil's eyes shone with excitement as he visioned new paths of ocean for his search. But Seiglid, at ease now with himself, only smiled and waited for what each tide would bring. As the days lengthened, restlessness among the untried boys became a scratching irritation which the older men must calm. Boys had been known to venture too soon, before the spring tides had worn themselves away high on the land. The risk then was greatest and mothers would look for their return in vain. To sober them, Fridonay, the blind story-teller, chose a tale of sadness and warning: gathering the folk to his side in the half-light of the tide-bound cave he began in measured tones to tell the story of Tsebbrid and his venture among men.

"Many generations," he recited, "have lived to swim the waves since this story first was told."

Seiglid closed his mind. "Why that story of them all?" he wondered, disturbed. His thoughts turned to his own son, born now, and living still on the land, for it was a story of the ugliness of men and the fate of one of the folk who had lived among them long ago.

Many generations of the folk have lived to swim the wave since this story was first told. In those days the folk were more numerous and their beaches in the spring time were like nesting grounds, where the young ones ran happily in the sun-soft sand. In those carefree times the Day Star seemed to shine with more heat and the waves were warmer. But even then the young men of the folk were attracted to the endless ice of the north in search of the laughing lights and many met their deaths.

Tsebbrid as a young man was tall and his limbs were straight. When the longest day came, he and his companions, all the youngsters who were born at the same time as he, swam away with the morning tide. Maids and mothers were left to weep and as always the young men wore stern faces to hide all that they were feeling. It is a hard thing to leave all that you have known but this swimming away to venture into new waters has always been our custom: only the best, the bravest, the most fit return to become the fathers of the folk. Very many are lost. They venture across many seas, along fjords and bays, over the endless ice or among warmer waves. It is their pride to swim alone, living as best they can until the time of the Equinox warns them that winter may catch them fast; then they turn homeward to their own beaches again.

When Tsebbrid did not return his mother bore it well and her daughters came close and comforted her. Those young maidens who watched for him in vain were content to see others of his companions coming home, their sleek heads dark against the waves, their sturdy bodies shimmering with the long sea water as they stepped out of the racing surf.

The winter passed. The folk lay warm and snug in dry caves, under hanging walls of stone. All through the darkness and the storms they sang and told stories, laughing and playing with the little ones. On fine days, when it was possible to go out searching for food, the women combed the sandy shores. This was a time when his mother's eyes looked sadly over the ocean, but Tsebbrid never appeared. As the waters swung closer to the sun once more, and food was plentiful, and the babies were born, Tsebbrid, like so many others, was forgotten and the tides came and went and washed away pain.

Three bornings had passed, and again young men were preparing for their venture. One dreaming youngster leapt up suddenly on the rocks and his companions rose too at the alarm in his face. Gazing over the water they watched with horror the ugly figure who staggered from the grip of the waves. His eyes were sunk deep in the bony sockets of his face, and his head almost bare of covering hair was pocked with scars. A shoulder also gleamed white with naked flesh and seemed crooked, swinging a withered arm. As the wretch stumbled in the last of the sea roll it became clear that he could not stand upright, but supported

24

himself by the knuckles of his good hand, and his legs bent weakly under his weight. No-one moved forward to help him. With eyes shifting and muscles alert for a signal the folk were ready for the running dive which would fling them all far away from this fearful creature. With a slow, crablike, sidling movement he came up the beach, then standing alone among them he turned up the palm of his useless hand and stretched it out to them in a gesture of helpless longing.

"I am Tsebbrid," he cried.

For many tides Tsebbrid swung between living or dying. He never spoke, but his gaunt face seemed at ease and though he often wept as the maids fed him or held him in their arms to ease his pain, rubbing and massaging his empty muscles, it was clear that happiness was flowing into him and at last he began to find his strength once more.

It took him many days and nights to tell his story, whispering in the stillness of long evenings, weeping in the cold of morning. It was a disjointed telling, coming back again and again to fear and betrayal, the meaning often lost in tears and repetition, but patiently the folk pieced it all together.

He had left on a morning tide when the air held a soft summer promise of rain and soon he lay on the long grey swell, with water falling about him, carrying a clear sense of the far-off cold. He had long since known that he would go to the north and he swam without a stop until the black sides of the Land on Fire appeared above the waves to the West. Here in the chill waters he found himself surrounded by joyous swarms of silvered fish who flashed and raced before him, tempting him to follow.

Between the Land on Fire and the Land of Ice flows a strong current of cold blue water, clear and shining in the sunlight. On its surface move great ice floes and mountains of ice. Solid and stately they slide on the long waves on a wandering journey southward. They excited Tsebbrid, who climbed onto a small island of ice and leapt about, shouting and rocking until he grew tired and slept at last. But the dance of the ice mountains is too slow for the sturdy limbs of the folk and Tsebbrid soon left his shrinking ledge of ice and travelled on with the shining current and its glittering fish, past the icy fringe of the land, going south-west. Old Three Fins found him and led him on. He is a solemn fish with his starting eyes but he knows the way to the warmer banks where the cold currents meet the Great Stream, and food of all kinds fills the waters. There, even in the long days of summer, grey fogs rest on the water. Tsebbrid would not lie on the slow swell of the ocean to rest but once again chose to sleep on ledges and cliffs of ice until to his amazement he saw one tip and fall. In slow silence the blue sheer side of ice gently bowed toward the water which seemed to rise eagerly to take it while, gleaming and cracking, a new white island shape appeared with water running in silver rivers from its sides. It was like a solemn dance from the beginning of the world when solid land first rose from the gut of the ocean and Tsebbrid drew breath in wonder until he realised his own risk and left the ice. It was a dangerous place to be in, with bad visibility both in the teeming seas and in the mist-filled air and Tsebbrid was uncertain where his venture would take him in this turmoil of waters.

Then the ship appeared, sailing in majesty from a low bank of cloud which hung pearl grey on the waters at dawn. As she moved forward, tendrils of mist hung still about her shrouds and spars and the wet wood of her sides glistened in the early light of the sun. She seemed to have been born fresh at the moment and from her bright deck came suddenly a lilting song played on a wooden whistle. On the instant Tsebbrid loved her and rising up before her in the water held out his arms in longing at her beauty. She came closer and closer then with a thud of heavy canvas and the amiable groan of swaying wood she went about and made away from him. Without a thought he plunged after her as so many of the folk have done. Without choice or reason Tsebbrid took up the stream of his fate and followed the tall ship.

Against the steady southern passage of the icebergs the ship forced her way, turning and tacking to catch the cunning winds. In her wake Tsebbrid leapt and plunged, carolling at her beauty. In exuberant wonder he swam ahead gazing up at her long nose and fin-like jibs. He flung himself under her sides and tore his fingers on her crusted keel as he reached up in love to stroke her as she swept past. Mad with pleasure he roared and sang in the sunlight until on her decks laughing men pointed and shook their heads at him. Why did he stay? How should he trust the men who sailed in her? But Tsebbrid had lost both heart and mind to the singing ship and nothing would turn him.

So they came, the ship and Tsebbrid, through the mists and the floating ice to a little ledge of land lying still above the waves. With a rattle and angry cries the ship shuddered and stopped, her sails bundled up to her spars; and while Tsebbrid swam backwards and forwards in distress men swarmed over the sides into a boat and clambered ashore. Staying himself against an anchor rope Tsebbrid watched them on the shore. He winced at their loud voices and watched amazed their flailing arms and striding feet. When the shooting began he fell from his rope with a splash and cowered on the sea-floor beneath the keel until his heart cried for air. On the land the men propped up their guns like branches and fired them again and again. When they returned they carried between them many great white bears, their silky coats ripped and slashed open, with blood and guts trailing dark on the ground. How piteous their black muzzles snuffling now in the dirt, how useless their huge claws against the guns on which they were slung. Tsebbrid knew that the bear, Akpotok, was bad-tempered and dangerous, yet he wept at the dirt in those once proud nostrils, and smelled at the men with

27

disgust. But he still stayed and followed the ship.

She seemed now reluctant to leave the land and followed the sight of the shore, turning at last to the south. The air was warm with the odours of the land, but the water was chilled by its streams and rivers and soon Tsebbrid knew that he was no longer in the open sea but in a wide bay, huge and almost enclosed. From the deeps he heard whale song and seeing their coiled backs slow rolling on the surface he was filled with awe; and with fear for their safety so close to men and their tearing, noisy guns. But the ship continued to stay close to land, her progress slow as she curiously nosed into every inlet and estuary. Excited every day by new happenings, more and more intrigued by the fearsome men of the ship, Tsebbrid nevertheless was aware that summer was shortening away to the Equinox and as he travelled south with the ship he wondered always when they would turn back.

A gun sounded from the ship. The raucous voices growled and spat. Tsebbrid shrank away into the waves, eyes only above the surface. Men's feet thudded on the hollow wood of the deck and the ship began to die, her sails hanging slack, the booms swinging. A gust of wind leaned her on her side as she drifted meaninglessly. With a clatter of blocks a boat was lowered over the side and with angry barks and awkward gestures men on the ship pressed others down into it. As if relieved of pain the ship came up to the wind once more. Men went aloft to smarten her and the blurred slapping of loose ropes and wrinkled sails sharpened into action. Clear cut against a lowering sky the ship sped forward once more and Tsebbrid with her — though more than once he stared back at the lonely boat left under the dark sky.

Curiosity sent him back. In the morning, grey and with gusting winds, he returned to the place where the boat had been. He could see clearly where its wooden sides had pressed through the water and he followed gaily, amused at these strange creatures, men. Why were they going into an open and bare estuary scoured by bitter winds when so near to the south comforting rocks

28

stood out? That they wanted shelter he was sure, with winter now so close.

It came into his mind to play with them, as he had played in his home waters with other creatures of the sea, and swimming under their slow tub he pushed and pulled, pressing them toward the safety of the cove. Then they struck him with an oar as he passed under the boat. A vicious jab, it snapped bone in two and opened all his heart in pain to let the sea water in his lungs. Senseless he rolled to the surface, belly up as a dead fish. Many of the folk have died so.

The men pulled him into their boat. It is part of their nature to act in this way: so often they destroy and, after, they are so distressed. Men are set far off from all that lives, they have built their boundaries and are wound within them. Tents and rooftrees they put up to hide from sun and rain, tatters and furs wrap out the air. Their feet tread in their own sweat and will not press upon the land they aim to love. And so, surrounded, they peer out with fear at all who are, as we are, won with wonder.

So Tsebbrid was saved by the men's remorse and sick with pain lay in their boat as they made toward the land.

When the sounds of the beach chattered in his ears Tsebbrid raised himself to look out. Before the white-topped wave could fall he was over the side and away. His left arm useless with pain, it was hard to direct himself through the wind-driven waves but he crept at last among sheltering stones at the land's edge and crouched there watchful. The men too crouched miserably on the beach. They had turned their boat over and sheltered under it while evening came, and with it the rain.

All night long Tsebbrid wrapped himself under hanging weed and tried to work warmth back into his useless shoulder. With the coming of the day the drizzle continued and the men left their shelter only to relieve themselves. Tsebbrid picked limpets from the rock at his side because he was hungry and dared not be seen by the men. As the western side of the world tipped up to receive the sun once more the rain slowed and stopped and the empty clouds swam up into the blue and floated high on the surface of the sky. Bird song, liquid and clear, filled the air and the warm, peaty odour of earth rose from the land.

Driven by his hunger, Tsebbrid crept among his rocks gleaning food. He felt the men's eyes on him, but they did not come near. As night fell he huddled again under the lea of a boulder to sleep. The tides came and went and Tsebbrid could not swim away. Now the sea began to freeze all along the beach and he watched the men watching him. One morning he woke and they stood at his side.

A man spoke curtly, gesturing with fingers to his mouth. Another leaned down and shook him where he lay under the rock and gestured in the same way. Panting with terror Tsebbrid tried to run into the frozen sea but they held him fast, grunting and gesticulating. Timidly Tsebbrid broke a small shell from its hold on the rock and held it out to his captors. Understanding their nods and pointing fingers he ate first, smacking his lips and showing his tongue to prove how good the titbit was. With difficulty a man snapped off another shell and scooped the soft sea creature into his mouth. He bit then spat, growling and gnashing his teeth so that Tsebbrid fell to the ground in terror. But the men tried the unfamiliar food again and with struggling faces swallowed it down. How much they ate! Cramming food into their mouths, six or seven shellfish at a time until they dribbled and gagged. Their fingers shook and trembled round their lips as they pushed every morsel in. It was not wise: among the nine of them many stomachs would not accept such plenty so that they staggered away retching and undone. But they would not let Tsebbrid go.

They tied Tsebbrid with a belt of leather around his middle to which they cleverly fastened a rope. Often in secret Tsebbrid pulled at these fastenings and tore with his teeth at the rope. But the fingers of men are long and cunning and Tsebbrid could not undo the knots that they had made. Whenever his teeth tore the strands of the rope the men would find the place and with rapid skill mend the break so that Tsebbrid could never recognise the place he had weakened. All through the long dark winter Tsebbrid was forced to search for food for the men, and their demands were enormous. In return they kept him warm.

Strengthened by the food he gave them the men had gone far out over the land and returned with many fallen trees. From this wood they built a hut and when the snows came and the white cold of the north was too intense to be borne Tsebbrid crept inside and curled up at the feet of the men. Though his heart longed for cleaner air he could dream at times that he was in a cave of the folk as he slept.

Men bring fire into their huts. It lives when they command it and they love to place food in the flames. They gave cooked food to Tsebbrid but it bit him with its heat and he spat it out of his mouth. He would not copy their ways. They took off their outer skins, and tried to cover Tsebbrid with them but he would not have it. Those furs and rags were an offence to him and he closed his nose at them. When the men laughed at him Tsebbrid learned that it was a pleasing noise and during that first winter he often played for them.

Spring came and, while the land brightened with colour after the numbing whiteness, the men began to die. Their flesh swelled and cracked and bled, their teeth loosened in their heads and their flux loosened to water. First one collapsed and lay until dead and then two more, the last crawling with sobbing cries from the hut until he could press his fingers into the earth outside, and there, weeping, he died.

While Tsebbrid watched, tethered and distressed, the men dug deep into their earth and tenderly placed the dead into the hollow they had made. Then piling up stones over the bodies they sang the parting songs.

Those who were left, though weak and very tired, revived as the sun grew stronger in heat and light and they tore up young green plants from the earth to eat

31

them, *since from the earth they gain their strength.*

Through the long summer days Tsebbrid watched the men and learned their ways. He swam for them, though they kept him captive by his rope even in the water, and caught fish for them. Knowing their need for food in such quantity Tsebbrid led them in their boat over to deep water and there he found Old Three Fins once again. Saying the right apologetic words Tsebbrid even caught big fish for the men, twisting and diving in the clear water in a game whose end he always hated as he handed the lifeless corpses into the boat. But he could not refuse to catch the fish because the men were cruel and Tsebbrid feared them even when they played.

Often under the hot summer sun the men would splash at the water's rim and then he loved to join them. They threw sticks onto the water and shouted with delight when he swam out and brought them back or dived deep for shining stones or metal discs that they threw down. But there were other games: Tsebbrid was tied by his long rope to a stake hammered firmly into the ground, then the men shouted to him to act. He never knew what they wanted and at first stood quietly, smiling and shaking his head. Then they threw stones at him. They threw slowly at first so that he had time to jump and twist clear. But laughing and shouting the men threw faster and faster and the little pebbles ricocheted and sang through the air until his skin was stinging and he had no more breath to skip and leap but fell panting on the stones.

Tsebbrid tried to listen to their words, to find out what they wanted of him and through that second long winter in the hut he began to understand. One man in particular, smaller and younger than the rest, took the time to teach him and tell him what had happened to them all.

It seemed that one of the men who died was his father, and a leader of men. (For they follow one man and will not yield to the woman who bore them as we do.) It was he who directed the ship, he was her captain, and he searched for a sea passage to the north-west

32

which would bring him out to a vast ocean. Why he wanted this, or why he was unable to read the currents and drifts correctly, but spent his search in wandering a land-locked bay Tsebbrid could never understand. Perhaps it was for this stupidity his men abandoned him, though his son said they complained of lack of food which was always a grievous wrong to them as Tsebbrid knew. However it was, the ship discarded her captain and these others, his friends, and went home. The boy was certain that she would return to find them all.

Spring returned but the ship did not. Slowly, as another summer passed, hope died in the men's faces and they no longer gazed eagerly over the water every morning. Their cruelty was acted out not only on Tsebbrid, but their words bit at one another, if they spoke at all.

Although they had lived in this land for nearly two years the men still seemed to be on it only, not of it. They had placed their hut on the ground just as they did their feet, without making any concessions. In all that time they had taken greedily, and given nothing in return. They had no words of apology for the deaths they caused, although with their cunning knots and ropes they trapped and killed numbers of little creatures of the land. They sang no praise of the trees that sheltered them with their bodies. Except in death they gave nothing to the earth but waste and filth.

They wanted to go home, the boy said wistfully, and Tsebbrid nodded a sad understanding. Although he could follow their speech he could not form his own lips around it and would not try for fear of the men.

Violence sprang up again and again like angry waves against a rock as the men's minds battered against the monolithic fact that they could never leave this place. Anger rippled and swirled about the hut just as waves do when the wind will not let the tide have its way.

Two men muttered and grumbled constantly, until winter was come and heavy grey clouds hung on the horizon. A cold wind picked up dry sticks and leaves and blew them across the rattling grasses iced in at the sand's edge. As if lifted by the wind one man leapt at the other. The cutting knife went up and down.

"He's slitting off his skin just as he did the little animals'," thought Tsebbrid miserably.

Men crowded round, their movements urgent yet afraid; then walked dully away leaving the dead body on the ground. A gritty snow began to fall, whispering up the beach from the frozen sea. There were no colours anywhere.

The snow fell and drifted over the land: drifted over the body they would not bury. It would keep until later. Listlessly a man took Tsebbrid searching for food under the snow but none of them would eat. Everyone was silent, moving only to sigh and be still again. Tsebbrid saw their tears for the first time.

When they began to eat the red meat, juicy, sizzling over the fire, Tsebbrid did not at first understand. Then in the movement of an eye, his disgust at the dripping blood and the tangy smell turned to horror. He knew what they had in their hands. And they were eating it.

The longest night came and went and Tsebbrid lay sleepless against the wall of the hut. Whenever the men moved their hands he felt nausea rising in his throat, mixed with fear. When they looked at him he read a terrible meaning in their empty eyes. He brought them more and more food but they would not always eat. And there came a day when there was no mistaking any more: the men wanted meat again.

With sideways looks and nods to each other they licked their grinning lips. One pulled out a knife and felt the point, then slipped it away again, his eyes cast down. Tsebbrid lay stiff, his bones aching from the trembling of fear. He could no longer face his fate and whimpered mindlessly for the open sea, for the freedom to enter his own ending.

He woke in a sudden moment in the black foetid air which was full of the men's outbreathing. The blackness rustled at his side and a breath leaned in his ear.

"Go merman, go for your life."

34

But he could not move, no air was in his lungs, he drowned in fear and his heart could not act.

"Tsebbrid," a whisper moved his hair once more. "Tsebbrid, go back to your folk. You are needed here no more."

Laying a grateful hand against the lips of the boy who gave him freedom Tsebbrid slithered across the floor. In a moment the cold, moon-filled air freshed away fear and stumbling under the weight of his joy he fled down the beach and over the creaking sea ice. His bonds were gone at last.

When Tsebbrid fell into the waters of that far bay spring was still delaying. How he swam those northern waters he could not say. As he reached the warmer Great Stream his crippled side was useless, the broken shoulder grating and collapsing, unable to bring him home. But the water held him day after day, carrying him back to his folk. If he did not eat it was because he would not; weakened as he was by sleeplessness and pain he could only drift and wait until he felt his home waters near him. Then came the final pull, and he was on his own beach.

Tsebbrid, crooked and old before his time, paced out his days on the beaches of the folk. He lived alone: trust had been washed from him and he was slow to smile.

As an old man he studied the stars.

A sigh greeted the ending of the tale, and a silence. The story was seldom told, and it left unease in the minds of the silkies. Always, down the years, the teaching was: leave the landsmen, stay hidden from their sight. But no mention was made of the harm that they could do. Now, was this it?

"What! Will they come and eat us!" cried Idranil. And he laughed.

But his laughter could not dispel their disgust at the ways of men and Seiglid shivered as if a hand drew the hairs upward on his spine as he thought of his child, who was also an offspring of the land. What harm had he created for the babe, bringing it so unseemly into the world? What trouble for the woman, its dear mother? What heartbreak for the folk?

Perrid, warm, full-fleshed, three times to be a father in this year's borning, caring equally for all his women, and for none, caught the frisson of Seiglid's fear and rolled anxious eyes at him in the shadows. The affair of the woman at the croft was no secret to Seiglid's born companions. Comfortable in the steady pattern of things Perrid shook his head: with one wrong step the dance of the folk could be disturbed, their patterned life of generations caused to break and change. But if it was willed so it would be. That much Perrid, already, had learned.

Before the longest day dawned, while the young men readied themselves again for venture, Seiglid brought home his son, placing him in the arms of old Marthy, his own nan, who wept over him, but silently vowed him all her love as she strove to fill the place of the woman who had borne him.

In the quiet kitchen of the croft the kettle ticked and sang over the peat hearth. The woman moved silently about, lifting the tiny clothes which hung before the fire and testing them against her cheek. He had come, as she had known he would, his face dark and angry as he stood in the doorway. She had crouched back from him as he swept into the room, looking fiercely round. With his cold hands he had ripped the child from beneath the covers. In the doorway he paused again, murmured soft words that she would not understand, and was gone. Now she sang happily to herself for she knew that after all her fears she had won: while the silkie had his child, with its webbed toes and thick hair, she had her own, his firstborn, sleeping peacefully in the quiet of the shelf bed.

Chapter Three
Manchild

In the quiet of the cave a sudden choking cry splattered up the walls. Roused, an aged grandad grunted and shifted himself; none of the younger folk stirred. With the cry old Marthy reached out, barely waking, gentled the youngster under her hand then drew him sleepily into her arms, rolling on her back to pillow him against her tired old breasts. She held him so, her arms folded about him, echoing a tradition of the folk, a memory of the time before thought, when it had been necessary to raise even new borns in the sea. Now not one of the folk even acknowledged that time, it was gone from all but the deepest traces of memory. For more generations than the mind could grasp silkie young had been reared in safety on the beach.

When the earth-born babe was brought to her it had been old Marthy's first task to teach him how to find ease and safety in the sea. He had moved happily from the first, his limbs free and confident while the water held his chubby body's weight. More sure in water, he wallowed still on land, crawling only to collapse. But he knew no fear and would forget to close his nose against the salt splash of the waves. Rhythms which in adult life would be second nature needed at first to be taught. As he grew he would press himself impatiently from her arms as she stood in the waves, and sink until his toes touched the sandy bottom at her feet, his tiny starfish hand against her knee as he gazed about. To her dismay

38

he never kicked away into the sea spaces around him, but when first he left her side, it was to walk into the quiet below the waves pull. To walk, as the landsmen would. And she snatched him up and swam with him, teaching his strong legs the rhythms.

Through his first years Marthy had kept his secret, hiding his strangeness: his slowness to swim, his easy balance on the rocks. She made a joke of his sure-footedness. Where others stumbled, older than he, to wail over their grazed knees and bruised hands, her land-baby rarely fell; but in the sea he spluttered still, mistiming the wave, inhaling the spray. He laughed at the worried pursing of her lips and dived again, determined to learn better. But in the night he often drowned in fears.

"He is anchored too tightly to the land," Laggidar, oldest of the menfolk said at last. "Free him for the sea."

Smiling gravely, Seiglid would not comply and placed his hand, protecting, on his son's nape. In the sandy hair a slim chain of gold winked in the sunlight. "It was his mother's gift. It is all he has."

A tremor moved the old folk as they looked down at the little one's insignia, but they said no more. The babe was motherless, a rarity among the folk, and everyone would give a little more to make up his loss. But it was hard to touch that chain, to weigh the stone it held. Poor little manchild, the Donilid, whose mother claimed him still. They named him Bridik, the Rock, but it was as Donilid he was known, fondly, their manchild, and if they laughed at his oddities it was only to snatch him up on the instant in love and contrition so that, not understanding, he laughed with them and was happy.

In the morning after his disturbed night Marthy led him early to the waves. The tide was still high and she picked her way carefully among the rocks to find some titbit for him, calling him to her side when he would have skipped away. The pools were filled, awash with fresh waves, and limpets still moved along their sides. His quick fingers, more agile than hers, soon lifted one away, but she had to reprove him, holding his wrist, until he had recited the proper words, the apology to the tiny life he had stolen.

"Say it carefully, my Donil," she shook him gently, "the creatures do not give themselves to us, it is we who must give gratitude to them."

But he was no longer listening, and she turned to follow his gaze out to sea. A broad-beamed fishing boat was making its way past their low headland, butting across the choppy seas, its bows hidden again and again in bursts of spray. Although still far off it seemed unusually intrusive, for there was little traffic beyond Sgeir other than in the long sea lanes which were well known to men.

Crouching into the side of the rock, grey-brown, hardly visible, Marthy reached out her arms for her nursling. But he was gone, and peeping out she saw to her dismay that he was scrambling among the tumbled rocks below the cliff face, trying to reach a vantage point. She called him but he would not hear her and with a sigh she began to follow.

Stooping to lay her hands for safety against the slippery surfaces, crouched and slow moving, Marthy — if she were seen at all — had every appearance of a grizzled old seal, humping irritably over rocks at high tide. As she groped forward she raised her voice in complaint: not for the first time she felt that the Donilid was growing too soon beyond her care. He stood now, in plain view of the fishermen, his hands splayed across his face to cut the sea glare as the flat grey light of the Day Star broke from the cloud banks behind the rocks, and silvered the waters.

"Look, my nan, the bravery of it! See how it smacks the waves aside. Oh, I want to stand there. Let me go on the burning craft that moves?"

But she beckoned him down fiercely, crooking up both her arms to him.

"What are you saying, you silly?" she hissed at him. "Come from their sight: men are there. It is a boat, a man ship!"

He laughed at the unfamiliar words as he slid,

dutiful, down into her arms.

"A man ship, a *donacru*, for Donilid, manchild," he cried. And when she frowned and pursed her lips his round child face became suddenly stern. "But Marthy, it is true: manchild I am, though always and forever one of the Folk of the Sea. Do you not see, my nan, their ships must call to me? And I, when I can venture, shall go to them."

"It is often so. The beauty of ships, sailing free in the seas, can catch at the heart of the folk and beckon them in their journeyings." Old Marthy, remembering the tales, shivered and tears shimmered her sight.

From that time on, though he grew away, left her side and joined the other boys of his borning, Marthy continued to watch over Seiglid's son. When heroes returned from the deep seas the youngsters would press forward to hear their stories. Unlike the others the Donilid knew his own father, but it was not his search he listened to with such longing. With misgiving Marthy watched him whenever the ships were mentioned, whenever one of the strong swimmers spoke of the wrecks that were to be seen in the clear southern seas.

"Like waves of dreaming they are, asleep for ten thousand tides. Stones lie in them, shaped and smoothed, metals wrought in ways of mystery to make walk-ways for men. Tall trees from the land they take to bend them for their will on the water, and they lie now, skeletons, at rest in beds of shingle. And through their halls, their cabinned spaces, swim the clouds of prettiest fish: spine fish, stiff fins erect, their backs alight with colour, or midnight fish, spangled like the heavens. Bird fish there are, and butterflies tame to your hand, that flitter in the ports and passageways, eye-patterned. The artefacts of men lie smoothed under the waves' hand, brittled to breaking in their burial time, their use all lost now."

"Then there is nothing for the folk there!" Marthy's sharp voice, trying to break the spell, bring back her Donilid from the men's world which held him rapt.

"Why there you make your mistake, you of all!" Laggidar pointed with gnarled hand. "You hold the found vessel, your bowl of metal to provide for the folk!"

A warm laughter accompanied his words, and Marthy flung her arms about her head in pretended submission, grinning her gap-toothed old grin. But her heart remained uneasy

She said nothing more, however, to the youngster as he grew. No babe of the Sea Folk should ever know fear on the beach. Thus as they grow they will step out breast-high to meet every wave. A cowering child would never live to raise another. Yet for all the care, the love that surrounds the little ones, danger lies on the horizon, waiting a fresh turn of every tide.

Summers came and went, sliding down the golden skies of autumn. Winters bleached colour from the world, shading everything in greys, laying rimes of white along the rocks below the cliff. But with every year spring returned, light strengthened and renewed, and in the sleeping cave proud mothers tucked their new infants up against their milk-warm breasts.

The days came when the last light of the setting Star pried even into the recesses of the cave. The longest day was near, time of pride and parting. Evening lingered long over the beach and when feeding time was done, before the dusk began to chill, the folk drank the last of the Day Star's light, and watched the children as they played. Useless boys dived, calling and laughing, beyond the breaking waves. Girls ran chattering among the womenfolk, or played their intricate games with shells, laying out their pieces, hoping to complete the pattern before darkness came and the tide returned to scatter their design.

Borry and little Vereen, solemn faces framed by their swinging hair, played turn and turn about. Colours, texture, shape and size all had meaning in their game, which grew and spread in regular shapes and spirals on

42

the firm sand. There would be no winner — it was not a game of strength and the folk have scant counting skills — but the design itself was for them completeness and satisfaction.

"Ah Borry! How were you hiding that?"

A sharp razor shell, purple dark in its curves, emphasised a darting line of lighter shards.

"I've made a jaw bone! See? there are the gleaming teeth and here you should make ..."

It was never completed. On hasty dashing feet the boys stumbled by, kicking up the shells thrashing the air with long gut-lines of weed. Borry wailed and hid her eyes, then ran weeping into Larra's arms to cry her disappointment out.

Vereen stumped patiently down the beach, kicked at the ribbed sand, then wandered ankle-deep in water watching the play of light on the bubbles of foam that swept around her feet, hiding then showing her tiny curled toes. When she stood still and wriggled her toes they sank into the sand and the waves came and weighed the sand on her until she felt she could never pull herself free of the clinging beach ... but out her foot came with a satisfying glop! And while she stood, hands on her dimpled knees, water filled the hole as if it had never been. She ran on, stamping on the water to see the lacy drops fly up, then with arms outstretched ran into the welcoming sea. Ducking under a breaking wave she bounced to the surface once again. On the wave tops she twisted and turned, her fingertips beckoning up bright drops to flash in the level light of the sinking sun. This water was a friend that she had never learned to fear.

The sea is unaffected: it knows simply its own occasions. At that moment, far off in the depths, a movement in some central trench set mud slowly falling, slid plates of ocean floor apart and moved the waters, as when the first whale breached in the creation's dawn. Far off from the folk a wave was made, a master wave, heavy in its power. Moving through the miles of spreading water it lessened and lost weight, but still it came on. It swept the rocks in that sun-drenched moment, rising up the cove, swinging the listless weeds, then took up the child and threw her down. Among the excited cries of the folk at the wave's fringe she was lost in silence, down in the deep before she could draw a breath. Rolled and pounded about, her bruised and sodden form was not released to the light for long moments. It was Idranil, her brother, who lifted up the floating, lifeless remains: Vereen was gone.

A sigh swelled to a groan as the folk moved aside to open a passage for the strong swimmer and his burden. Ready tears sprang in their eyes, and the oldest shook their heads in sorrow. A life, still fresh and young, had been taken. This was not the accustomed way. An old, completed life could be swept away, in sleep perhaps, overnight, or on a halting breath in a cold midwinter. That was a necessary step. But this, this was hard to bear. Even so her passing would not go unmarked: there were the ceremonies to perform. After whispers of consultation gnarled grandsires led the way, directing, advising. Little Vereen, lost now and cut off from their love, must be settled back into the sway of the waves.

Swimming upright in the water the folk took her body away over the sea, beyond the reach of the daily tides. The womenfolk sang songs of farewell, holding out their arms, their hair floating around them; men bore the little body with only fingertip touch, mourning deep in their throats, catching up and filling the parting songs with harmonies. Into the night they swam, down a long moon path until at last the place was reached. Long sea streams would carry her now, down and down into the womb of the world.

"We are born out of the water carried in women, so it is right that we go back to water borne by men." The old grandsire on the beach was pleased with the turn of the words. "Born out of water," he repeated. "Borne back by men. So it must be. This is the tide of our lives which we cannot resist — birth to death, birth to death."

He raised his withered old arms and swung them in an empty gesture until they fell useless into his lap once more. He bent his head and gazed at the upturned palms.

"All our lives we follow tides and drifts, forces we cannot see," he whispered. "We can never know where the current comes from, nor where it will bear us to. It may bring plenty leaving us with full bowls and glad bellies, or take away everything we have and make our hearts hollow. But no matter how we may long for it the same tide will never bring back what it has taken. And if a tide brings us sadness it cannot be washed away on the ebb." He looked up at the earnest faces of the folk gathered on the rocks around him. "All this, my people, is the pattern of our life. The waters about us move in their patterned, pre- ordained way: the very stars on the surface of the skies have their ordered movements to perform, and so do we. We cannot see the pattern, any more than one drop in that ocean can see the meaning of the Great Stream which brought it here. As we tumble into dark troughs, with no glimpse of the future or the past, it is easy to despair." He shook his head. "To despair," he sighed again.

"Must we be always swept on, against our will?" a voice asked out of the pre-dawn dark.

"Our will?" The old one was angry. "Our will? What is our will if not to comply with the pattern, to live best that which we are, fulfilling to the limit of our being the fate which is ours — to be the Folk of the Sea. Do the seals cry out against fate, or the birds tell the wind their will? May whales wander from their solemn journeys in the deeps and still survive? It is their will to be themselves: and so they are." In his passion he set his hands upon his thighs, leaned forward, head jutting.

"And if we cannot find ourselves?" cried Idranil. "What then?"

"It is for that search alone that you will spend your youth in venturing, my son. Not to find the limits of the eternal ice, not to waste your strength in search of warmer waters. Though you may follow the whale or yearn for wings on the wind it is your own self that you will come to know. And then you will return. Or die."

45

Tiring, the old one shifted his bony hams on the rock and bent his head upon his knees. It was over, but no-one was ready yet to lose this moment in sleep. In the world-awareness that sudden sadness brings, they wanted somehow to piece together a truth which would bring comfort.

"A story, Fridonay!" they called. "Tell us an adventure!" And, lenient as always to their wishes, the little man came forward in the growing light and began in measured tones to tell a tale for children:

In early times, when the seas were warm and the folk lived thick as smelt in the sea, their limbs silver and bronze, then there lived a boy of the folk, Balidur, who was an urchin, full of a fine mischief.

This boy Balidur was sturdy and straight-limbed and his face was open and his eyes full of light. He was a boy, honest and fair in deed, who never knew worry or care, but as a little one grew, close and comforted, strong at his mother's side. Gentle he was and tender, guiding the steps of little ones but never heeding the words of the old: for within him lived an imp who wanted to laugh at all that he should have held good.

The old ones spoke to Balidur, his nan and the grandsires saying, "Never hurt the birds, our friends. Never give them cause to fear us." But at this Balidur laughed:

"Why should they fear us?" he cried. "They can lie on the wind when we are tied to the waves. Let them rather learn to listen to us, who sing daily with more meaning than any bird, who cries his single song on the wind and then it is heard no more."

So he laughed and would not see what the grandsires wanted to tell him, that we are all equal under the same light. And the nans told him "Love all creatures, Balidur, for we are all spawn of the Day Star". But he

46

would not heed them, and saw in all the seas only matter for laughter and fun.

On the beach of his borning he came one day upon a large white bird. Afraid and forgotten was that bird, and white in every feather as a flake of snow. But Balidur, full of evil and fun, wanted to spoil the bird and took in his hands black lumps of clay. While the bird looked sadly on him Balidur held firm its feet, and while it could not fly spread black earth upon its wings thinking to make it heavy as he was, to make it cling to land and never more venture over the water. But the bird, staring sadly on him all the while, folded its mud-heavy feathers to flight and lifted away from Balidur, and the beach and from the folk entirely. No-one saw it more for the bird knew shame with its mud-dark wings; and fear also, for no longer could he hide when on the snowy wastes of the north.

But Balidur cared nothing for the bird he had harmed in his youth. With his straight limbs and his charm he went on to hurt others, members of the folk, even the maids of his own borning, until none would be his close companion.

"Leave us!" said the grandsires. "Go now on your venture, for here you hurt every one you touch, and our hearts are blackened by you, even as you blackened the bird in the time of your childhood."

Then Balidur went venturing, and far he swam and wide, proud in his head and too strong in his heart for any maid of the folk to hold him. So swimming he went due north, to try his pride on the ice.

Cold is the sea of the north waters, cold and hard. Ice fingers hold that sea and stretch out, unforgiving, to capture any who linger after Equinox. Yet Balidur lingered. He had seen no bear, the laughing lights had eluded him as they do so many who venture north in pride. Seals slipped away as he approached, and no birds came.

At last the narrow grip of winter stretched across the snow, and wind from the Ultimate North scoured its surface. White drops were everywhere, up, down, *before and behind, wherever he turned Balidur saw no surface any more, no sea, no snow, no sky. All, all was white.*

That white of the Ultimate North is all light. It is every light you ever saw, and it pierces the eyes as a beach grit would, ending all senses. In a white blindness Balidur circled, knowing no sense of homeward, lost and alone.

Then came the Bannern, friend of the folk. Flying ahead of him Balidur saw the dark mud wing that he himself had made. But our bird held no hurt for him. Steady he flew, turning and returning until Balidur set after him. Then steady and slow he led the white-blind boy out of the snow, back to the sea, and gave him again to the waves, his home.

"Go with the water," he whispered to the youth. And Balidur came home. Great the joy at that late return. Full the thanksgiving of mother and sister, thanks to the Bannern, whom none will ever harm again. Remember the Bannern, friend of the folk.

The old story, a well known part of childhood, comforted them all, and they smiled and nodded, watching the story teller, their own lips framing his words.

Distressed Idranil closed his mind: sameness was not what he wanted. The old one's talk of a patterned existence in which to lose one's will had irritated him. It was always the religion of the old, that everything was pre-ordained: this way they could bear to look back on their past and feel that there was no other life they could have lived than the one they had. "So soon to leave it all behind, it must be comfortable for the old man," thought Idranil, "to feel that he has successfully completed his pattern. But what lies ahead for the young folk, how can he expect them to accept his doctrine? At every step there is a choice, so how are we to be guided?"

He walked slowly away across the damp sand, worrying and dragging at his own thoughts as small waves worry at a rock, trying to find a firm base or topple everything down. Soon Seiglid joined him. Idranil turned away his head:

"I go on today's tide." It was his usual forthright way, to speak out his immediate thought and to act on the instant. "To be a listener here is more than I can stand any longer. My little sister's death means more to me than a wind pattern on the ocean, and yet that old grandsire may maunder along, passing us the droppings from his constipated mind, and I am too young even to hiss at him. Whatever else I gain on this venture there will be self-respect."

"Where will you go?"

"North again. I've always planned that. I have this longing to see the White Bear once more." He said this with a shy sideways look.

"Old Akpotok?" Seiglid was startled. "But you know: 'One blow from his claw and you'll be no more'. Aren't you afraid after all you've been told?"

"I? Oh yes, even I tremble, I promise you! But I would like to see him all the same. And I would like to swim again below the white underside of an iceberg, to go to the herring beds and see the Bluebacks in their thousands flashing silver in the sunlight. The Snow People, too — there's a mystery. How would it be to spend a winter with them inside their little round huts of snow?"

"Seriously? You would go among men?"

"Perhaps the Snow People are not really men. In the stories they seem like us."

"What, with a face as wide as a walrus's and great flaring nostrils!"

"No, no, be serious," Idranil's sudden laugh was a cough of bitter amusement. "All men are not alike, any more than we of the folk are. I would like to meet them, see how they live, perhaps have one of their women."

49

He glanced speculatively at Seiglid. "And you? What will you do?"

Seiglid stepped gravely aside, giving himself time to think as he selected a smooth flat stone and tossed it across the tranquil waves that lapped the shore under a solemn grey sky. His eyes watched his companion's face.

"I search," he said. "This beach is often a lonely mooring to me: somewhere, beyond the horizon, I hope to find another, warmer, thronged with folk. Our own sea folk I mean, our family and kin. I will have no more of men. Be guided by me my friend, no good will come of your desires."

He had never spoken so before. His own venture among men so many years ago had brought him no harm. Indeed, his son, manchild, stood tall on the beach, ready now for venturing, indistinguishable from the youths of his borning. There was no threat there. And others of his getting were playing now on the sand. Seiglid began to sense the time when he would welcome old age, would settle in peace and remain idle on the shore, telling his tales, repeating the old mottoes.

But Idranil still bent before the abrasive force of fame, pushing himself further in every journeying to find and know the people who fascinated him, shaping himself for legend.

Yet year by year they eluded him, for he would not dare to face their busy settlements, the throb and scurry of their working summer lives. And could not brave the terrible winters to find their snow-rounded homes. He had trod their lands, sniffed out their hunting sites, but had never caught up with the people he was seeking. He must wait, he believed, for the season to be complete. In fact, in his ambition, he was to break their pattern when he found them as surely as if he had stamped in a child's game of shells.

Chapter Four
Idranil and the Snow People

When at last Idranil saw them, suddenly on the ridge above him, he knew that they had been there for some time, watching him. He had been aware, perhaps, of their attention and had been performing for them. However it was, he stood now gazing upward, his hands still full of flowers, shyly smiling, welcoming the newcomers in whose land he was the stranger.

They remained unmoving. Laughing at himself, at the strange sight that he made bedecked so with flowers in his hair, around his ears, and in the rough hair of his chest, Idranil strolled slowly forward, lifting his hands to them, empty palms upward. The short-stemmed flowerlets tumbled to the ground around him. The slope was hard damp earth and loose stones yet Idranil forced himself, walking lightly, to appear carefree. He was afraid, but must not frighten his visitors.

The people watching him might have been made of stone; their faces expressing nothing, their eyes bright but pebble-hard. They were a carved part of the hillside, watching in terror the weird figure walking up to them.

It was a child who broke the tension, wailing in anguish into the skirt of his mother's long fur parka. She snatched him up, clamping her open hand on his face, her own eyes wide with fright. Idranil called out lightly, gaily:

"Don't be afraid little one. I won't harm you!"

At his voice any courage that the women and

51

children might have pretended to deserted them completely and they fled out of sight down the other side of the ridge. One old man remained. Arms held out in unmistakable welcome he called to Idranil in his own staccato language, his voice deep, charged it seemed with a sense of ritual and circumstance. If Idranil could only have understood what was said then he would have avoided pain later. His distress need never have been.

As it was he came closer, looking with a calm trust into the old man's face. It was a face puckered and creased by the years, dark eyes glittering in the radiating lines. He spoke slowly, clearly, smiling. He had no front teeth. A gesture of his head set his thick hair swinging. He seemed to indicate something which was to be seen behind and below him. He grinned again and again, repeating his welcome. Idranil stepped forward and looking down saw for the first time the summer camp in the next quiet bay.

It was not surprising that he had missed the little family settlement. The three tents were all strung together of animal hides, the browns and greys exactly copying the drab shades of the landscape behind them. Everything, the tents, the land, the people themselves, had a rubbed, used look alien to Idranil who, like all silkies loved cleanliness and the brightness and sparkle left fresh by moving waters. But these were the people he had sought in every venture he had made and he was determined not to turn away yet.

Whatever their initial fear had been the people were quickly reassured by the old man's words and he seemed by his tone and his gestures to imply that Idranil was his own creation brought out of nowhere to delight his family. Rapidly the welcome took on a festive air: food and drink were brought and offered to the visitor. Soon everyone was squatting round him smiling, nodding and eating. Special titbits were held out for his pleasure and Idranil ate the food which the Snow People eat.

Whenever Idranil looked back at his early time with

the Snow People he found it difficult to order or contain his memories for he could not then speak with the people nor understand their meaning. It was, as far as he could judge, not long after the time of the longest day, but so close was he to the Ultimate North that the day never ended and although the gleaming Star was tempted toward the horizon it never disappeared from sight. For this reason the people sleep only when they feel the need and the rhythm of day and night which the sea folk know and honour was lost to Idranil, who found himself confused and sometimes ill at ease. The food he was given distressed him also since he could not know what he was eating and felt at first a distaste for the red blood. In time however both of these difficulties faded, and he spent his time working to learn the speech of the Snow People so that he could begin to know them.

The women were patient and kind, nodding and smiling at his efforts and mistakes while they worked. Their work was endless, cleaning and drying skins of a creature Idranil did not know, the creature they called *tukto*. *Tukto* was everything to the people — their home all summer, their food and their protection from cold and the hard ground. One of the first presents the people gave to Idranil was foot-wear made of *tukto*: a pair of boots to save his tender feet. He wore them proudly, stamping confident on the hard earth, walking dry through boggy grasses. When he swam he found them useless, for they filled and sank so that he must dive for them, but he knew in his heart and mind that while it is for Sea Folk to understand the sea, here among the Snow People he would try only to know their world.

Twilight came and the nights grew rapidly. Idranil knew that soon he must leave: cold fogs clung to the waves and drifted over the land, the trickles of melted snow which wandered across the earth were disappearing and soon the night-time must equal the day. It was the end of venturing and time to turn toward the home beaches. When he spoke of this to the people

Idranil was confused by their replies. Everyone was calling on him to stay, their emotions were strong, written in tears upon their cheeks and he found it hard not to weep with them, yet promising to return he remained firm for home and his own folk.

Then during a lengthening night-time, as he lay in the fur of *tukto* that he had chosen as his own sleeping place Idranil felt a woman of the people slip into the furs beside him. She was naked and smooth to touch.

The girl pressed against him, she lay her hand across his heart. Easing herself upward, her breast against his shoulder, she pressed her warm mouth to his ear whispering and tickling him with her plea:

"Stay with us, *kabluna*. Stay, Netchilingmio," she murmured, using their name for him, "and make us happy. Make me happy, Netchilingmio. Make me happy."

Her warmth overwhelmed him. The night was long and they lay content under the covers. When at last he drew his body from her Idranil had surrendered. He would stay and winter with the people of the snow.

Night after night Idranil lay with the girl Aputna, and during the day she often stayed at his side. She made him a parka of *tukto* with a white fringed hood, and coverings for his legs from fur of Akpotok, the White Bear. His feet in their overshoes were warmly stuffed about with grass which Aputna dried for him each day for his comfort. To have a woman among the Snow People is to have a wife, one who cares at all times for her man, one who will if need be die so that he can live. These were the promises she made to him, under the coverings of *tukto*, when the oil lamp warmed the black dark of the tent, and with her promises and her care little Aputna drew Idranil closer to her and taught him love.

Ice began to grow on still waters and frost lay day-long in the shadows. Then the wind came.

It threw the clouds headlong across the sky and ripped the still mists off the headlands. The waters of the fjord fled before the wind and hurtled about the once quiet bay, climbing up the beach in confusion. The men hauled their big umiat up from the water's edge and folded away their smaller kayaks. Racing overhead the wind dragged winter across the land and the waters.

In the tent at night the wind searched for Idranil, causing him to sink more deeply into his furry bed. He heard in its roaring cry a voice chastising him:

"Idranil, you have left the sea, you are mine now. You are mine, you have no waves to hide in ten feet down. You are on the land, Idranil, you lie always on the surface, you have nowhere to hide. You are mine, mine, mine."

The voice fell to a whisper and Idranil lay deep in his furs, trembling. Then with a shout the wind was back again, clapping the hide walls of the tent, strumming the guys and sifting a fine drift of snow across the sleeping people. The walls of the tent were alive, leaping and shouting, drumming louder and louder. They cracked forward and back with a noise like a whip snap, then with a rasping cry the hide split from top to bottom.

Instant black night filled the sleeping space as the lamp was hurled away by the impatient wind. Groaning the tent filled, lifted and fled before the baying gale. The people snatched helplessly, impeded by their furs in which they slept naked. The white ghosts of the hairless men leapt here and there capturing their lives once more. Women lamented and babies screamed. Dogs joined the uproar snarling and biting at the end of their tethers. The wind screamed upon them, jubilant, and raced up among the stars.

Half unrolled from his *tukto* fur Idranil scrabbled with his fingers at the bare ground. When he raised his head the wind ripped at his cheeks, pummelling his face as it had fought the tent. Grit, snow and small pebbles flew against his head and shoulders. Sobbing with fear Idranil tugged at the fur, dragged it over his head, rolled it about his body. The wind sidled beneath him, pressed against his back, deafened him with its clatter and shout. Deep in his own darkness Idranil groaned aloud, gritting his teeth against fear. His bones

55

cramped with cold, his head aching at the insistent noise, he longed for quiet deeps, for the long wave his home.

Slowly the reluctant morning came, the distant east bright brittle yellow against the dark land and the black clouds overhead. With daylight the wind dropped and silently the snow began to fall. In the few hours of daylight the people gathered up their scattered camp. A meagre shelter was made and, as the fall deepened, snow was piled against the walls. With the coming of the snow the cold was not so brutal and the old people laughed with joy and cackled to Idranil of the comforts of winter.

The snow houses were built in the lee of a rock ledge above the rim of the icy sea. They were strong and compact, each sheltering five or six. A tunnel under the snow was the entrance, curtained inside with *tukto*. On a sleeping ledge at the far side was the communal bed of furs. A single oil lamp burned continuously in the house, warming the people, thawing their food and lighting the constant darkness of the long winter night. Here they sat, ate, sang, slept, passing the leisure time of winter in comfort and gaiety. Work was at an end, only pleasure lay ahead for the family who had a good stock of food and fat laid in.

Idranil joined in their singing, weaving through their chants the lilting songs of the silkies. Songs of the long wave that he loved, and of the freedom of the sea. At their request he told them in their own tongue of the liquid light of the shallows and the dark blue of the deeps. He described the racing Blueback shoals shining under the waves and the glittering krill that swing and sway below the moonlit surface. He told them tales of the venturing men of the Sea Folk, of the laughing lights that led them northward, of his own earnest search. When they asked him about the seals he sang their mournful song, and he told the children's story of the Bannern, friend of the folk.

With snow covering the ground outside, smoothing out the rocks and wrinkles, travel was possible once more. Friends arrived, their sleds packed tight with old people and children. Brothers and cousins met once more and round the cosy oil lamp damp clothing was thrown aside and happy people told their stories of the summer and its labour, of trading and of hunting. Outside the wind tugged fretfully at the falling snow, whipping it this way and that, piling unnecessary drifts then shifting them again. Within their houses the Snow People stood up to dance and lay down to laugh and love. The best of the year had come.

But for Idranil the menace of the wind was as real as ever. Whenever he went outside for welcome or farewell he felt its presence, screaming across the empty white darkness from the Ultimate North. The fingers of the wind could search him out wherever he lay and in the sweaty heat of the sleeping snow house he felt the mocking stroke of fear between his shoulder blades and shivered and grew chill, even in the arms of his loving Aputna.

She laughed at his fears: yet he noticed that she was not immune when her father was late in returning. With his dogs and sled he had been visiting his brother's wife's family and when the time came for his return a blizzard filled the air with blinding white.

"He will wait till the wind dies", she smiled, to hide her fear.

"The wind cannot die," Idranil muttered. "It only waits."

But he did not know why.

After the storm the landscape was changed once more. The drifts which had been familiar took on new shapes, and the inner ice was scattered and broken along the beach. Out over the fjord the sea ice creaked and snapped as it settled into new formations. Idranil gazed sadly through the twilight, longing for the movement of light on restless waters.

Then the light was gone completely. Total dark lay on land and ice. Journeys were over unless the moon was seen; when clouds hid her face the whole world was no bigger than a lantern glow. Fear waited for Idranil in the surrounding dark and he felt his body weakening as he cowered inactive on the sleeping shelf. When the people sang to the loud bang of drums he nodded and smiled: in the silences he heard the slow sobbing songs of the silkies. The dark was his dread, and out of the dark leapt the wind.

The beginning of light in the morning sky brought no relief to Idranil, although with the rest of the people he stood in the trampled snow between the houses and lifted his face toward the hidden Star. As the light grew he was told he must join the men: a new kind of hunting was about to begin.

It seemed that, against their usual custom, the people were going out to hunt on the sea ice. Their usual prey, the *tukto*, lived inland; it was not for him that they were preparing their weapons. The talk was of a sea creature, the name unknown to Idranil, or possibly never spoken. The hunters' eyes slid toward him as they talked and muttered. With smiles and nods they encouraged him.

"We go out to the sea. We will take you back where you came from, Netchilingmio."

"You will not know your sea now, it has become so hard."

Yet when they had moved out over the tumbled ice of the tide crack Idranil felt a thrill of recognition. Where the snow was blown back and the ice lay clear and clean it was as if he walked on the solid ripples of an evening calm.

He had little time for memories: the sleds rushed forward, the men ran over the wind-blown snow shouting and cracking their whips over the lead dogs. As Idranil could not keep up the pace Piautok, one of Aputna's brothers, waited for him and tucked him warmly onto the sled under a *tukto* cover. Under the twilight sky they raced along the fjord, ice particles glistening in the air about them. Then one by one the other men spread out over the ice calling farewells as they went and asking for good luck in their hunt.

Idranil and Piautok curved away across the ice until suddenly with a word of command he halted his dogs. Even on the bare ice the sled dogs could find shelter: after a rapid drink of snow they curled under their own tails to wait. Piautok had found a dark water hole in the thick ice, shrouded with damp snow. Approaching quietly he gently slid a long shaft of white ivory down into the water below. Then he too squatted down and waited, turning from time to time to flash a delighted grin at Idranil, useless on the sled.

Silently, alert to the faintest signal, Piatok stood up, his spear held above his head, his eyes never leaving the snow hole and its tell-tale shaft. A sudden jerk above meant movement below and Piautok's spear flew downward. In moments he was struggling to drag a dark glistening body through the hole. Idranil stood up in horror. It was a seal.

The seal lay dead on the snow, sea water glistening on her smooth sides. Idranil reached out to touch her but already the rime was forming as body heat died and the merciless wind laid its hand upon her. Idranil felt tears rise in his eyes at the memory of her gentle grace now gone, and he hid his face in his hands to escape the prying wind. Piautok clapped him gleefully on the shoulder.

"We will do well my Netchilingmio. See the one we have caught. Many more of your people will follow."

"My people? Why do you say that?" Idranil felt a chill of apprehension around his heart. True the seals were dear to him, as to all the folk, and his name linked him closer to them. He looked down again at the stiffening corpse beside him. He had never seen such beautiful markings: body silver-grey, head, shoulders and sides dark with a pattern which seemed to carry some message, if he could only understand.

"What do you mean? What do you know of my people?"

But Piautok had turned again, poised above the breathing hole, waiting for another peaceful, unsuspicious creature to surrender to his spear. Idranil leapt forward snatching at the wand as a warning but Piautok was too quick and with straining muscles pulled out another streamlined body to hump onto the snow beside the first. In a rage of pity and distress Idranil punched and pummelled the man at his work until Piautok gravely held him still, then placed him firmly on the sled and strapped him down with a dog's harness.

There was no more luck that afternoon and in the heavy darkness they made their way back across the ice guided by lanterns hung up at the settlement. Soon above the rushing of the sled Idranil heard the triumphant cries of the other hunters. Then the wind picked up their voices and roared joyfully at their success. Idranil crouched miserably on the sled and covered his ears. The derisive wind sang and shouted to him, plucking at his clothes and clapping the covers about with glee.

When the men were to go out again they came to Idranil with troubled eyes.

"Come with us Netchilingmio," they pleaded. "Bring us luck once again."

"How can I bring you luck?" he replied, "when I do not wish you to kill the *ranarn*?" He used the name the folk use, which the people did not understand.

Then they began to explain to him.

"You are Netchilingmio. You live among those people. You are the *angagok* of the Netchilingmiut and they must obey you. Where you go surely your people will always follow as they did in our first hunt."
Idranil shook his head. They were using words he did not know and he could not make their meaning clear in his mind.

"What do they call me?" he asked Aputna in the night. "What do they expect me to do?"

"They call you by your name," she replied. "The creatures they caught, the *netchil*, they live in the sea even as you did. You are Netchilingmio."

She spoke the name clearly, slowly, and at last he understood: Man of the Seals. It was true, it was his own name in the language of his folk. How had these people known it? And what did it mean to them?

"Our *angagok* gave you that name when you came to our shores. He knew that even as you had come here, so would many of your people. We abandoned the lands where *tukto* is to be found once you had come among us. Now our hunters will be successful among the seals."

"That is foolishness, and you a fool to repeat such nonsense." Idranil flung away from her. The snow house vibrated with the renewed strumming of the wind.

For days the wind blew, angry and impatient.

"It will wipe everything away", thought Idranil sadly, "but the wind cannot take this thought from the minds of the people. They truly believe that I bring seals to them and I cannot prevent it."

"Do not grieve for the Netchilingmiut," the men said earnestly. "With these skins we can win many comforts."

"We do not have to work these skins as we do the *tukto*," said the women. "Once they are clean the men will take them to the *kablunait*, the men with big ears, who will give us sharper knives, longer blades. We will have flour to cook again, and many comforts."

"Who are these big-ears?" asked Idranil. "Why must they have seal skins?"

"That I do not know," Piautok told him. "In the hut they collect these skins and in their iron boats they carry them away. They hunt among the ice floes south of here and carry away the seal pups in their thousands. How anyone can use so much fur I do not understand."

"Perhaps they use the oil to light their vast settlements."

"There is little oil in a seal pup. I do not think it can be that."

"While they take so many young ones there are fewer seals here for us. But they do not care how we live."

61

So the men discussed the strangers, the landsmen, shaking their heads in bewilderment at their excesses.

"I can understand," said Idranil at last, "how you make your lives here in the snow. These big ears I do not understand." And he puzzled often in the night, trying to fit his mind to a problem no-one can make clear.

Across the crusted snow came the wind, lifting the ice crystals and sending them scattering across the land. Harsh, abrasive, the blown ice grit scoured the land leaving nothing for the people. From the beginning of time the wind had blown, tearing away comfort, ripping up everything the people had made, burying them without trace under its trailing blanket of snow. Beneath the snow there was shelter, but the wind lifted the covers once more and hurled its burden on, promising and threatening in turns, subjecting the snow and its people to a relentless caprice. In such a bitter world the Snow People had to find warmth where they could. Idranil did not grudge them the seals, though he sickened at slaughter. He could not believe with them that his presence persuaded the seals. The creatures lived out their lives too, and part of their life was to be hunted: if they were wary they would survive, if they came to the breathing hole where Piautok waited they would surely die. This is the bitter truth of their way of life under the waves, under the ice.

The men were waiting to hunt again, and Idranil was willing to go with them, but still the blizzard hurled around the snow houses, blurring sight.

"Does the wind never stop!" cried Idranil, despairing.

"Angagok can stop the wind," one man affirmed. "He has the way."

Startled Idranil and the younger men turned to look at the ancient figure huddled in furs on the sleeping ledge. It was the same who had first welcomed Idranil into the homes of the Snow People.

It was a devout mystery which the old one acted out. With an antique fur pulled over his head he resembled a weird creature of the wild. In one hand he held a short, smooth piece of wood, in the other a flat drum. On the grey and beaten snow between the houses he began to dance; and brittle bones tied about his legs clattered to his stamping, and his weathered old voice was whipped away into the wind. Wind and voice became one, rising and falling in a wild chorus. The clap and snap of the drum was the batting of the hide tent walls, the sigh and moan of the stamping watchers echoed the tune of the wind playing across an empty pot. The rattle of the dry bones mingled with the patter of ice particles hurled across wastes of frozen snow. Snowflakes passed to and fro across the darkness before Idranil's eyes, the song mounted in frenzy until his head rang, shapes came and went, indistinct, outlines seen through water. The snow houses rippled and ran to the horizon. The song sank to a murmur and grew sly and evil. Then came a shout, a scream of pain. Every man hurled his spear into the wind, the women crouched at the mouths of the snow houses and battered the air about them.

Who screamed? Who saw the wind die? But there it lay beneath their feet. In the stillness the snow fell smoothly. In the silence of the calm night air the stars pricked the sky. The people walked back dazed to their houses, none looked in another's face in the clear yellow moonlight.

After sleeping the hunters made ready. Dogs clamoured in harness and the hunt moved out once more over the now quiet ice. The light was stronger now, in a few days the Day Star would break free of the horizon. Where it lay concealed the sky paled from grey to blue to a glowing gold and gold-flecked little clouds flew low in the sky. The air was still and the ice gleamed in the light. In places pressure ridges threw long shadows toward the racing sleds. The light picked out the sculptured waves and troughs of the frozen snow and everywhere was a tingling beauty which delighted Idranil's heart. Against all belief the people had vanquished the wind. They were his friends, nothing was too good for such valiant friends.

Once more Piautok and the others crouched at the breathing holes. Now Idranil had no thought of halting them for deep inside he felt a power which he had never known before. The people were right: he could call the seals.

Standing on the solid ice Idranil stretched out his hands over the surface, he lifted his face to the light horizon and he began to sing. Love was in that song, and death. Love for the seals, for their strength, their flowing beauty under the wave; and death that waited for them above the ice, where their bodies were clumsy with weight.

Idranil sang, and all his longing for his own folk was in that song. Its sobbing cadences echoed to the high black cliffs along the shore and in the empty brightness of the shining air his song took shape. The flowing notes curved and swam before him and he saw their power. The song throbbed within him, pulsed in his head, vibrated through his finger tips and pounded down through his feet, down into the ice, down into the water below. And the seals heard. And the seals came.

One after another they flocked to the breathing hole, urged by the trembling arms of the men they seemed to leap from the water to the land. There came no pause, no rest, and the song flowed on about them. Over the battered, blood-stained snow the song flowed; Idranil, blinded by his power, sang unseeing, unending, calling the seals. Into the undulating call of his song he wove the seal song of the islands and the haunting cry swept across the ice, irresistible, until the night came.

It was full dark when, by lantern light, the men began to load the sleds with their catch. Weary, they could not lift the seals alone and each had to help another until the heaped-up load was complete. The dogs struggled to grip the icy snow but the load was too great; they fell and slid, barking and snapping at one another in frustrated rage.

"We cannot return with so many," said Piautok. "We must make a cache."

After more delay the dead seals were piled again, all

64

anyhow on the messed snow. They made a huge dark boulder against the ice. With less of the heavy bodies to haul the sleds were able to move at last and the men started back. Out of the darkness a little snow began to fall.

Looking back, the dark outline of the piled seals soon became lost under the dusting snow.

"We will know the place," said the men sturdily.

The way ahead dimmed in the whiteness, the soft flakes flying in every direction. Up and sideways they flew in confusion. The dizzying flakes brought a strange lassitude to the men who stumbled wearily along beside the dogs. One man fell and his heavily laden sled hit him. With his leg broken he had to be piled above the seals and the pace was slowed again. Secretly, shiftily, the wind began to rise.

"We have gone too far," one man gasped, "We have passed the houses."

"No, it is farther yet."

They went on in fear. The wind in its revenge was losing them in the blizzard.

At last every man agreed: the settlement was behind them now and their way was lost. The only course was to stop and make camp.

As the night lengthened cold crept into the bivouac. The unconquered wind rushed in and away, laying ice on the eyelids, sealing mouth and nose. Desperately the men fought against sleep, shaking their heads until the icicles clinked around their hoods. Utter despair gripped Idranil, weakened he lay behind the men and waited for death. He knew now what he had done and life, once so dear to him, had become a burden. If there was power in his song he had no right to use it for destruction. In his madness he had delayed his friends with such excess that this was to be the end of it: the men were dying and out on the ice a useless heap of dead flesh was all that remained of creatures who yesterday had the freedom of the seas. And the wind yet blew, derisive of the silly play of yesterday. Against the wind, elemental from the beginning of the world, there

65

was no power on the earth or in the air, and the only haven was below the sea.

. As light crept back across the sky Idranil rose up, stepped past the frozen forms of his companions and walked out onto the ice. In the blizzard and the darkness the men had travelled in a wide circle which led away from the settlement, away to where the fjord widened out of sight. Far away, faintly, Idranil sensed the open sea. Slowly he turned and faced their icy gaze.

"The wind is the only enemy. Only the wind has power and you should fear it, for the wind will never die."

Then he went out over the ice, walking back toward the distant waves.

Chapter Five
Homecoming

At the time of the Equinox the sky drifted down and lay upon the water. Fog. Weightless, yet it flattened the waves. Odourless, it caught in mouth and nostrils, rasping in spite of the damp. It seemed a friend, curling down against shoulders or thighs like a bed companion, yet it was a worse enemy to the Sea Folk than the battle of the gale, more treacherous than shifting currents or a sudden cross-wave. For returning heroes there would be no stars to guide them; for the weary swimmers their only clue would be sounds and scents in the water. Yet the pressure of the Great Stream comes from behind a returning venturer, giving nothing of home.

When morning crept only sluggishly into their sleep and the sour, sunken, rusty smell of the sea fog smothered over mouth and nose, women woke in alarm. Chattering and calling, palms turned up in anxious gestures, they ran wildly stumbling about the beach, trying to find a break, to see the welcome blue. But the sky was no longer high up on the air, it had sunk floundering to pinch at knees and ears with its cold, giving nothing. The cold cloud turned breath to steam, gathered as tiny water drops on hair and eyebrows. Young mothers, their babes but this year's borning, became hoar and grey. Old grandsires coughed and spat, their lungs turned liquid by the vapour.

"Get out to the Point! Feeding must wait! Go out for a warning." The old voice cracked urgently, hollow under the dome of the fog.

The women, even the oldest nans, strode into the even swell of the sea, walking purposefully until mist and water swallowed them.

They swam close together, calling as they did so, keeping contact in their blindness. The currents at the mouth of the cove were subdued by the weight of the cloud but still had to be negotiated with care. The women of the Sea Folk knew this entrance well, as well as any venturer would: they had been taught its vagaries as little children, learning the sea with their born companions. While it was not for them to travel the wide world once they were grown, nevertheless they also had this duty beyond the confines of the cove: many times in muffling fog or blinding rain they had made the Point their lookout to guide the wanderers home.

The Point was a lonely stack which extended beyond the southern cliffs of Sgeir. It stood in deep sea water and was their last bastion. To the north, flatter outcrops hinted at land, showing themselves only at low water. Many an exhausted venturer had swum wearily into the sea wrack of those skerries and rested briefly from his long journey before making the treacherous passage to the home beach at the time when the tilt of the tide could wash him in. But any swimmer who passed to the south might continue for a day and a night before he found another landfall. And then, bone weary, he must face the Great Stream once more and return.

So now the women, their long tresses sinking and rising with the wave, swam to the stack which was to point their heroes home. The sea rode by its base in a long-drawn pattern of rise and fall, a sullen sweep which made it easy to beach on the flat ledges from which the Point grew. The younger mothers crouched and found a foothold, then standing square, before they had even shaken the salt sea from their hair they turned and with encouraging cries, with outstretched arms,

68

fingers catching, they reached into the water for the old nans who were swept in on the next wave to stand arms akimbo, heads thrown back, and drink the welcome air. Then, paddling and splashing, they edged about the rock, their laughter echoing in the enclosing cloud, until they found the safest spot. There they rested, combing out their salt-tangled hair. And there they began to sing.

It is one long song, the Homecoming, of summer warmth with its land smells, and the winter comfort of bodies entwined. It is a song of longing for suckled safety and the promise of surrounding arms. As the women sing it they seem to weave a spell of steadfastness in a changing world, of certainty to strengthen halting steps. And their menfolk, hearing it, are drawn toward the land.

Landsmen in their sea lanes are too far off to hear that song. But some have known it, and in their delight will turn toward its sound. Few then return to tell of what they heard for in their ecstasy they would drive their boats onto the rock, and the maidens of the folk, still singing their wooing song, swim out to receive them and carry them down in gentle arms to their final rest.

Far out on the swell, Callidray, that strong swimmer, heard them, and sinking to swimming depth once more, adjusted his approach. With the turn of the tide he knew the wind would freshen and the last shreds of fog would be torn away. But he seemed also to sense brisker weather behind the wind and hoped, as he dived once more, to be safe inside the cupped hands of the home cave before the storming winds could search him out.

Home time was close and he lessened the distance with dreaming. So many homecomings remembered, so many women giving themselves, in love perhaps, but in excitement too, which he understood. Emotions were heightened as the menfolk came in, the young swimmers feared for, the strong ones now so dear. Callidray had known times, stupid to deny it, when the maidens had fought to be at his side, when he had been

69

forced to choose one or another from a circle of smiling, panting faces. No more now: he, and they, were older. Yet, as he surfaced once more, he bared his teeth in a smile: it was a good time, the return, with the old ones scurrying to comfort and the arms of women soft yet certain to protect. There was one he would look for, Larra, she'd had, he thought, his child. A yearling now, would it bear any semblance of himself? No matter, he'd love it a little for her sake. And love her too. When he rose into the air he heard the singing once again and was tempted to turn southward and seek out Larra herself, before another could be first, but his weary limbs demanded sleep, strong as he was, and he trudged on until cross-currents and surface rills told him the rocks were at hand. Then he surfaced for the last time and calling to get his bearings, he swung into the cove where water lapped quiet at last against the land in a gentle sound of home and of peace, and so he was pitched ashore by a slow rolling wave.

Pebbles clattered under his sea-soft feet and above him on the beach he heard the urgent shushing of the old grandsires as they scowled about, cupped hands to their ears. Soon their dark shapes appeared in the soft whiteness, and Callidray called, naming them. Shrunken now with age the old men clustered about the swimmer, pleading for news of the seas which they had abandoned, trying feebly to give support. Stumbling and awkward on the motionless shore after so many months of sea swell, Callidray laughingly hugged the creaking old frames and slapped the stooped shoulders, never dreaming of his own decrease.

They led him up the beach, scooped out his sleeping place so fresh and clean, and decried the women who were away leaving this hero unfed. But Callidray, laughing still, shook his head at them. Easing into the soft, white sand he fell instantly into sleep and dreamed, as he had waking, of the soft arms of women.

But his sleep was short and brutishly finished: "Wake! Wake, strong one, and swim for the Point!" The old men mopped about him, moaning and wringing their hands, while infants, wondering, sucked their fists to their mouths. They had no idea what to do without their women-folk. Custom had deserted them and they turned helpless toward the younger man's strength.

The saddened autumn evening, freed at the last from fog, glimmered bloodshot on the horizon, but overhead black clouds boiled. A harsh wind scoured the sea though no rain fell, and waves tossed about in confusion.

"The women are not returned, and the wind is rising!"

Callidray nodded, and held the old ones aside with his outstretched arms. Head back he sniffed the wind and sensed its warning of the storm which was biding in the north, waiting for its cue. Swimmers, he saw, must ride the last wave before the light went, or wait out the storm hanging safely over the deeps. Passage into the cove would soon be impossible, but the womenfolk must be secured.

Even as he tested the wind, as he walked to the water's rim, the first heads began to appear. First the old nans, side by side and cackling in relief as the water swung them up the shore. Then a bevy of young maids shepherded by their mothers and aunts. Stronger women, muscled almost like their men, followed this flock, but seeing them safe ashore would have turned again to the waves.

"Where are you going? What new fear calls you?" Callidray strode waist-deep to their side.

"Our sisters stay for us. While we were leaving we heard a cry, and Larra and Sareev remained singing on the rock to guide him in. We have to go back to their aid."

"I too. I'll come with you."

They ducked their heads in thanks then turned to the waves, their dark eyes calm and fearless even though the wild surface swung about them in a zagging lack of pattern and form in which they might be lost forever. Once outside the cove the wind swept away their words, and their hair clung darkly across their faces.

71

Callidray felt he had never known these women before and rejoiced at the heritage of the folk which gave such courage just when it was called for. What mothers his sons had! He tried to give them a shout of praise, but water filled his mouth and nose and he feared that they in their fresh strength might yet have to come to his aid, and so kept quiet.

Once they had gained the Point Callidray and the women joined the two who strained there against the wind trying to see the tired youth whose call they had heard. Tossed by the unruly wind the surface seemed to seethe and rage and among the foam-speckled wave sides it was impossible to make out any solid form. Light was draining rapidly from the sky, colours were bleeding out of the clouds, and still he did not appear.

Then, almost at their sides, it was his outflung arm that they saw, breaking the surface and imploring them. He had come so near, but in the next wave-fall he would be swept on. When they saw his open mouth, his staring eyes before he sank again, they knew that he was done.

As they watched in horror it seemed that the water, in which he could have lain safe, was towed from under him by the towering rock: as if its roots drew in the base of the wave and with it the gasping boy. He was rolled helpless into the dark shadow and above him the wave, unbalanced by the encroaching land, toppled and fell. The crashing surf of that fall thundered in the watchers' ears and Larra cried out, her hands to her face.

"The land will break him!"

Sareev bit her knuckles but could not turn away.

Like a lifeless mass of brown weed they saw the lad lifted again in the safety of the wave, lifted and swept away from the cruel rock. But danger still stood in his path, the tidal surge of the Great Stream must carry him on and the crags still waited to crush him. Without thought Sareev launched herself into the receding wave. In unspoken accord a second woman dived at her side.

"Wait!" cried Callidray, restraining the other women and watching closely under the shadow of the wave's arm. But as one pebble bounces across a pool so they dived in sequence, and their heads and limbs were a chain across the unsteady seas. They rose from their dive directly beneath the drowning youth and raised him in the circle of their arms. He heard their wind-whipped voices encouraging him and drew the darkening air deep into his lungs.

Callidray saw them for a moment, then the wind-raged wave curled over and they were gone. In the rolling interface he searched for them, sensing where they would appear. And so he loosed himself from the rock, let himself be swept away yet remained upright in the wave, feet, arms and eyes searching. For long moments land was lost and his companions hidden under the green swell, then his heel crashed hard, his groping hands caught hair. With his last strength Callidray lay his back against the wave and he pulled. Pulled them all away, away from under that beetling height which, seen against the scudding clouds, seemed to lean forward over them in its eager attempt to crush out their tiny lives. He pulled because life swung there in the balance, and life was all that the youngster had. So he pulled Larra into his arms, lay on his back under the pelter of the waves and pulled. And the women, true to their design, held the young life safe, and the lad was given regularly into the air, and he lived.

In the frothing scurry of the waves how they laughed and gasped at their success! They lay on the wave's broad back as if on the safety of the home beach and they embraced the boy, stroking his cheeks, his hair, his long straight spine.

"Thou art swimmer truly," cried Callidray, stealing the words of the old ones which would welcome him to the beach.

But the youth, his face drawn, only retched and sobbed. So they turned him about and drove him through the foam to find their passage home.

Of that last effort the youth knew nothing, never saw the gaping white teeth that filled the mouth of their shelter, never felt the rip of a tide driven to savage fury by the wind. Entirely spent he rested in the arms of his kinsfolk and by their skill was drawn up into a quiet space between deep rocks on the beach's rim. There, for the first time, they recognised their prize: it was the manchild, Donilid.

"Better to have let him be caught up by the land that longs for him," Callidray shrugged, spurning the broken youth with the side of his foot. But the women denied him, and all together they drew him out of the last spinning of the waves and struggled up the sand with him, up onto the still shore.

"Happy the return!"

"A swimmer thou art, indeed!"

"Had you success in your venture?"

Among the voices on the darkening shingle was one younger, stronger, and Callidray turned away to smile into his beard. It was Perrid, companion of his own borning who spoke the words, Perrid, full-fleshed with rounded, pouting cheeks and soft lips etched pink in his smooth face, the laughter-maker of long ago. Yet as the days passed, and the swimmers strode home, it was clear that now they gave him respect, while Callidray looked in vain for his fellows to wonder at new ways, for of Idranil there was still no sign, and Seiglid would never return again from his fruitless search. And it had to be admitted: Perrid knew his role.

"You are returned," he told the youngsters gravely, "and now you take women of your own. You make, in your ecstasies, new children of the folk. But are you, all honestly, fitted for this? You, Pletrid, who tell of fear when you saw the water-spout? Did you not agree when you went out that the sea would rule you? That fear and danger must be your portion if you are ever to learn, ever to know yourself? Now you have seen with your own eyes what the risk might be. Yes, I see you find that hard, but think my son: would you rather stay here and be master only of these few pebbles? No, don't answer! Think now for next year's venture. And you, our Donilid, how many lives do you feel are worth your

74

safety? So many were risked, child." He held out fingers to count off with a thumb. "Wait out a storm in patience boy, your rash presence has little value to us else."

"I thought I could do it," the man-child muttered.

"Then you thought in pride, boy, and that pride of body's strength is only a weakness. Come near and hear the story of proud Vilidorn, and of the humility he learned at the last."

It was with a murmur of approval that the folk gathered to Perrid's side as he took his place on the Elder Rock: in him the traditions would go on, the old stories like this of the Sea Serpent would continue to be told.

Once in a warm sea time there lived a man of the folk, mighty and strong. Vilidorn was his name. His pebble-hard muscles stood out on giant limbs and his proud head stood high on his sturdy neck. Across his massive shoulders, matted with curling hair, his strength moved in rippling show, and knotted ropes of mighty sinew were his arms. Straddled firmly on his powerful legs, feet rooted in the bedded sand, this man was a rock of fortitude and stubborn will.

A hard man was Vilidorn, and proud. He laughed at the trembling efforts of the folk to topple him, and could hold three adversaries at a time to submission beneath the waters. In wrestling and grappling no-one was his master. It was said his strength outmatched the very waves.

On days of storm, when mountainous breakers roared, it was his habit to defy the sea: standing motionless in one chosen spot he would shout his challenge, his full beard shaking off the spray, his red mouth laughing. Though the waves burst above his head he would not surrender, only with the dying of the storm would he step aside, kicking the last wavelets beneath his heel. Deriding their weakness he left at last and went to venture on the ocean path, calling his challenge across the deeps.

"I am Vilidorn, strongest of the sea folk! None can hold me against my will!"

Fish rushed away beneath him. Sea birds cried, raucous, above his head.

"Be afraid!" they seemed to say. "Beware, for one may come from the darkest cavern of the deep, whose strength you cannot guess!"

Vilidorn sensed the awesome fall beneath him, and he tried in ever farther dives to sound the creatures of the deep with his challenge.

"I am Vilidorn and you cannot hold me! I do not fear your year-long dark."

So then the serpent rose to the surface, its shiny length thrashing the surface, searching for Vilidorn.

The looping body pulsed over Vilidorn's flesh, huge suckers clung to his skin, and now he felt it draw him down. Around him its many folds throbbed and flailed as Vilidorn braced his legs and arms to force aside the pressing coils. Around his ribs one squeezing circle lay, another turned and knotted about his legs. With panic strength he ripped the slapping tail from his neck and felt the tearing of his own flesh in those thousand sucking mouths. The water clouded before him and through the murk he saw the serpent's glowing eyes and grasping beak.

With that strength which was once his pride now dying to hollows in his arms and legs yet Vilidorn struggled on to halt his enemy. Blood from his many wounds swirled in the sea about him, like shadowy serpents trailing out his death. And yet he fiercely placed his foot against that hard shell beak, stamped back his heel into a yellowed eye. It was his final thrust and blackness pressed upon him as he felt his last air crushed out of his folded lungs.

And in that moment the grappling coils were torn away and he was freed.

Up! Up to the air again! Helpless as the weakest of the

folk Vilidorn lay on the wave tops savouring life, and heard the sea birds cry, joyous, above him and watched the dash of silvered fish below.

"Be grateful," they seemed to say. "Thank the friend who came from the deeps to your salvation."

Then, marked across his huge brow by white craters of torn flesh from the struggle he had won, the massive head of Serbadon, the toothed whale, rose from the waters, and his quiet eye sought out Vilidorn.

"Know yourself now, Vilidorn of the Sea Folk, and put away your pride."

"My life is yours, lord, and in your generosity my only pride," replied the weary man. "How can I serve you in all the days you have given me?"

"When your strength returns you may serve me, and you may help my unhappy people: return to your beaches and watch there for my brothers. Alone and melancholy they swim onto the land to end their lives. If you can, with your strength, take them back to the deeps to die in dignity; stay by their side until the last, and try, Vilidorn, to be sure that none of my people shall ever again drift unfriended into that final abyss."

"Trust me in this," swore Vilidorn.

At that solemn pledge Serbadon sighed heavily and rolled down to the lonely deeps once more.

Then Vilidorn came again to the beach of his borning, silent and understanding, to begin his lifetime duty. So it is to this time still true that no whale will die alone if Sea Folk can be by; for this we owe that great mind in the deeps who once saved proud Vilidorn."

There was matter also for Callidray to think on in that tale, and he nodded soberly to his old friend across the heads of the people. The blind Fridonay was gone to the waves, but here in Perrid the custom of the folk was safe. Plump and comfy as a woman, yet he had their inner strength too, and knew himself.

So with stories and legend, myth and rumour, the winter would pass. The womenfolk would give themselves as always, and the men, young and old, enjoy their comfort. Storms attacked and snow concealed the beach, rain often drenched the women as they gleaned food in the pools and puddles and after being hidden from them for a long cloud-time the golden Day Star would again shine flat across the shimmering wave tops in a last gleam before drowning.

In the darkest time of midwinter Perrid had drawn Callidray aside.

"Venture no more, my friend. Only we are left," he said. And Callidray gave his words solemn consideration, for Perrid was speaking of what they two owed to their beach and to their kin: their knowledge must not be lost with all those others of their borning.

But, before the obligations of old age could bite at muscle and thigh, there was another homing still to come, bringing old stories to life on the clean-washed morning when Idranil walked up the beach and into the legends of the folk.

Such rejoicing there was then: feasting and abundance, and singing of another, wilder, style, with rhythms that demanded a response. Now the spring days were lengthening, the Day Star gaining strength, and in the veins of the youths and maidens of the folk new desires were throbbing. With the return of a hero long given up for lost the old folk too felt a new pulse of life, and the singing swelled to the beat of their clapped hands, to the hollow, bird-like calls they were echoing. And with the music the folk stood up to dance.

In the dance the women are the sea wave, hands joined they rise and fall along the beach, whistling in their teeth the whisper of shingle under the wave's hand. Then the strong swimmers stride out, heads back to breast the wave. Their bodies are sinuous to show their swimming over the sweeping wave, and the women, drawing close, caress them as they pass. The dance tells of ventures proved and the brave lives of the swimmers, but it also calls to mind the coupling which is to come after, and celebrates the survival of the silkies. Untried boys and maidens never take part in the dance: it is a holy time.

Bridik, who was the manchild, had danced the previous year. Now in the long wave of women there was one whom he searched for in confidence. With this celebration of the spring, of Idranil's unlooked-for return after a winter among the Snow People, the Donilid planned a ceremony of his own. As the dance reached its climax, broke and died high up the shore he drew the maiden away into the shadowed soft sand above the storm drift. There, cuddled close to an old nan, a tiny girl-child lay, a babe of this winter's borning.

He lifted the child and placed her in her mother's arms, where she sighed and pouted, stretching restlessly. Then he took her tiny hand and felt the anemone grip of her fingers.

"Marveen, she is mine, no need to deny," and his teeth gleamed white in the sheltering dark, laughing at the shyness which made mothers of the folk shrink from the fathering of their babes. "It is a fact clear to everyone who sees her," he whispered, and spread out the little fist to splay across his palm.

"They will grow, Donilid! Her fingers will grow to be like the other children's as she swims."

"No my dear: she will remain like her father. She and I are other than the folk."

As he spoke he felt in the springing hair at his neck and loosened the thin chain he wore. Loosed it and lifted its yoke from him. The shaped stone hung weightily between his fingers.

"The woman gave me this, my mother. Now it goes to the new babe, to Giersi."

The child's mother shuddered and wept, trying to thrust the thing away, but he overcame her. Cupping the little smooth head in his hand he slid the gold across her brow, over ear tips to nestle in the baby folds of her neck. And the girl child opened her eyes to gaze and gape at him.

"Go well," he murmured, though the greeting was more fit for a son. Sadly he stroked the young mother's worried frown away, smoothed her tensed shoulders, arms burdened with his child. Tenderly he held them both against his wide chest, but the caress was brief. Even in this time of hero's return sadness of parting intervened. On a smiling sigh the Donilid put the two aside and walked the glistening moonpath on the ribbed wet sand.

"So. The world stayed for Idranil and brought him home at the last. He'll never journey again. But I? Where will my last venture take me, and where will my end be?"

As he looked, staring painfully into the west, a thin cloud drew haze across the moon's bright face. The silvered path became diffuse, a future with no track or reason. He could not guess what was to come.

PART II

Chapter Six
McBride

McBride was driving down Route 3 in a rage. He didn't know it but he was a danger to everyone else on the road. Even to himself. All the way from Boston he had been fuming, muttering, swearing aloud, desperate to put into words all the fury that he had bottled up during that ridiculous interview with one of the powers of M.I.T. So they were sacking him! Alright! He was glad to go. He thumped the wheel with the palm of his hand: "You can all go and do yourselves!", he shouted, then braked wildly as a Pontiac sedan appeared from nowhere under his front fender. "That goes for you too, Jimmy," he added viciously. But he slowed down: that was the third close call in half an hour and the odds were running against him. He became aware that the outskirts of Plymouth had rushed by on his left. There was a shack near here where he could pull off and stop for a coffee. It was time.

"So Feinstock, you're finished with me? Fine, Feinstock. The spoken word has no meaning in your country - it's what I'd always suspected." He drew himself up, he bristled in the driving seat, a small man, but large in his anger. "You consider that I've written nothing of value. I have not fulfilled my proper term at Woods Hole. (Where I have been messing about in boats all summer.) Very good. Big Brother has obviously been peeping over my shoulder for the last six months. And you claim this is not a totalitarian state. Why - you're in slavery here, slavery to the dollar. Jack Kennedy is just as bad as the rest, over there in his spread at Hyannis Port. You're all the same, Feinstock, you're a bad taste in my mouth and I'm happy to spit you out at last, Happy!" His old Ford rolled off the highway onto the clinkered forecourt of a fast-food cabin just short of the Cape Cod Canal. "Happy," he reiterated, reached out of the car window to open the door and stumped over to the hut.

He was a stocky little man, thick-set and belligerent, and had lost his usual balance. Throughout this, his post-doctoral year, he had done his best to seem at ease among the strangers and among the scientists he had come so far to meet. But he had no knack for friendship. He was happier at his research, a study of the nutrient levels in the well-lit shallows between high and low tides. He found the microscopic creatures which were his subject easier to predict, to analyse. Among his fellows he felt at odds, irritated by the preconceptions, the irrational thought processes of all those ignorant of his special subject.

He walked back to the car a few minutes later, ruefully studying her decaying bodywork. She'd been nothing much when he got her a year ago for a hundred dollars over a couple of bottles of Gallo wine, but the salt spread on Boston's icy streets every winter had brought about a final rot. She would never pass inspection again this year.

"I'll dump her right on the sidewalk outside M.I.T.," he told himself with a grin, "or drive her into Harvard Yard just before I get on the plane." A glad thought.

So it was over, it was time to go. It was as it should be: this had never been the right place for him, he was no laboratory scientist, although Woods Hole was a happy experience, and the Cape a world he would like to know again. He had been looking forward to a winter here. He drove on over the canal and turned south, through Mashpee and on toward the beach. Below the road to one side they had already flooded the low-lying cranberry bogs to protect the ripening fruit from a sudden frost. Soon they would be harvesting, shaking the tiny bushes until the ripe berries came off the stalk and floated to the surface to be gathered in by wide rakes. He thought of the coming feast, Thanksgiving, and sighed: he would be gone before then. Before Halloween too if possible; he'd celebrate at home in Scotland this year.

Anger returned, tinged with self-pity. So it had all come to this: his years of study were nothing now. His career finished. He could no longer think of himself as a researcher. If he were, when the breakthrough came he would not have hesitated, so fatally as it turned out, before informing the world, the rest of the so-called scientific community, of what had happened. What difference? They would never have believed in time.

He drew off the road again, and leaving the car walked down to the beach. Standing looking out to sea he knew a moment's wild longing to fling off his clothes and wade in to swim out and beyond Nantucket and on into the world. It had always been this way: when people failed him as they so often would he turned toward the ocean to find peace. He could look back over so many moments of crisis and distress in his life, but the even pattern of the waves, their hushed retreat after every thunderous rush upon the land, soothed him, gave him the hope, the optimism to go on. It had been no easy life he had set himself, but all he could remember, from the very first, was his determination to learn the secrets of the sea. His earliest home had breathed the sigh of the waves. Day and night he had been swept by that insistent rhythm. Everything he desired, or so it seemed, lay there at the water's edge and as he grew he ventured to learn more and more. Without books, without any teacher but his quiet mother he had acquired the understanding that was the basis of all his studies since. Everything had led him here, to this shore and to this failure. He sighed on a long gasp of despair, the responsibility swamped him, but the wind from the sea calmed him at last and, walking along the beach he was able to relax a little.

He came across the track of a horseshoe crab, a wide

83

shuffle over the sand, and followed it down to the water's edge. The tide was going out fast and soon she would be left behind. He stood watching her, fascinated by the incredible age of the species. For more than three million years creatures like this had struggled for life along the shore. It was an encouraging thought. He bent to pick her up, slipping his fingers under the broad shell-like prosoma which had sunk slightly into the wet, puddled sand. Ignoring the wriggling pairs of legs and the forward lash of the long telson, or tail, he carried her into deeper water where she instantly thrust away from him over the bottom sand and out to sea.

"Off you go," he told her, "this is no place for you either. We're both better away."

He waded back to the shore and sat down on a wooden break-water post to remove his wet shoes and socks. He squeezed out his flapping trousers, tipped the water from his canvas shoes then wrung out his socks and stuffed them in a pocket. Barefoot he strolled on, checking the sands around him and searching for calm. The damp sand was chill underfoot and the sun was losing its warmth when he at last started back to his car. He walked briskly. One last visit to the laboratory, he'd clear up there this evening, then back home and book a flight out of here.

In the corridors of the Oceanographic Institute at Woods Hole the heating was on. Although most people had left for the day there was often someone working all night. He went almost furtively to his own small office, not wanting to talk to anyone. Molly Christoff startled him as she stepped suddenly from a door just ahead.

"Oh Don! Hi, working late?" She stood hugging her stack of books, effectively blocking his escape.

"No. No. Just looked in to pick up a few things." They would find out soon enough that he'd been asked to leave, but by then he would be gone.

"How's it coming along then?" She'd no idea what he was supposed to be working on but always tried to be friendly, which irritated McBride who had only one use for women.

"The work is fine, just fine," he lied abruptly.

"You're worrying too much," she said, reaching out a hand toward him, being aware, being feminine. "Is it still that creature, that pet of yours that you had? I'm so sorry. What was it now, some kind of seal I believe."

"The books all tell me he must have been a manatee."" It was impossible to keep the bitter irony from his voice.

"Really? So far north too. They don't usually leave Florida." She moved to lean against the wall. Obviously settling in to make a night of it, McBride thought viciously. "Aren't they the creatures sailors are supposed to have lusted after — you know the origin of the mermaid myth? I believe they have these great mammary glands and the sailors all started dreaming of breasts."

"They have no more breasts than an orang-utan, but unlike most women, they've a great deal of maternal love. We could do well to study them more closely instead of making up damn fool stories about them."

McBride stamped past and into his own room, aware as he slammed the door of her parting murmur: "My, my, he's certainly upset." He was a fool to snap at her like that but if this sort of silly reaction was all that people could come up with when they thought of mermaids, just wild imaginings of sex-starved sailors, what kind of reaction could he have expected if he had walked in here and told them about the silkie? Who in any case was male?

"They'd have laughed me out of here, never mind throwing me out."

He collected up his two or three reference books; folk lore mainly, from the Western Isles of Scotland, and books on anthropology. Unable to find a bag or cardboard carton to carry them in he tipped out the waste bin and piled them in there, filling it up with the tapes his friend had made through all those long, humid summer afternoons. They were his testament. He eyed the big Grundig tape recorder wistfully for a moment, then packed it up and carried it along too. It was an

85

awkward load and he didn't bother putting it down to shut the door behind him but shouldered his way out into the evening parking lot and dumped everything in the back of the car.

The headlights lit up the Old Cape Cod house as he turned into the front yard. Built about forty years ago the design was one that had stood the test of centuries of winter northeasters. Like oilskins, its long sloping roof protected its back from the gales so that the second floor had windows only on this, the landward side. It was a wooden frame house with weathered wooden shingles, repaired in one place with corrugated zinc. Paintwork was peeling and the window screens of yellowed nylon all needed repair. He walked down the side of the house, appreciating the damp scents of autumn on the sharp evening air, propped open the screen door and went back for his books and the waste bin. Once inside the big back porch he set the things down on the floor. On the floor beside the thin mat which was the only bed the silkie had wanted. This was where he had spent every moment of those few weeks, within sound and scent of the sea which was his whole world.

McBride squatted beside the mat as he had done so often before and, hands clasped under his chin, went back in his mind, remembering, reliving, shaping and trying to find the meaning of all that had happened.

End of July, or was it the first week of August — he'd have to check the calendar — he'd arranged to go out in the boat with Stan Leamus. Stan was a regular old Down Easter, made out of harshly angled bone and a leathery brown skin. In spite of the heat of the day he wore his woollen shirt of an astounding, unheralded plaid and his trousers hung apart from his body on ancient braces. His concession to the airless heat was to remove his knitted sleeveless sweater which lay in the cluttered little cabin among nets and pots and oily rope. On his bare feet a pair of old tennis shoes, on his head an erstwhile baseball cap. Behind heavy-rimmed glasses

Stan's eyes wrinkled to inspect the hazy distance.

"We'll catch nothing in this glare," he said yet again, the pessimist.

The sea was like a sheltered pond through which at long intervals passed a heaving swell so slow as to slide unnoticed beneath the hull.

"A day like this and I feel I could walk on the water," McBride cracked open a can of beer with the triangular end of the can opener and placed it in Stan's outstretched fist.

"It'll storm by sundown. Thunder's building up," Stan announced, and sipped distrustfully at the beer.

One of the pleasures of an outing with Stan was the ease of not speaking unless you wanted to. In hours of silence McBride had helped the old man set his lines before dawn, or taken an evening tide to haul in lobster pots. With hardly a word between them they could spend a day digging clams (though never a Sunday) and then sit silent on Stan's back porch of an evening while his wife cooked up a chowder for them. It would not be true to say they were friends for both were lone men; but their lives touched.

"What's that?" McBride pointed.

"Looks like seal."

They watched the sleek dark head on the surface. Seal can often stray into Cape Cod waters, where they will lie lazily sunning themselves before taking to the northern seas again. McBride put up his binoculars to compare this little one with the grey seal of his home waters. There was something wrong.

"Take a turn over there, Stan. There's blood on the water."

As they drew close McBride leapt up onto the cabin roof for a clearer view down into the water. He saw the sluggish movement of limbs.

"It's not a seal, it's a man!"

As Stan eased back on his throttle and guided the boat round on a wide curve about the dark stain spreading in the water McBride dived from the roof. Between them they lifted the thickset figure from the water and lay him on the decking. A deep, jagged wound had slit his inner thigh and arterial blood was pumping weakly over the boards. McBride felt unhesitatingly for the pressure point and twisted a piece of twine into a biting tourniquet. Then he pulled off his soaked T-shirt and pressed it over the wound, trying to draw the gaping sides together as he did so. He was aware throughout of Stan standing above him watching, and of a sense of the other man's disapproval. He looked up, puzzled.

"If you listen to me you'll leave that and throw him back over the side." Stan turned his head and spat largely.

"What do you mean?" McBride was angry but he remained on his knees, holding the pad in place.

"Take a look at that. And use your head."

For the first time McBride studied the injured man, and suffered a shock of surprise. McBride was a hairy man himself but the figure that lay in the well deck beside him was covered; covered in a brindled brown hair that was a furriness over his shoulders, the backs of his arms and hands, his chest, back and buttocks. The outer parts of his legs were also thickly covered, the whole shining wet, sleek and streamlined. McBride touched his shoulder and felt a momentary disgust which shaded into fear.

"Is it a man after all?"

"Use your head," Stan grunted again. "Where did it come from? And where did it get that cut?" With a foot he turned over the creature's helpless hand showing a watery brown stain on the pale palm. "Rust. And that's a cut, not a bite. He was diving a wreck and something shifted on him."

"Diving a wreck? But there's no boat. He's no gear."

"You're right there's no boat."

They both looked out over the tilting surface. There was no horizon, the sea shifted to haze and the haze became the sky. There were no boats.

"Tell me what you're thinking, Stan. I don't understand this."

"I think what you have there will bring you no luck. We would be better never to have seen him."

"But what is he?"

"I don't give any credence to the idea that they search for the souls of doomed sailors, but they're said to swim in the wrecks. I've never seen one before, and I wish we'd never seen this." Savagely he opened up the throttle, he was heading back to land.

McBride said nothing, he'd sailed with fishermen before and knew their superstitions.

"It's a silkie, that's what it is," he said finally. "One of the seal folk. He'll do us no harm. Do you have a needle on board? I have to stitch him up."

In the black japanned first-aid box he found what he needed. Already he knew that he could not call a doctor to the strange creature he had saved.

Off the coast where McBride's rented cottage stood Stan lifted the inflated dinghy from the roof and dropped it into the water alongside without a word. McBride lifted the unconscious figure into it and paddled away. He regretted Stan's disapproval, but he was going through with this all the same.

Often in his home in the Western Isles of Scotland he had heard stories of the people of the sea, the seal folk who walked like humans on the land, but could swim like the seals once back in the water. As a boy he had searched out the people who knew the stories and whenever he was at a ceilidh he had encouraged them to tell of the old seal-hunting days, and of the King Seal who could assume human shape and was known to have been the death of many hunters. In spite of this vengeance, the silkies were considered by all to be good folk and able to grant favours. Nevertheless the boy McBride was aware that his mother hated the old tales and was frightened by them all, and with an older wisdom he never questioned her and was more quiet with his enquiries. It was certain that many of the old people of the islands believed in the Sea Folk, but their lives had only recently touched the twentieth century and they were still filled with unproven beliefs. He remembered the Mary Bean he himself had carried for good luck; and the prayers of his mother.

It seemed that the oldsters of Cape Cod were the same: Stan had obviously been raised on a diet of evil spirits and witches with no gentler side to their nature, like the old woman of Nauset Sea for instance, who lived in the wreck of a whale and enticed ships onto the shoals with a lamp hung up on its tail. She was a witch who made a pact with the devil for dead souls: Goody Hallett they called her and she had lived near Chatham! What a mixture we are of fear and disbelief, McBride thought, and he felt again the unstoppered surge of fear as he touched his patient, lifting him from the dinghy and carrying him between the dunes to the house.

The fear — or was it exhilaration? — enlivened the following days as he fought to ease the suffering of the creature he had carried from the sea. Antibiotics worked their miracle: the small quantity of sulpha drug he had on hand was sufficient to banish any fear of infection, but the wound was still a very serious one. A branch of the femoral artery had been damaged but he had been able to stop the bleeding there and had drawn the wound together, giving it a chance to heal; nevertheless he was afraid that major nerves and tendons were severed, for there seemed to be no movement at all in the leg or foot.

The silkie lay still on the floor of the porch, his nostrils flaring at the terrifying scents around him, trembling constantly at movement and noise. McBride tried to soothe him, sitting calmly at his side and, forcing back his own aversion, stroking the oddly furry arms and shoulders of the creature as he would a frightened puppy or child. As he did so he observed him closely, noting the heavy muscles over hip and thigh, the stubby hands and splayed feet. Would he ever swim again? McBride tried without success to feed his patient but everything was refused, and he would have thought the will to live was gone if it were not for the desperate pleading in the liquid brown eyes which seemed to fill the silkie's whole face.

By the third day McBride was ready to despair. Although he had trickled some water into his mouth the silkie seemed unable to drink and only gasped and moved his head fretfully from side to side. Any food he was offered he pressed aside weakly with his tongue. There was little hope. When he went out onto the porch that morning McBride's heavy mood was not lifted by the sight of a friendly figure sitting there.

"Hello Victor." He stood dully at the sick creature's feet, hands in his pockets. "I don't know what to do."

"He is dying and you don't know what to do? Tell me." Victor stood up. Six foot three, he seemed to fill the porch, and a warmth and compassion flowed from him to revive hope for the helpless creature who lay between them.

"I found him in the sea, it's his home. The leg's badly cut but will heal. It's that he cannot live in this shock of strangeness. And he will not eat."

"Food. Yes." Victor looked searchingly down at the drawn face and hurt eyes. "I'll get him food. Wait with him." Then he stepped quietly away, gently shut the screen door and ran down the back yard to disappear among the dunes.

It was on the dunes McBride had first met Victor Wasielewski, a gentle, sensitive man whom the gibes and Polack jokes of his boyhood in Milwaukee had injured deeply. At school he had frozen into a dumb non-participation which had earned him the label of "unteachable". As he grew in size his earnest parents feared that he might become violent and kept him often at home, encouraging him in intricate work with his hands. On their deaths, one following the other after only a few months, he had used their small savings to establish himself in a couple of rooms over a garage near Sandwich and there he worked up his growing reputation as an artist, welding metal and driftwood into shapes evoking the lightness and freedom which he sought. He seemed simple-minded for he expressed himself poorly in English, but he was an aware man, with a gift of stillness.

He returned within half an hour carrying a couple of baitworms, a tiny transparent crab, some dog whelks and slipper limpets from the breakwater pools, all lapped about in sea-water inside his hat. With a stone he smashed the shells and drew out the tiny creatures still alive. Taking the silkie into his arms as if he were a child he slid the wet succulent morsels between his lips, crooning his satisfaction as each was taken eagerly and eaten. But halfway through this feast the wild one turned his head away: it was not his habit to fill his stomach after a long fast and also the opulent smell of the big man was overpowering him.

As the silkie sank into a satisfied doze the two men left him and walked the beach.

"You were feeding him wrongly," said Victor. "Why was that? Did you really want that he should live?"

"Yes, or I believed that I did."

"It is not the same thing. To save him is one thing, now you have to love him."

"That's what I cannot do. It would be easier to hate. I feel sometimes that I agree with Stan, I should have thrown him back. He will do me harm. I know it."

"Is that why you fear him?"

"I'm not afraid of him, but of what he means, what he is. A whole species living secretly in the world. It's like the Lost Tribes, Atlantis, Twenty Thousand Leagues under the Sea all rolled into one! I'm a scientist, Victor: I should be rushing to make this amazing discovery known to the world. But I'm afraid of what it means. Here is my chance of fame, of a voice, and at one moment I'm thrilled, excited, ready to shout on the housetop. Then it all evaporates and I feel only anger: why me? Why did he have to come to me?"

"He is the two halves of yourself: of all ourselves. The light or the dark, love or hate, innocence or fame. You don't know how to feel about yourself so you don't know how to feel to him."

"That's right. At this moment I could go either way:

look forward, or look back. I am Janus, trying to look both ways at once."

"Janus?"

"The god of the doorway: he'd a face either side of his head. We think of him with every New Year for January's named after him." He sighed. "I don't know, frame or innocence, you say. Victor I'll tell you this — after the creature's well he should go back to the sea. I will not have him made a specimen or put on show." Then he sickened of himself once more. "Oh that sounds very fine: when he's well. And I don't even know if he'll ever swim again."

But after Victor's intervention the silkie's condition began to improve. Two and sometimes three times a day McBride went down to the shore and returned with a pan full of molluscs or other littoral dwellers for him to eat. Very small fish he enjoyed too, politely tearing off the head and tail, then wiping the rest firmly between finger and thumb. One day, to please him, McBride brought home a small lobster taken fresh from the pots, which he ate with delighted skill. He seemed rarely to need a drink though the heat of the day was often a trial for him and he loved to suck on ice cubes. Morning and evening McBride brought home buckets of sea water and, protecting the injured leg, doused his friend thoroughly, splashing and laughing together in a game they both loved.

His friend: for this he had become. With returning health the silkie reached out more and more to McBride for contact and company. When the man was gone from the house he would return to hear sad keening sounds from the porch: sounds to which he was in time able to establish a pattern.

It was Victor, who visited almost daily, who first remarked upon something of which they were both hesitantly becoming aware.

"He understands what I speak to him! Look!"

"Say to him," McBride murmured involuntarily.

"Yes, I will say to him and you will see." Victor took up a food morsel from the pan at the silkie's side and concealed it in his vast right hand. Closing his left fist in the same way he held the backs of this hands uppermost toward the wild man. "Which one?" he asked "Which hand?"

"But your movements make the meaning clear," grunted McBride as the smiling creature reached out shyly to indicate the right.

"Yes, yes. Now see." Victor shrugged this off impatiently and took up another piece. This time he hid his hands behind his back in the age-old children's game, concealed the scrap and offered his hands again. Again the other reached out and again he was right.

"He smells it. He's a very well developed sense of smell, I'm sure." McBride sniffed at his own hands. "That stuff smells strong enough for me to recognise it, let alone a creature that's lived wild all his life."

To their surprise the silkie muttered in his lilting way, jerking his head toward his right shoulder. With his finger and thumb he pinched his nose closed and was able to keep it shut as he took his hand away to beckon Victor to play once more.

"There. What can you say now?" demanded Victor when the ritual of hiding and choosing was over.

"It's like a trick, Victor, like teaching a dog a trick. We haven't necessarily proved that he can understand that we use language, that we communicate. And yet, you know, I want to agree with you. I think he knows."

He stared kindly at his patient for a moment then gave a nod. "I'll feel a fool but I'm going to try the old 'Me Tarzan' routine."

Still staring fixedly he jutted his thumb into his own chest.

"McBride," he announced clearly. "McBride."

The silkie watched him warily. McBride repeated his embarrassed performance. A thinking pause. Then: the silkie raised his own thumb in the identical way.

"Bridik."

"What did he say!" McBride exploded.

"He repeats you. Do it again."

Again the jutting thumb: "McBride."

94

Again the hesitant mime: "Bridik."

"Not bad for a first attempt," cried McBride excitedly. "Now you try, see if he can get his teeth into your name."

Victor bent eagerly forward and pointed to himself, "Victor," he announced with clear Polish inflection.

Solemnly the silkie turned to him, pressed his thumb once more against his chest. "Bridik."

"No. He's not got it." McBride was disgusted at his own credulity.

"Wait, wait," patiently Victor tried again. And then again.

"Maybe we've got it wrong," said McBride slowly, as all three sat staring expectantly at one another. "McBride," he announced once more. Then leaning across laid his hand on Victor's chest. "Victor." He turned to the newcomer, placed his outstretched palm on the furry chest. "Bridik." He drew a deep breath. "Now you Victor."

With firm gestures Victor completed the round.

"Now you Bridik."

Both men could feel their own hearts beating as the stranger leaned forward.

"Bridik," he said as before. "Ikbrid. Iktar." He looked anxiously at each of them as he haltingly made the round. But there was no doubt: he had spoken their names.

The euphoria at this discovery was astounding, the two men felt themselves to be flooding, overflowing with information: names, labels, signs and signals were flung back and forth until Bridik was panting in his effort to keep up, to achieve the sounds with which he was being battered. At last, laughing and breathless the two men flung themselves down on the floor of the porch, surrounded by discarded objects whose names they had been stabbing at their pupil. Gladly the three of them beamed on one another: it would be slow work, but in the end they would understand.

More confident now, Bridik searched in the pan of sea water at his side and held up a whelk.

"*Kotipka*," he said clearly.

The two men looked at one another.

"Of course," cried McBride, "he's telling us in his language now! Oh why did we never think of it? He has his own tongue."

"He also has speech! McBride, think of the things he can tell us. He has lived all his life in the oceans, he has seen what we can never have seen. How much we will learn now!"

McBride felt again that touch of fear: so much that we do not know. In a moment that could all be changed. Sitting here at his side was the Unknown, the Creature from the Depths: it was as if melodrama was suddenly becoming real. Everyday things became intangible; misty barriers between himself and a world which until now he had only glimpsed. At Woods Hole everyone's mind was delighting in the latest project: a three-man submersible capable of depths of 12,000ft. Once that was launched even the deep floor of the mid-Atlantic would be opened up for their exploration. And yet here was a voice which could flesh out those images from below the surface, fill in the colour to what, even after the closest research, could only be a line drawing.

"I'm afraid, Victor, afraid of where all this is leading."

"It is leading only to better understanding. Understanding between ourselves and our friend here, understanding for all men of the world they live in. This can only be good."

"Only if men are good, Victor." McBride shook his head. "Do we have the right? I mean, can we in all conscience take this man, whose people must have lived undetected all these years, and change him into one of us? We should rather become one with him.

"Oh I'm really no scientist Victor. I'm afraid to see Bridik here, and all his folk, sacrificed on the transitory altar of progress. It isn't that we will learn from him, our minds will not be broad enough to include his. He will be forced to submit to our idea of life. Look at the reservations in this country, look at the eskimo, look at my own crofting folk: progress is a wheel that rolls over them all. And achieves nothing for them. No, Victor, I'm scared. I'm scared. Let him be well soon. Let him go back to the sea he came from."

"And this is all you fear?" asked Victor quietly, after watching his friend silently for a moment. "You no longer fear him?"

"Yes, I fear him. But that is something personal, something between him and me. I fear what he is bringing, and I don't know what it is. I fear him. And yet I'm learning to love him. I could love him like a brother." And he laid his arm across the silkie's shoulders. "How long before we can speak to one another, Bridik? How long will it take?"

Slowly a plan evolved. McBride began to make daily notes of all that he could discover about the silkie — weight, measurements, data of all kinds. He searched for books of history and folk lore, unravelling the mystery of the Sea Folk into the written word. Day by day Bridik learned to express his simple needs; at the same time, to a tape recorder, he recited the stories, the myths, the history of his folk. His delight at hearing his own voice from the machine was tempered with a sadness. He longed to be among those folk and sometimes, chattering idly in the cool of the evening, he told of his distant home across the grey Atlantic, and spoke of his kin, naming them sadly: of old Marthy, his nurse, long dead and returned to the wave; of Seiglid, the strong swimmer who had fathered him; and of his own girlchild, Giersi, a babe when he left, solemn-eyed, splay-fingered and like, so sadly like, the children of the men who now befriended him. And they sensed his longing: it was time to swim once more to the beaches of home.

To please him his friends took him at dawn one day over the dunes and down to the sea. With tears he lowered himself into the ripples at the tide's edge. Beyond him waves curled grey-green and translucent, sand particles danced in the trapped light within the waves. The white tops curled, crumpled and swirled around him. Lunging quickly in spite of his useless leg, Bridik snatched up a rolling shell before the wave could drag it back, held it up in triumph and then discovered to his disgust that it was empty.

"Pah-pah-pah-pah," he muttered, making spitting movements with his lips, a trick the other two had picked up, meaning the thing was useless.

Reaching up he grabbed McBride's arm at the elbow and levered himself to his feet. Staggering as the sand washed from under his one good foot he gestured a welcome.

"In. In to water," and he grinned broadly in McBride's face showing his small even teeth. Here in his own element he could be bold enough, they discovered. The wound had healed well and was firmly strapped. It would come to no harm. Before they were waist-deep Bridik had left them. With a quick twist he was among their ankles and then away.

Through the clear water they saw him for a moment: he swam with a strong fluid movement of the lower body and leg, similar to that of butterflystroke, his arms bent up against his chest. Then they lost sight of him and became anxious at the length of time he remained submerged. But he reappeared after long minutes not even breathless and swept back to them on a wave.

"Leg must learn," he said reprovingly and made his useless sign once more.

Then using the force of an approaching wave he butted Victor's stomach with his head, slithered round his knees and upset him into the water. Laughing at his friend's surprise, McBride was unprepared for the silkie's speed and was amazed at the furry stroke which took his legs from under him also. Floundering and splashing the men fought their way back to the air. Somehow they would have to explain to Bridik that they could not stay below as long as he could.

"He'll have us drowned!" cried McBride searching furiously. Before he knew it he was down again but had the satisfaction of feeling his toe hard against furry flesh. When he surfaced Victor was holding a screaming yapping Bridik in a great bear hug. Early bathers, had there been any on the beach, would have seen two men playing with their big dog but would have been surprised to hear what they were saying.

"Give over Bridik, do! I must have air — in water I die."

"So — nose close!"

"We cannot, Bridik. We're not made that way."

"No? Eyes close — yes? Nose close — no?"

"That's right, Bridik." Victor put him down. "You must take care of us now. We can stay under water only a minute, a very short time."

"Under water? Under?" Bridik laughed at the odd expression. "In. In water. Please come in." And he was gone once more.

Their efforts to follow him were futile and caused him much amusement, try as he would to hide it. McBride's kicking breast-stroke he was sure was a joke, but he soon was trying to copy the powerful crawl that Victor demon-strated. With amazement he learned that neither one could swim face up below the surface and he circled them again and again in this position pulling faces and making unmistakably rude gestures until they were shivering with cold and pulled him out of the water to help him back to the house.

"We'll come again tomorrow."

"They began to make plans. Men always do.

The next morning Victor phoned at first light. He was hoarse and feeling full of cold. He would not swim today. By evening McBride felt it too: a wretched, scratchy cold in the head, one of the most irritating complaints. It has no cure.

In the morning Bridik was sneezing, too. By nightfall he was feverish and recognised neither of his friends. A respiratory infection, nothing more: but in one who had never before been exposed to such a thing it ran a desperate course. By the second night McBride could no longer bear to hear that laboured breathing and flung himself on the telephone.

"Doctor. Be quick — he cannot breathe. His heart will not stand this much longer."

The doctor came, unalarmed and too late.

When he saw the still figure huddled in a corner of the shadowed porch he shrouded it compassionately with a blanket.

"You made a mistake calling me," he tried to sound kind. "You should have called the vet."

Stan came round as soon as he understood what was wanted.

"You'll throw him back now then," he said, watching McBride's granite face.

Victor carried the lifeless form in his arms like a child wrapped in a blanket. They paddled the inflatable out to the boat waiting in the dusk.

"We'll have to take it miles out into the stream," said Stan. "You don't want it washed back onto the beach."

"No danger of that." Victor unstrapped the sack he had been carrying on his back. "I have this to give him."

It was a seal, carved from a piece of black soapstone. He placed it with the body in the blanket and tied the last stitches.

"Now he won't be alone."

It was the dark of the moon. In silence they slipped him back into the waters, then turned toward the land beyond the horizon.

McBride finally left the old Cape Cod house in November. He was able to book a flight on the twenty-second and so left before Thanksgiving, which seemed appropriate. He had seen the last muddied tragedies of fall and now was turning to his old home where he would be able to make a start on the work ahead. Winter was coming as he drove back up Route 3 heading for Boston and Logan Airport. Once on board the plane he fastened his seat belt and took out some papers. It was the article he had been preparing during those long days of summer. Around him passengers were talking about something which had happened in Texas that afternoon, but he paid no attention.

Throughout the flight he corrected and annotated the article which now he would let no-one read. Finally he wrote across the bottom:

"We shall none of us be put on show, but we are all of us specimens."

Chapter Seven
Seal Woman

All day, under the tilting sky, Giersi lay on the rough black rocks high above the gheo as she watched the seals on the tiny beach below. So steep and close were the cliff sides that only at midday could the Day Star's light penetrate into this narrow slit. The sea constantly shifted and rebelled, gripped by the long fingers of the land. The empty cries of the gulls echoed meaninglessly overhead. But the gheo was neither empty nor sad. At the water's side a seal family was settling in.

Throughout that summer Giersi had followed the seals, watching them and learning their ways, leaving her home beach among the folk to lie on the bare rocks with the yearling bulls and cows who rested there after their journeying. Sniffing at them, touching them if they permitted her, she tried to learn where they had been, to discover what they knew, until tiring of her questions they slumped back into the sea and went away. Once or twice old friends had returned, grinning at her and questing over her face and hands with out-thrust whiskers, but they were proud of their own independence and like everyone else had little time for her, pushing her irritably aside if she went to swim with them.

Giersi, manchild's daughter, sighed. Among the silkies too she was only an irritation: no-one wanted her to swim the waves for it was a maid's place to stay on the home beach in the curving shelter of the cove or under the warm dark of the cave. But she, restless, longed for the clean white-grey cloud above the endless waves, the long calm swell in the early dawn and the clarity of spindrift swept into her face by the travelling winds. Now every day's end brought more desperate longing as the spent Star sank glowing into the distant horizon and the golden stream of light lay tantalising at her feet, stretching across the far seas. She too, like the female seals, would have gone venturing with the menfolk but she was forbidden: she must make her place among the maids, the mothers and the old nans. This year was particularly hard, for the young men of her borning were all away venturing, and when they returned she must consent to love, and begin to make a baby for one of them. The idea filled her with distaste, she dreaded to lose her freedom, so recently found.

She had always known that she was different, and that where she searched for love she would find only a sort of fond impatience. When the folk gathered on evening rocks or in the winter cave for a story telling, she had searched in the faces about her for a warmth that she could fold to herself; but the smiling faces were filled only with a general caring. And though she wriggled close she felt all her own angles and awkwardness; she could not round her body into the comforting arms but held away, aloof. From the first moment when she had any awareness of herself as a single being she had known that this self could not be one with theirs.

"See the pretty new babe," they gloated, but she always turned away in disgust at the wet and wrinkled little faces and would not learn to give the love she waited for herself.

"You shall carry my bowl for me," they coaxed when she would not forage with them, but naughty and disobedient she ran between the rocks to follow the silly boys, and to watch their wild antics.

"See what I have," she would call to them. "Come and see what I've caught."

They gathered round but scorned the tiny fish and

laughed at the broken shell that had looked so pretty in the water.

"I got it from a cave below the farthest rock," she told them. "Down dread deeps it was."

They listened wide-eyed at that, a maid telling of ventures. It did not occur to them to withold belief: to the folk truth is as open as daylight, making everything clear. There is no pretence to cloud understanding, to take away trust with its threat of dark and storm.

So they heard her tale and repeated it and the old ones took her sternly to task. Standing in the circle where she had hoped for love she found derision: gnarled fingers shook at her face, cackling laughter crackled through her. Naked, stripped of her special difference, Giersi, manchild's daughter, felt for a moment ashamed. Where she wanted love she now imagined hate, and knew she would never share her mind, its wild images again. Turning away she scrambled out of reach up rocks where they could not follow. That was the splendour of her difference, her long nimble toes and fingers with which she held bird-like to the crannies dizzy-high above their heads. She was spanked when she came down, punished for the fright they had suffered. But again and again when she wanted to escape she climbed.

"Just like her father," scoffed one old nan, and Giersi froze high up on the rocks above and would not come down all night long. Her father, the Donilid, where was he, dead in the sea? She had never known him and like all the other little ones loved to guess, gazing in awe at the tall heroes as they stood lazily about the winter beach, waiting for the spring and venturing once more. But as she grew tall, and taller still, it was clear that none of these men of the folk had fathered her, and she yearned for him, though all she knew of him was the strange stone she had worn all her life, chaining her to him.

At last old Larra had told her:

"Your father was gone from the folk long before he left on his last venture. His ways were never our ways

104

for he loved the land and, manchild, searched always in the ways of men. It has been his death indeed and he will never return. Try to forget him child, for his was an unhappy life."

But at times she wept for her lost father, and she wondered at him all that night on the lonely rock face. In the morning she came down changed and aloof. She was like her father and would no longer try to obey the dictates of the folk if her heart turned her away. Like him she would go her own way. It was then that she began to follow the seals.

Here on the high sun-warmed rock she was at peace. Below her was a life of real freedom and as she lay watching she felt part of it, tied more strongly to this family of the sea than she was to her own folk.

The first to arrive, some days before, was the big cow seal who now lay contentedly sleeping in the lee of a weed-fringed rock below the inquisitive swirling of the waves. How can she sleep below the surface? thought Giersi enviously and watched smiling as the drowsy creature rose to the surface and lay calmly panting without opening her eyes. After four or five breaths she closed her nose once more and sank into her sandy bed without seeming to have woken. Her little pup shifted irritably on the rough sand high up the beach, but obedient to the ways of his folk he did not cry out, only waited patiently for his mother's return.

Shortly before the pup's birth the master bull had arrived. It was his self-appointed task to guard the tiny beach and tirelessly he swam back and forth on the verge of the open sea. He challenged any who approached his beach and only after his close inspection had a second cow been permitted to swim into the gheo and climb the little beach to wait for the birth of her own child. Giersi herself had avoided his notice by climbing up from the far side of the narrow headland: at this time of year she knew better than to approach the bull seal, even if he should prove to be an old friend: his teeth and temper were fierce. The second female, now lying at ease on the beach, would shortly give birth, most likely at some time during the night tides. The little white-furred baby would be dearer to Giersi than any infant of her own kind and she ached to come nearer to the seal family and to win their trust. She swam homeward through golden evening light, planning and dreaming.

In the last calm, before the waves fell down on the land, she held herself still and gazed at her home. The low rock had little to catch the eye, rising only head high above the highest waves at its northern end. In the memory of the folk more than one winter storm had swept across that barren heel of land. The south-facing shore was higher, its rock face dropping sheer into the water and on down to the deep roots of land below. The western tip of these heights contained a shell-sand beach which rose up from an outer ledge of rock exposed only at low tide. The rocks were weed-covered and treacherous to those who dared to enter in harsh weather: only the deep water channels were free of the eddies and cross currents which could rip away a weary swimmer just as his home beach seemed to welcome him. The land was tipping to receive the tide as Giersi swam in and the rocks were all submerged, but even so she followed the appointed approaches as she had been taught when, as a tiny maid, she had learned respect for her native sea.

There would be no food for her at this time but she had fed during the ebb at the distant gheos and now wanted only to slip into her own lonely sleeping place. It was many years since she had left the tangle of limbs and bodies where the others of her borning lay, though she liked to hear them near her in the night. She slept alone, nearer to the mouth of the cave, and when the tide was high loved to watch the ripples of reflected moonlight above her head. Waking or sleeping, through every moment of her life breathed the sigh of the sea as it collapsed upon the land.

Giersi lay in a soft hollow of sand left in the cave when the earth rose up from the womb of the ocean. She listened to the soft rush of pebble and shell beneath the wave's hand and seemed to hear her own name:

"Giersi. Giersi."

Truly someone was calling her and she sat up quickly. A hand touched her hair, fingers flickered over her shoulder and caught her hand. She knew her friend.

"Hancid! I didn't even know you had returned. When were you come home?" She laughed in delight.

"Hush, hush. On the morning tide, but you were already gone. Where do you go? What's this I've been hearing all day about you and the seals? Are you still in trouble, Giersi?"

"No, no trouble; don't worry about me - what about you? Where were you this summer? Have you new stories for us? How good it is to have you back."

She raised his hand to her face, rubbing her cheek against him. Once, long ago, she had hoped this one would prove to be her father. How foolish she was as a child! He was not old enough, and now that she was grown she knew him as her friend, sometimes her only friend.

"You will hear all that in time, there are stories enough. My worry now is for you. You have set everyone against you, ignoring the nans and babies both. No-one has a good word to say, Giersi. It's all the seals, the seals. Why is this? What are you doing?"

"They are true sea people, Hancid. They interest me. I love them." There was a defiant emphasis in her words, she never gave love away. She tried to whisper to tell him how it all was until he laid his hand against her mouth, then with a finger behind her elbow beckoned her outside. The sea was sullen black with a tumbled fringe along the land. The moon was down.

"You know nothing of the creatures, it is all in your mind. You see a family — mother, father, babes — but it is not so. The bull seal wants his women for only one purpose then he will leave them for ever. The mothers feed their babes for only one moon's passing and then

107

they too will leave. They live their lives out in the waters alone, Giersi. They have no old folk to advise and love them, no born companions they can trust. Their freedom is a selfish thing and they are vicious to protect it. There is no love to be found among those people of the sea, Giersi. You should stay among the folk and learn to love there."

But she would not hear him.

"You've been told to persuade me. To help to make me consent. I won't, Hancid: this is not my place."

"And the gheo you visit is not the seals' place either. What you are watching is foreign to their ways. Come with me and I will show you the seals you are learning to love. Come."

Bitterly he turned away down the beach and with sure movements entered the water and swam away. Brave as she was Giersi had never swum alone at night. Close behind Hancid she could follow his wake through the water, feeling its ripple against her shoulder. There was no light anywhere for a long time.

The dawn was not all that she had imagined it to be: only the sky lifting from the water as light began to stream in. A damp breeze slid across the surface and rain was close. Swimming at Hancid's side she was finding it hard to maintain the steady pace his many years of venturing had taught him and she longed for the air sooner than he did. But she gave no sign as they swam on under the heavy swell and leaden skies.

The island when they reached it lay like a fat woman at low water, hip and shoulders rising roundly from the waves, the waist a low valley between the two. The exhausion of journey's end almost overwhelmed Giersi, but Hancid swam on, circling to the eastern beach. Here, as they approached, the damp breeze reached them across the island and the smell of the seals was pressed into nose and mouth, eyes and face.

"Fagh! Oh, Hancid what is it? Why does it smell so bad?"

"You'll see," he replied grimly. "Come."

Only stark necessity had forced him to bring her to

this place, he hated what he was doing but knew that she had to learn.

They stepped awkwardly up the beach, finding their way between the cows who lay there with their pups. Frequently they were met by an angry hiss as the seals reared up at their approach.

"Be careful not to go too close," murmured Giersi, "They like a whole body space clear around them."

"Then they haven't enough room here," snapped Hancid, stumbling wretchedly as his feet slipped in unnamable slime and he stubbed himself painfully against stones.

Suddenly a huge bull rose up in front of them, blocking their way. The white hair of his head showed him to be a senior, used to long years of dominating the cows and younger bulls of his beach. With a snarl he loped towards them, bouncing and crashing down the beach.

"No, no. Be careful," screamed Giersi and lunged toward the rocks at the side of the beach. Hancid stumbled and fled toward the sea where the master bull halted, searching for him with bleary coated eyes. The beach was now a scene of panic with many cows humping toward the water or striking out with agitated flippers at the press of neighbours too close to their young. Two little pups, white coated, lay crushed in their blood, where the rush of adults had trampled them.

Looking numbly out to sea, Giersi made out Hancid working his way round to the rocks where she crouched, sobbing at the horror of what she had seen. But he was not finished yet. Cautiously he led her up into the grassland behind the beach. Here, though less crowded, the scene was the same. Cows reared up aggressively as they approached, even snarling and snapping at them. On their guard now for the big bulls they were able to avoid surprising them as they slept and they kept to the higher ground, away from the muddy stream where younger bulls wallowed and eyed the cows. On all sides Hancid pointed to abandoned pups: some were long dead and black flies hung in a visible stench above them. Others, abandoned at birth, lay like helpless infants in soiled and wrinkled bags of fur, too weak to lift their heads, their eyes dulled by dirt and disease. Too many small bodies lay crushed and broken under the awesome weight of adults.

Giersi could walk no farther but fell to her knees in the mud and slime of the beaten grass.

"Why have you brought me here? What do you want to prove?" she cried. "This is not their true life; they are forced to live like this. There is something evil here, Hancid. No creature chooses to be degraded into this. The island is too full. Can they not move to other, cleaner beaches? Hancid, what does this mean?"
Hancid, what does this mean?"

"There are no other beaches, Giersi. Have you never wondered why the folk live as they do, on one sparse rock, when there are oceans all round the world where they might go? There are no more beaches for the people of the sea, the landsmen want them all. And so your precious seals live here for only a short part of the year, angry, aggressive and vicious. Soon they will leave it all and go out into the waters unloving and alone until it all is forced upon them again next year. Stay with the folk, Giersi. They will never abandon you like this poor creature." With his foot Hancid stirred the mute body of a day-old pup huddled against a tuft of rank grass for shelter.

The pup's fur lay in empty rolls along its narrow body, the soft white hair rumpled and damp. At the nudge of Hancid's foot however it rolled on its side and brushed an agitated flipper at him.

"This one has some courage left to fight against his fate," Giersi smiled through her ready tears. "Hancid, let us interfere. He has the right to life, or death with dignity. Let us take him to the gheos and give him a new chance."

"He will die, Giersi, he needs to be fed. Without his mother's milk he will die in a few days. Leave the seals, Giersi, and come back to the folk."

110

"You are so sure you are right. Can you not see that I am right in this? Help me Hancid, we must bring him away, that is the only way that I can forgive you for having brought me to this evil place. I hope never to see such a sight again, only by saving just one can I bear to think of this. Without this one alive I think I must come here to kill the rest, to save them from this disgusting lie, which is never life."

She crouched beside the lonely pup and lifted a heavy stone in both her hands. It swung above the helpless creature and through tear-blind eyes she took her aim. The pup's dark eyes widened and two oily tears trickled down its face. Giersi hurled away her stone and sobbing laid her face in the damp fur. Alarmed at her violence Hancid began to help her away, afraid at last of what he had begun. Slipping in the disgusting mud they staggered away, then Giersi looked back. On the slope behind them the little pup, weeping piteously, was slithering along to follow them.

The long struggle back to the folk called for all the strength Hancid had left. Only just returned from venture he longed to lie at ease among the folk, yet here he swam the long waves once more with Giersi half sinking at his side as she helped the pup along. He, it was clear, had never been in water before, but he swallowed his fear and fixed his liquid eyes on Giersi, ready to follow her to the world's end. In the first wave he automatically closed his nose, though after watching old nans with the babies of the folk Giersi was ready with finger and thumb to pinch his nostrils together. He also had some idea of swimming but his awkward tail swung from side to side with no real purpose and he lost his way. It was soon obvious that his wet fur was weighing him down and without his baby fat he had little buoyancy or protection from the cold. Then Giersi took him in her arms and swam on her back, holding him close, and the feel of his warm breath against her cheek gave her strength to go on again. But at the last it was Hancid who brought them both home, swimming in the face of a wind which made the surface a nightmare of chopped waves and flying spume. With the baby seal he could not dare to dive deep, and he doubted whether Giersi was even conscious when they came to the home channels.

Her harsh face turned aside all the well-wishers who crowded the beach and she walked between them, the pup in her arms, to her bed in the cave sand. Wearily Hancid shook his head at the query in old Larra's eyes.

"We must wait a little longer," was all he would say. "We must wait."

With the first light Giersi was away again, the exhausted pup at her side. She took him in her arms and tried to teach him to hold to her shoulders or to grip her hair. But though he pressed his flippers against her neck he was too weak now and soon fell back.

Once at the narrow cove she had a new problem: would the old bull let them through his guard? She approached anxiously but found him occupied with another threat. A young male seal was cruising at the entrance watching the first cow who, though aware of him, lay sunning herself on a rock, refusing his advances. Choosing her moment Giersi thrust the little pup before her and slipped in among the encircling rocks. Slowly, with calm, sure movements, she walked up the beach and laid her little one beside the pup who rested there to wait for his mother.

She was a long time returning; she had fed her child at first light then gone back into the sea. She would not leave the water until the rush of the tide brought her up the beach in the late afternoon. While they waited, Giersi fondled the older pup then rubbed her hands in the little one's drying fur, transferring some of the familiar scent to the newcomer. In the middle of the day bright sunlight lit the beach and the two seals shifted awkwardly, unaccustomed to the heat. As the day began to die the older pup started to lose heart: he threw back his head and wailed. Then the mother lifted her head in the water and searched about for her child. Beside her the other cow lifted to the surface. The pup wailed again. Satisfied the second cow sank back to the bottom:

her tiny pup had lain silent all day in the shade of the cliff and Giersi had been shy to disturb it, knowing it could be no more than a day old like her own.

The first cow slowly swam toward the beach, a widening ripple stretching back behind her dark nose as she quested about for her son. He, unaware of her approach, cried again, putting up his head in a pathetic display of loss and loneliness. Then the little stranger reared up too, opening his mouth as wide as he could:

"Borhaab," he bawled, and with a comic look of astonishment at his own daring sank back on to the sand.

The mother paused, sniffing suspiciously, and Giersi lay still, one hand silencing her tiny pup. The other infant moaned again, he could smell his mother's nearness, and she was compelled to come closer. Her damp nose tested him, querying the sense of strangeness she felt. He seemed intact, and impatient too; with a sigh she rolled onto her side baring a nipple low down on her smooth body and her son began greedily to suck.

Giersi waited until the two were at peace then slowly, carefully lifted the little one into the lee of the mother's warm belly. She placed his nose gently against the second nipple and waited.

Little Borhaab knew what was happening instantly: beneath his searching mouth the nipple suddenly appeared from its pocket of fur and immediately he seized the first feed of his life. His foster mother raised a languid head to sniff at him, but, so close to her own, she caught only the familiar child-smell. Giersi she ignored as she sat there, bright tears of relief standing in her eyes: the pup had taken his chance, he was going to live.

As the urgency of feeding relaxed the mother began gently to pat her own child with a lazy flipper and to scratch fondly in his fur with her long black nails. The little Ronarn wriggled against her side in delight and the two breathed quietly into sleep. Borhaab edged over against Giersi who curled about him, hiding him from

113

the searching wind which had crept into the narrow confines of the gheo. Out on the open sea the waves were glowing with the Day Star's dying but Giersi felt no more the longing to be gone. While the master bull patrolled back and forth she slept untroubled on the open beach.

During the night both cows had left the beach to feed and sleep in the warm comfort of the water. On the night tide they came in to feed their young and Giersi was woken by Borhaab's wriggling efforts to reach his foster mother. Again at first light he fed and while the cows sank back into the water and the pups slept, Giersi was able to search for food for herself about the rocks and pools laid bare by the ebb.

For the first three days in the gheo skies were clear and the weather remained bright, although a chill wind sidled in from the sea at the end of each day. Giersi, who had never spent a night away from her folk until this, would have found it too cold to sleep if it had not been for the warm body of Borhaab huddled against her. With every feed his loose coat seemed to fill up as he grew his comfortable covering of blubber, and his silky white fur shone as she stroked and scratched him.

During this time a third cow came into the gheo, heavy with her unborn pup. In the early dawn her tiny daughter was born, so quickly that Giersi was scarcely aware of what had happened. Straight away the little one began to suckle, then patiently lay still while her mother humped away down the beach to lie at ease in the water.

Only as the pups grew older did their mothers show more than momentary interest in them, and the master bull, who may or may not have fathered them, seemed unaware of their lives. When the good weather broke and wind-whipped waves set higher and higher up the beach the mothers appeared anxious, the two recent arrivals even going so far as to place themselves protectively in front of their offspring as the sea hurled itself up the beach. As the sandy space grew smaller Ronarn's mother climbed up behind him and taking his hind flippers in her mouth pulled him higher up out of danger.

When the dark ferocity of the storm broke over them Giersi was terrified: at such times she and the other womenfolk all cowered in the cave. The lightning blinded her and she wanted to run wildly about as the thunder bounded back and forth between the cliff sides, echoing and grumbling. Somehow she remained still, braced upright against a rock, Borhaab in her arms, as wave upon wave broke over her head and smashed against the roots of the cliff, ripping back sand and stone to rattle against her legs. Out in the turbulence of the narrow bay she saw the three seals; one was wedged on a high rock, her child sheltered by her sturdy body; the other two swam the storm, one cradling Ronarn in her arms, the other nosing her baby away from the bruising rocks. She seemed clumsily unable to grip the tiny pup in her flippers and as the fury of the storm grew, her efforts seemed useless.

A feeble daylight glinted on the rainwater that poured down the cliff face, and the laden clouds seemed to shut off the gheo beneath their metallic weight as they hurtled before the wind. It was not until the day's end that they started to split and tear under the wind's constant driving, and a pale yellow sky could be seen high beyond them. Although the rain stopped with the dark, the wind continued to shriek and cry in the rock crevices and Giersi could find no shelter from the tossing sea. When morning looked wearily into the cove from under the sullen clouds the small curve of beach was changed. The storm had built up a drift of sand and shingle in front of the cliff and in the hollow behind it lay a bedraggled white pup, battered and drowned.

Giersi stood aghast, then fled out into the bay searching for her friends. The cow and her little pup had left their perch on the rock, Ronarn and his mother were nowhere in sight. Giersi stumbled back up the littered beach to Borhaab.

She dragged the other dead pup down the beach and

swam out with it until the pull of the tide took it. Then in the sandy hollow she scooped out a bed for herself and her seal pup. All day they lay there sleeping; rousing only to gaze out to sea searching for the missing seals.

By midday the youngest mother and her pup had returned. Later the other cow came ashore alone and lay awhile in the breaker's foam. She showed no sense of loss and soon would leave the beach. Of Ronarn there was still no sign though Giersi once thought she heard his hungry cry. His mother came heavily ashore before the evening high water and permitted Borhaab to feed for a few moments. But she was restless and frequently made as if to return to the water. Each time, however, she returned and raised her face to Giersi's, her wise eyes pleading for some kind of understanding.

Giersi stepped beside her to the water's edge, then crouched down, her hand on the uneasy cow's head. For a long moment they watched one another's eyes.

"Very well. I am with you. Let me help,"

Satisfied, the seal turned into the water and swam off.

Giersi followed. Out to the point of the narrow bay they went, then the seal swung round and held herself up on her tail, her nose and whiskers questing the air. Giersi looked up but could see nothing. She scrambled among the weed-hung rocks, the waves sucking angrily at her arms and legs. At last her agile toes found a hold and she climbed free. Standing on the rock she searched about in the failing light. A wave fell back with a chuckling, gurgling sound but there was something more. A spluttering cry, watery, half-submerged on the other side of an ugly boulder.

It was not in Giersi's nature to leap the open space between. She lowered herself into the angry water under the huge rock and began to edge round, her feet searching for a hold hidden beneath the water and weed. She slipped and for a moment her foot was trapped and she must bend and squirm, her head below the next flowing wave, to free herself. Carried out with the wave she clung to the side of the rock and pushed herself round. In a moment she was face to face with Ronarn.

Caught between two boulders above her head he had been trapped by the retreating tide. Almost unconscious with fear he hung now close to drowning as the sea returned. Giersi wedged herself into the gap below him and with her shoulder eased him upward as the next wave came gushing round the rock to cover her. Close to her cheek she felt the pounding terror of his heart but again she was able to lift him clear and as he breathed more easily he began to grow calm. Her own arms and legs were strained to bear his weight but first she knew she must still his fear. When at last she could hold him up no longer she gentled him with words:

"Soon all will be well, little one. Only wait while Giersi comes to you."

She pulled herself up through the gap in the rocks until she was above him. He was heavier than her own pup, almost too much for her, but as the next wave filled the hollow she seized his hind flippers, his cold, fleshy feet and dragged him back, freeing his tail. Then gently she nudged him down the smooth back of the rock and so out into the sea once more where his mother waited.

All the seals lay on the beach that night. Whenever Giersi opened her eyes she felt confident, calm eyes upon her. Contented, she buried her head against Borhaab's side. She was a part of the seal family and they trusted her.

After the storm it seemed that her life among the seals changed. The cows relaxed and left her alone. Even if she came close to them, in water or on land, they no longer brushed her away with irritated gestures. The old bull ignored her as ever and the young challenger, who had fled before the storm to open water, was uninterested. But the youngsters were ready for any kind of mischief.

First they worried at the pieces of driftwood washed up on the beach and when Giersi finally threw the water-worn stick into the sea they hurtled after it to play. They nosed the stick about, dived under it, bit it and threw it up with their flippers. Then Ronarn would swim off with it, only to be chased by the younger Borhaab who would catch at his tail, snapping and swirling in the water until his foster brother turned to chase him. They hid from Giersi among the rocks, then burst out on her grinning, their rows of pointed teeth glistening below their stiff dark whiskers. When she grabbed at them they swam away, but one was always glad of a ride home on her shoulders if the chase went too far.

Though at first they tumbled awkwardly in the water, soon they were her equals, diving and rolling confidently five or ten feet down. Once or twice they chases shrimps or little fish but Giersi was not sure if they really ate their prey. At the end of every game they pulled themselves happily up the beach and eased themselves into a sleeping hollow, content to wait for their next nursed meal.

The weather remained calm and mild, the high clouds a shelter for their games and growing. Ronarn was first to lose his shining white coat. For some days his mother had contentedly accepted the master bull's advances and their mating was a slow and stately dance in the offshore waves. Now she was preparing to leave and the old one vented his angry spite on the precocious junior bull who finally gave up hope and retired, leaving him the two anxious younger cows.

Within a couple more days Borhaab also assumed a tattered, patchy appearance as his silky white baby fur dropped away and the handsome mottled grey of an adult seal began to show. Giersi watched with alarm: her baby would grow and go away. The hair rubbed off first from his head and hind flippers and Giersi scratched at the place, easing the itching that he felt. He loved to be made much of in this way and rolled over, stretching out his chin for her attention, but in shock she stopped. When at last he turned an inquisitive eye toward her she humbly resumed her grooming, but spoke as she did so:

"You wear a strange sign, my Borhaab, here about your neck. In your fur you carry the sign I have chained to me. See? This is my stone." And she held the broken cairngorm she wore in front of the seal's eyes. "See Borhaab? It is my father's stone. Has he marked you too? Shall we be joined by this strange sign forever so that you will not leave me?"

The pup sensed her sadness and rolled upright, his eyes moist with distress. Laughing she held him close, but every day brought nearer the time when he would be gone.

With a humble forethought Giersi led Borhaab away from the gheo when his moult was complete. They swam side by side in the long waves and, though she was leading him, he often swam ahead, glancing back with wise eyes as if he knew all that was in her mind. In this way she brought him to the home beach.

There was a gladness at her return, but tempered by unease at her companion. Few of the silkies had time for a young seal, some even claimed that he would steal their food.

"No, no," cried Giersi. "He fishes for himself now. He will take only what he needs from the wide sea, he will not forage here."

But she always knew that Sea Folk were hard to persuade and that in bringing home her seal she was defying tradition.

"See how gentle he is," the folk used to murmur when he pillowed his head in Giersi's lap. But they would never fondle him or make him welcome. Was it their lack of love that made him leave? Later, during the dark winter days, Giersi would let this bitterness flow through her.

Whatever the cause, in the end the day came. More and more Borhaab had swum alone but this time, before he left to fish the high tide, he fixed his solemn eyes on her face. Somehow he seemed to know that this was the real leave-taking and sadly he gazed about the empty beach as if printing it on his memory. Then with a long sigh he gazed out to the far horizon.

At that look of purpose Giersi knew.

"Why must you go? I need you. Only stay a while."

But as she pleaded she knew her own pride and despised herself. Of course he would go; it was his life to go, to be a seal, and hers to stay. There was nothing to be said. One last time she leaned her cheek against his smooth head, caressed his warm skin. Once more his whiskers reached the hollow of her neck, his warm breath was in her ear.

Then:

"Goodbye," she whispered, and without a backward glance walked up the beach. Borhaab watched sadly, yawned away the tension of the moment, and gave himself to the sea, his home.

Chapter Eight
Hunter

Through the long winter darkness Giersi suffered alone. Now and again Larra sat at her side, smoothing her hair and patting her weary shoulders, but the contact brought no relief and night after night the girl's sobbing troubled the folk in their sleep.

"We can only wait," said Hancid again, but Larra felt fear seeping around her heart. They had waited so long, but it seemed that patience was not enough. When the folk gathered in the cave for the stories and songs that ease winter's night away she took her place beside the the girl and lay her arm about her to give her warmth.

"Sing for us, Giersi," she whispered and felt her sadly shake her head.

The young men, grown since their ventures in the wide sea, told of the sights they had seen, the dangers they had known. Useless boys, waiting their turn to prove their worth, sat near their heroes, eyes glistening in the dusk. Older men were called upon to add their deeds to the histories of the Sea Folk and time and again the old ventures were rehearsed once more: of Tsebbrid who went among men; or of Idranil and the Snow People.

"Why?" The folk marvelled as so often before. "Why are the landsmen so strange? Why so angry with all other creatures? What do they fear?"

"They fear death," murmured an old grandsire. "They believe they should be immortal and regard death with a panic dread. They spend life attempting to avoid its end rather than enjoying its flow. In an effort to live for ever they even attack one another."

"But surely," queried one youngster, "that is a story from the past, grandsire. Can men really be so evil?"

"My own grandsire, when just as young as you, boy, had occasion to watch the antics of men. What he saw then, long before my borning, has been told to one or two of you here, and been believed."

His listeners nodded solemnly, and gleaming eyes turned towards the youngster, who prompted:

"I have never heard the story, grandsire. Would it please you to tell us once again?"

His good manners placated old Perrid, who settled his back against a rock and began to tell the story of the sinking of a gigantic ship among the distant icebergs.

"All this," he finished, "my grandsire saw with his own eyes and heard with his own ears: the men as they entered the water gave up great cries and screams. They gripped at one another, struggling to climb up into the air. But they could not. The hangings and covers which they wore were filled with water and this pulled them down. In little boats some bobbed about and my grandsire swam among them. But when he approached there were angry cries and someone spat noisy fire at him. This is the sorry way of men when they face death. They have no courage for the open seas."

Old Perrid, his white hair a snowy cover on neck and shoulders, nodded his firm belief in the inferiority of men; but certain of the folk were bold enough to disagree.

"It is true that in their big ships they cannot know the seas as we do, but I do not question the courage of those who go alone on the water, without machines to help them."

"And I have respect for those who paddle in a small curragh. I remember once ..."

So story followed story in the winter cave; of summer seasons spent in venturing and of bravery in winter's storms. Outside the cave days of icy brilliance were lost to days of fog or sleety rain. Wind-driven waves thundered along the shore and foam rolled and tumbled on the beach. Whenever possible the women crept out to gather food, as the days grew shorter and the cold more intense.

On the shortest day the proper ceremonies were observed and the well-remembered words rehearsed until the Day Star lifted on the rim of the world and it was certain that spring was on its way. Then there was rejoicing in the cave: music and laughter rang out over the tossing waves and for the first time Giersi felt a little hope begin to warm her.

"Surely, with the spring the seals will return."

And she began to sing again for the folk, weaving into her music the song of the seals. It was the time when maidens sing, waiting for their babes to be born. It was a time of rejoicing and ritual as the women folk prepared, and the old men recited the mystery of the world's beginning and the coming of the Sea Folk.

In the beginning the whole world was water, liquid yet still. Below the silent water lay solid rock, earth's centre, and above the smooth surface of the water lay the air, unmoving. Above the surface of the resting air lay the motionless stars. The whole world waited, lifeless.

Then from his home in the bottomless deeps the lordly whale rose up: Balengorion rose up from his birthplace in the deep and his black back split the shimmering surface, and he blew.

So for the first time the air began to move, drifted here and there by that first breath of life. Then Balengorion curved down again to the dark depths, but as he curved away his tail rose up high above the silent surface and with one stroke of his mighty flukes a wave became. So for the first time the water began to move, driven back and forth by that first stroke of life.

Beneath the rocking waters and the whispering air the whale lay, and the dark of the deeps was no more than the dark of the air above, for there was no light in the world. Then the whale began to sing. Balengorion's song is a mystery for he sang no words, but as he sang, in answer to his song, so for the first time the Star began to rise, called up into the sky by that first song of life.

In the wonder of that light the seas began to spawn. Swarming life filled the waters, swelled by the power of the new Day Star. First the tiniest specks of living things appeared, then the krill to feed the whale. And the whale still sang and the Day Star shone and sea creatures grew, and the sea was the womb of all the world.

Out of that womb swam a second star. It was the moon who tore herself free from the solid depths below the waters to swing in the night sky searching for light. Night after night she curves across the sky in the track of the Day Star. But she has no will to stand beside that light. Her shores are all dead things and in her yearning she calls the earth to join her search. By day and night the land she left tilts at her bidding and in the caves she deserted lie the captive seas.

Out of this catastrophe was all land born, when the seas fell back to fill the empty chasm where once the moon had lain. Since that time we of the sea are ever subjugated to the imperious land.

Yet the Day Star's light continued to bless sea and land alike, and on the land creatures began to crawl. And the whale still sang and the Day Star shone.

On the dry land began Man to apear, solid and earth born, longing for a sea season; Man the Avenger, aggressive and angry. In the ranks of Man grew Parscid, Protector. At the hand of Man he saw the world perishing; he saw pain and persecution.

Parscid walked on the shore in deep thought: his was the time of decision, of midsummer venturing and the time to know himself. In his mind troubles lay thick as smelt in the sea.

124

Parscid waited, surrendered to the Day Light. He waited for a silence to show him the way. Then from the deeps he heard the song of Balengorion. The song of the whale was calling him, catching him, never to return:

"Come to the deeps, Sire of the Sea Folk, come to the open wave, to moon tide and star time. Come with your daughters to the cool wide sea where peace and possession is waiting for you."

Parscid heard the song and gladly deserted the world of men. Happily he left the earth whose stones had become too hard for him. Parscid, Sire of the Sea Folk, led his family into the waves. So he gave us our freedom: to be one of the people of the sea.

Heavy storms were still punishing the beach, and Giersi often gazed beyond the sheltering rocks that held the cove, while the great breakers roared in, streaming such manes of spindrift above their mighty shoulders that a haze of spray reached to the far horizon. Through the droplets daylight was diffused and vague, giving little sense of time or direction.

"Where is the little one in this roar and rush?" she sighed. "Is it well with him?"

The rage of winter eased. Distant rocks were seen clear above the waves, and the startled cry of the seabirds was heard once more on the beach. Youngsters were primed for venturing and, anxiously watching the preparations of the men, exercised in the shallows and practised their skills.

The seals returned to haul out on the rocks and wait for the warmth, but Borhaab did not come.

"No lost venturer was ever watched for like this," the maidens of Giersi's borning giggled behind her back, their own babies now on their hips.

Hancid, before he left, drew her on one side.

125

"Giersi, it has become a madness with you. Forget the seals this year and give yourself to your own life. Sing and swim in the shallows, sweetheart. Enjoy the summertime and let me be sure of your happiness when I return."

Giersi frowned at his words but he would say no more, only laughed and then was gone.

Among the womenfolk Giersi sang the farewell songs and stood at the outermost Point to watch the youngsters, three who swam this year on their first venture. Nearby mothers and sisters wept once the boys were gone into the wide waves, but Giersi gazed dry-eyed across the dazzling waste of water. One dark head broke the surface suddenly, returning, and she felt a sadness for the shame of his womenfolk.

Then he was closer and she saw with a tension of unfounded gladness that it was the dark nose of a seal cutting an arrowed wake into the cove. Abruptly he stopped, held himself upright in the water and snuffed at the air, searching. His dark, round eyes found her where she stood and with a rush he was on the rock beside her, his head butting at her legs, an old trick, forcing her to sink to her knees at his side. Moaning with pleasure and excitement Borhaab had come back.

The summer skies widened above them as they played in the waves. Again Giersi slept in the open beside the seal. As a result of his travels he had grown muscled and firm. His puppy stage was gone and he was a seal almost full grown. His gleaming coat was dark, marked in every way by grey. When they swam together he was now clearly the master, stronger and faster than she. When the chase went too far for her she was glad at the end of the day to lay a hand on his back and so ride home.

He woke her with every dawn, snuffing at her face until she bared her teeth at him, then he knew she was awake and fuffed fish-scented breath over her, demanding that she join him in the water. With every high tide he left her to hunt his food and when he returned he found her gleaning the rocks after the ebb.

126

Then, sated, they lay down together in the warmth of the day, soaking the light into their skins. He could lie for long periods of time and often she was the first to seek the water once more. Then they swam together, diving and curving beneath the waves. She would hold his flippers as he lay backward on the water and together they would dive, testing one another: who would remain the longest? Try as she would, Giersi had to surrender first, even when she practised like Borhaab to expel all the air around her heart and lungs and dive empty. It was no use, her need for air overcame her and she must burst to the surface or choke under the heavy water.

Borhaab surfaced with her, laughing, his pointed teeth bared in his grinning face, his whiskers bristling with amusement. Yet he was understanding and sympathetic, knowing immediately when she tired and circling her anxiously if he thought she was in trouble.

He showed her a game he had discovered: climbing a smooth rock then sliding again and again into the sea. The seal had no manners but pushed her roughly away as soon as he was ready to go down and often they hit the water together in a flurry of arms and tail. At day's end Giersi would have returned to her own sleeping place, but Borhaab was forbidden by the folk who feared for the five new babes, and if Giersi walked away her friend wept desolately and she could not leave him.

At last the old ones came to her in a group, stern and forbidding.

"This cannot be, Giersi. We may not bring seals here among the folk. There is no custom to assure us of their behaviour."

She shook her head at them, hid her tell-tale face in her hair. But she heard their whispers:

"Manchild's daughter ..." That label again, from her childhood, stirring her pride if they only knew. But what was this?

"...always their way: to keep animals in thrall."

What did they know about it? Borhaab was not her slave, he was free, free of the water as she was herself.

"The young seal must travel once more, child, and you must take your place among your folk. It is time, Giersi, to put away such things."

"If he leaves I go at his side," she answered slowly. "I gave him his life, I have a duty."

"There is truth in it," cried Larra. "If he were an errant boychild she could do no less."

"But this is a seal. She has no duty here."

They discussed her as if she were no longer with them and Giersi slipped thankfully away. Their journey began with the next tide.

It seemed natural that Borhaab should lead and as he swam southward Giersi followed gladly. At first they played as they swam, but Giersi tired and there was no land in sight. She learned to rest upon the ocean, just as she had learned to sleep on the open beach. Always, with the seal, her life was being extended beyond the confining customs of the folk. She learned to eat as he did, finding food beneath the waves. For her taste there were little shrimps and other hardly formed crustaceans; for Borhaab young fish, squid and even octopus. Eating was a diversion in their long swim. Day and night they journeyed, and another day and another night. Borhaab seemed to know where he was going, although whether it was the currents that guided him or the stars Giersi could never tell.

She was weary when at last the land came into sight on the southern horizon, but she had become used to the rhythms of travel and felt that she was able enough to go farther. The flat rocks fringed with swinging weed were Borhaab's destination, however, and here he hauled himself out with a long sigh of satisfaction. It was an empty enough spot, the rocks stretching away to a long line of low cliffs where few birds nested. Where the cliffs dipped to the water's edge lay a small village, but it was far off and the men lived quietly there.

That evening Borhaab led her closer to the village and taught her to find lobster pots on the end of their lines.

These he could open with his skilful nose and Giersi was delighted to reach into the trap and pull out the inquisitive creature caught inside, which they took back to their rock to eat.

The next day Giersi would have gone to the traps again but Borhaab refused. Watching from the water she saw the fisherman's little boat chug out, and realised the intelligence of the seal who had kept her safely out of sight. Other seals knew this coast and swam close from time to time, but Borhaab sang to them, warning them away from his territory. When they hauled out on nearby rocks Giersi went to meet the newcomers, but Borhaab was aloof, he had company enough.

One bright afternoon, when small wavelets chuckled at the undersides of the rock and the air was warm with the scent of grass from the cliff tops, Giersi lay and lazily watched the seal playing in the water below her. The pool was light clean and she could see him twist and turn in an imagined hunt. Suddenly he appeared with a sly look from under the edge of the rock. A quiff of bladder wrack was plastered down on his head and he cocked a look at her that was at once so quizzical and so smug that Giersi laughed aloud. Then Borhaab began to idiot about, shaking the weed and pouncing on it, tossing it up with his flippers then diving down with it in his mouth. He swam off on his back with the seaweed on his belly, then rolled away slapping at it as it sank. He worried at it like this for a long time for her amusement, then suddenly swept up to the surface just where she sat and beating the water with his flippers splashed her thoroughly, forcing her to come and join his play. He was full of mischief, holding her legs with his flippers when she tried to swim, curving underneath her when she was afloat to lift and tip her.

They splashed all afternoon in their happy game, then lay breathless on the rock. Neither knew that they were being watched.

The spitting crack and the thud into Borhaab's flesh came simultaneously. He lifted himself up startled, then grunted at the hurt in his side. The bullet had torn a lung and blood bubbled on his muzzle as he breathed. Giersi watched in alarm, saw the fear and the pain in his dark eyes, and knew.

She lay one hand gently on his neck as so often before and with the other cupped water from a pool to clean his nose and mouth. His eyes were dimming but did not leave her face as she sat to wait with him for this death which seemed to have come from nowhere. His breathing hurt him and he lay his head on her legs, comforted by her presence at the start of this last journey, feeling safer because he was not alone.

Giersi watched in terror the man who walked down the front of the cliff, but she was determined to remain at her friend's side. His second shot whistled into the water below her, a third snapped shards of stone from the rock at her side, pricking her hands and face. In a hysteria of fear she dived and swam, still unable to believe that she would never see Borhaab again.

He had been lying in the grass on the cliff top all day long, and was bored indeed. Time and time again he would roll onto his back, pull the magazine from his jacket pocket, snap it into place and roll over again propped on his elbows aiming at imaginary targets. He prided himself on his speed with his new weapon, so much more deadly than the old shotgun of his father's with which he had first learned to shoot, trailing around the countryside at home about Arthurstown, hunting a rabbit or a pigeon. Now he was on to the real thing!

As soon as he saw the seals in the water below he had lined up his sights on them, edging closer to the cliff for a wider angle. Sure it was worth a shot, even at that distance, for the rifle had a range of eighteen hundred feet. He would wait while they played in the water there, but if they should happen to be still then the luck was in it. As they stretched on the rocks in the afternoon sun he eased the safety catch forward for single shot and picked a target behind and just below the larger creature's right flipper.

130

He knew the shot was good for he saw the animal jerk as the bullet penetrated. Yet the other did not try to escape, which was strange. Once below the cliff top he snapped off another shot standing, but it hadn't the precision and his third only ricocheted off the rock. The smaller creature went for the water at that but the bull was certainly finished. Rifle crooked in his arm as he had learned to carry the old shotgun, he hopped out on the rocks to take a closer look at his bag.

The seal rolled liquid eyes up at him, lingering and still alive. Quickly, too quickly for thought, Michael Shea swung the butt of the rifle. Once, twice and it was finished. Within fifteen minutes he was pulling the skin free from the last clinging shreds of blubber. He washed his hands in a pool and cleaned his knife. The seawater settled, rust-stained; the blood darkened in the sunlight and the carcase shone white and greasy. Michael climbed up the cliff path, pleased with his catch.

"You've never taken a seal skin?" Uncle Jimmy Cregan greeted him, wide-eyed.

"Sure and why not? There's a bounty on them, worth five or six pound where I come from."

"There's no luck in it, killing a seal. Sure doesn't the seal stand friend to man in the water? It's the Seal King's anger you're bringing on yourself now: isn't that the truth of it?"

"Away with you, there's nothing in that kind of talk."

"Well just don't be bringing it in the house then. I've no use for it at all."

Michael shrugged, and stretched out the skin behind the low stone wall that stood between the cottage and the road. He couldn't decide whether he was going to keep and cure it or whether he would take it to his father in the South for the reward: he needed only the snout to claim the money. It could lie there for now and he would see.

With his hands clean of the blood he went into the uncle's house for his tea. Sure this wasn't indeed his uncle, no brother of his father. But the old man had given him refuge when he was in trouble, and wasn't he caring for him and cooking for him and all?

Michael sat reading the paper by the fire until the meal was put on the table: a plate of egg and chips, wrinkled and overdone. Beside the plate stood a cup of rust-brown tea, strong and pungent, and sweetened with condensed milk. Michael bent his lips to the steaming rim.

"Oh the dear God! Will you look at that." Cregan was standing white-faced at the window. "It's herself. Come for her skin."

"The what?" Michael strolled across to look out.

The sun had just set, and dark against the glowing sky he saw a figure, face shadowed, shawled in black. It was Giersi.

"I said there was no good would come of it. Its her skin she's after and she'll never return without it." Cregan babbled. The old man seemed half demented at this evidence of superstition which stood outside his window. "Go out now and give it to her back and get rid of her."

"Whoever she is," Michael's voice shrilled with irritation, "tell her to take herself away out of here. The whole village will be on to me in the next minute. Go out and tell her now."

But Cregan would not move and in the end it was Michael himself who stepped out into the still summer evening. The girl's voice was no more than a whisper to him but in that silence it hissed and muttered malevolently.

"Have you no English?" he asked her, for he could understand not a word.

She spoke again and lifted an arm beneath the blanket she had taken from a neighbouring line. She pointed at the seal skin. Her eyes were hollow pits in her sorrowed face.

"Sure I'll take the muzzle and you can have the skin," said Michael, placating her.

He drew his knife and knelt to the work. In that moment she was at his side, her fingers in his hair, her cry a long ululation of misery. Michael leapt away from her touch, his eyes wide, seeing her arm, her shoulder, covered in hair, thick, like a seal's He stumbled away from her, his mind racing. There could be no truth in the old stories surely, yet she stood before him.

At her step he backed away, his trembling lips tried to form words but he could get no breath into his dry throat. She came closer again and his lungs flattened on a loud gasp of dread. Then he shied away and began to run. He found only one way, from the cottage to the cliff top again, and arms outstretched he compelled himself along. His feet were heavy, treading wildly, and he stumbled against the tufts and tussocks of grass that pressed close to the path. He fell against brambles, or against gorse and sobbed at the pain; but she was behind him still and he dragged himself away and on. A stone leapt from under his foot, cracking against his ankle bone and he almost fell. Then pushing himself up with his fists, like a runner off the blocks, he was away again, aware of the uncanny figure that plodded behind him.

Giersi had no plan, no clear notion of what she was doing. When she had returned to the rock and seen the heap of bloody offal which had once been her Borhaab she had screamed on a long keening note and a blackness had descended on her eyes and mind. Hunting dimly through this fog of sorrow, shock and pain she had followed the track of the man. Somewhere the seal, her friend, still existed and there was only one way to go. She had no understanding of the terror her accusing presence had created, but she followed like fate, waiting for the outcome.

The man was running to the sea and strangely she heard again old Perrid's words:

"They fear death. They have no courage for the open seas."

The man was running to his death then, and it was fit that he should. Giersi followed, watching blankly, mercilessly. The covering that she had stolen fell from her, her long hair streamed out behind her. She ran crouched and silent while the man sobbed and moaned in terror. When he began to slither on the wet rocks she stood watching. He threw a helpless look back over his shoulder: she stood there, the seal woman, naked in her fur, her arm up, pointing to the spot where he had taken the skin. Out there the water covered the rocks now and he watched its oily swell and retreat.

"No. No." His voice trembled, shrilled. "No. I can't swim good. I can't go."

She stepped up to him, panting from the speed, and he saw her even white teeth, her glittering eyes.

Weeping with fear, the strain and torment of the chase now undermining him, he scrambled and fell to the water, rose and stumbled on. At the rocks' end the waves went over his head. In desperation he wriggled upward, mouth open, hair streaming, but the water in his pockets and his shoes pulled him down again. His hands clawed at the surface above his head, he rose once more and drew a rasping breath. Then he sank.

Belching bubbles reached the surface, a wave slopped under a rock in echo. In the quiet distance a dog barked and was still. Giersi waited while dusk gathered closer, then wiping the tears from her cheeks in a cleansing gesture, she slipped easily into the comfort of the waves and swam away, turning her harsh face toward the north once more, toward the islands that had once been her world - hers and the seal's.

Chapter Nine
The Islands

Dusk had settled down early: first in the corners and passageways, then spreading into streets and open places. When the lamps were lit the dusk was defiant darkness in every hollow between the slabs and cones of yellow light built by the shops and the street lights. Streets glistened under a slime of forgotten rain and oily puddles shimmered as a gusting wind whooped by the buildings. Grey cloud swung low over the roofs and trailed a raining mist in the chimneys, tipping an afterthought of raindrops against umbrellas and hat brims. Voices and footsteps rang hollow, as if enclosed, as the people of Mallaig hurried home to their toasting tea.

The steamer was gone to Armadale hours before, and the last train was off to Fort William. In the harbour, water slopped awkwardly at the sea wall and only one late fishing boat was still unloading. Heavy men in dun-coloured sweaters and long thigh boots moved through light and dark, work almost done. A clatter of empty boxes landed askew by the old fish market wall, dislodging the drifted figure resting there.

His greasy rubbed raincoat was stained from sleeping damp, his boots stuffed with paper against the cold. A fence of whiskers surrounded his face, which he jutted toward the rattle and wet like a terrier on a rabbit hole.

"Are you there then, you old sea crab?" cried one of the men.

"What's he after?" asked the boy.

"Are you searching the silkies yet? Did you not find one now, McBride?"

Muttering, the old man gathered up his nest of tattered plastic bags and carried what was left of his life away to the emptied town. Tomorrow he would try for the islands again.

For twenty years McBride had searched. Following first one clue, then another. Ideas danced in his head confusing him and he tracked back and forth on a lost trail. The images of what he had once seen and understood about the folk became muddled among present worries. Then he took whisky and his mind cleared of it all and for an hour or two he knew himself again and seemed firm of purpose. But the morning brought self-doubts and hatreds and he was away again crossing and recrossing water and land; submerging his despised self in order only to watch, and to listen, as anyone would late at night and the family not yet home.

At first he had settled in his island croft within sight of a wide, white shell-sand beach. There the wind from the sea honed his brain, scouring it for action. For those first years his yearning mind scrabbled at the little language he had left: the tapes Bridik had made.

In order to make a start he first had to transcribe everything, listening again and again to the unknown sounds and forcing them to conform, to submit as combinations of the twenty-six letters which were all he had to work from. The most difficult to reproduce were the complicated long drawn-out vowel sounds of the folk, changing as they did in accent and pitch. Some of the sounds he recognised as words Bridik himself had taught him and on these he built his notation forms, but he knew there was room for wide errors and that often he was far from the uniformity that he needed. When at last he was satisfied that the written forms were as near to accuracy as he could hope to achieve, he began a statistical breakdown of the material, noting first the frequency with which certain terms appeared

136

throughout the text. He made notes of the position of certain words in relation to one another, and was able to discover which words were paired or permanently linked.

Once the unknown was reduced to mathematical proportions he was able to draw up a table or grid from which he was led to an understanding of the form of the grammar which governed the language. The folk used a system which was very like one, so he had read, adopted by the Eskimo people: adding or subtracting a seemingly infinite combination of suffixes or prefixes. Once certain of these were known it was possible from their position in the linkage to infer the meaning of others. If these held up in another context he had added a further point in his vocabulary.

Translation was slow at first, involving a great deal of guesswork, with later substitutions as new meanings became clear. He found that there was no difference marked in gender, though masculine and feminine names were always recognisable since the males all carried the -id syllable while the female names involved the softer rolling -r. This led him to difficulties in translation, some of which he never solved to his own satisfaction.

The tapes contained a collection of the songs, myths and legends of the folk, handed on in an oral tradition from generation to generation. Only rarely did Bridik seem to forget, or need to correct himself in his recitation. His story of the Bannern, a black winged bird which McBride took to be the shearwater, was a simple tale for children; but many of his songs were more complicated, using a poetic form which McBride found hard to reproduce. One mournful song in particular he was able to mould into the form of a sonnet, which he called Solitude.

All waters of the sea together flow
But I, alone, am here with none beside
To watch with me the ebbing of the tide
Nor hear the seabird's mournful cry and low.

None hears with me the far off rolling call
Of waves that pace out life's eternity;
And life, that changes like the rolling sea
Rolls by, as lone I stand till lone I fall.
The wind drones by and leaves me in its wake
And, sweeping on, so life has left me here
Upon the sands, shed, like a fallen tear,
By the remorseless sea: or like a flake
Of fallen snow, which lies upon the ground
To melt away, unknown, unsought, unfound.

Another song, with a more cheerful air, entirely
defeated his efforts:

Khermara rode out to conquer the sea wave,
Khermara rode out to ...?

Led by the laughing (?Northern?) lights
Led by their ?windglow
Khermara rode high
To the spindrift and snow
Khermara rode out etc ...

One hand caught a ?bright star
The other a moonbeam
He/she ?straggled his feet
Over ripple and ?ream

The ice of the moonbeam
Burned ...?
The ... star glittered
And slid in his/her fingers ...

No, it was useless: the terms were too specialised and in
any case he could not tell whether Khermara was a man
or a woman. If, as it seemed, the song told of a venture,
then it ought to follow that the hero was male since it
seemed that the women of the folk were all content to
remain quietly at home. But the name, Khermara, was
not a male name? McBride set the puzzle aside, perhaps
another story would help to unravel it.

He turned to one that he recognised: a ballad that Bridik had sung repeatedly before allowing it to be put on tape, as if he were practising it. The tune hung in slow minor sequences and there seemed no pattern to the words. The grammar was complicated by the fact that, unlike any other in the collection, this song or story, whichever it might be, was in the first person. In his own mind McBride had for a long time thought of it as Bridik's Lament.

When I was a boy, round-faced, light-limbed, gladness surrounded me as water the world. I never thirsted then for happiness nor felt it hold me up. I went with sure step among the folk, knew their love without earning it and their care without keeping it. This is the smooth-rubbed image of childhood which we cherish, looking upon it late.

Night-time, in a dream-time, waking I see it all again, all the warm remembered mellow memories march before my eye and I want again to be there, to know once more that cool confidence. Why, when I was there, did I wish myself away with longing for elsewhere? Within me were two folk, one wanting the still and steady land of infant safety while the other, yearning, whined for the wind-drift wave and a wondered going where all of the future is only beyond the next steep-sided water slide.

I am twice-formed, once for land, and water for the other. My father being of the folk my earth mother minded my going forth on the foam. She cried, they say, "How will I know my babe?" and from her store brought out a shaped stone, stamped it under her shoe and made my half. With a tiny metal chain she chained me to this piece of earth and I, willed to wear it, suffer its long legacy of loneliness. One half I had, and she held the second.

Whenever I swam the wave the stone seemed to draw me down and diving I returned to the old world of men though I stayed in the seas as my folk had taught me. Land-longing came from that stone, and it drew me searching year by year closer to the world of men. I wanted my mother, earth woman, to know me and I searched for her beach on all sides of the ocean path. See me, earth mother, see your stone that I wear, seek me a place in the world of men.

Their shores and their ships I have studied and learned. Now, housed among men here, I lie alone and ashamed. Mine was a water world, free, undemanding; mine was a hammock of peace which I long for again. To be back on the beach of my childhood: Marveen and Larra, Seiglid and Idranil, Hancid and Pletrid, my friends and my loves.

Giersi my daughter will grow comely in maidenhood. Her father they say has died in the sea. She wears the chained stone now, will it tear her too? Or will she, a woman, rest calm on the shore of it? When will she miss me, at star time of evening, or in the slow progress of dawn will she cry for me? Did she ever know me, wanderer that I was? Would she want me? Now?

Land-locked, at last I have all that I longed for, but even the longing is not taken away. Will the tide never turn to bring me back, back to these well-rubbed memories I cherish: when I was a boy, light-limned in gladness?

A night and a day McBride worked on the words and on the sense of what Bridik sang, and as he did so the old fear rose in him again until he found he was gasping, drawing in sobbing breaths as if he had been running, had outrun his strength. Abruptly he left the worktable and the glow of his lamp and pushed his way out into the grey dusk. The wind blew as always on the white beach and he pulled open his shirt allowing the chill to touch his neck and chest. The wild thoughts which tumbled in his head seemed likely to stun him. There was an answer here, but it stuck in his chest like a hastily eaten meal.

He walked, long strides, head back, arms gesticulating. He lurched along. Away. He was getting away. This was what had been behind him ever since the first moment when he held his brother in his arms in the waters off Cape Cod. He had known even then, and he had been afraid. His brother: that creature whose arms and hairy back had given him horror, his own hair prickling at a touch. There was no doubt now, the words were there making everything clear.

McBride fell at last and knelt in the sand motionless staring at distant seas. Years ago, as a child, he had lived here in the croft with his mother in the arm of the isolated bay. A little footpath went between the heather to the pebbled edge of the beach. How the seas roared then in the winter, neighbours never coming near for days during the big storms; and in the summer also they were often left to themselves. For his schooling he was sent away finally to the mainland and she, his mother, was truly alone. She became strange then, and often toward the end would sit slack-handed on a wooden chair in the doorway watching the waves beyond the headland. Days would pass and she never spoke but sat listening to the pain and to her past. When they sent her to the hospital at last he carried her himself into the boat, lifting her up high against his chest for she was no weight at all. She smiled finely then and whispered to him in the Gaelic tongue but he could not hear what it was she said. Afterwards the hospital returned to him all her belongings: a nightdress, stockings, the chain was there then, he remembered. Now where was it put away?

With a sigh he stood up and returned home through his own churned footsteps. He turned up the lamp and began to search. With a little scarf pin, a propelling pencil and the glasses she always refused to wear, the chain lay in an old chocolate box lined with lacy paper. The chain — and the stone.

It swung from his fingers, a fine gold chain threaded through a broken celtic cross of polished cairngorm. His mother wore it always; when it was broken he never knew. Until now. A metal ring had been embedded in the top of the cross and through this the chain was looped. It hung awkwardly now for it was snapped through the centre of the cross and only one loop of the enclosing circle was whole.

"She must have threaded the chain through the circle segment of the other half," he said softly; and felt sudden tears hot in his eyes, straining at his throat. Holding the broken cross he sat down again at the table. The worn stone's autumn colours glowed in the lamp flame. He laid it on the page:

She cried, they say, "How will I know my babe?" and from her store brought out a shaped stone.

There it lay, the shaped stone. He was sure of it, had known it from the start. Bridik was his own mother's child. He himself a brother of the silkie.

The search began that night. A lone man all his life, McBride had already felt the rejection of his fellows. He would ignore them altogether now, his place was with the Sea Folk. Who his own father was he never knew and no longer cared. If one of the folk had claimed his mother he now would claim the folk.

The next morning he placed a padlock on the door of his croft and walked away. A long journey was before him and he covered it step by step. From Barra Head to the Butt of Lewis he came to know the roads and the byways, the tracks and the paths. He crossed the Cuillins of Skye. He travelled from North Uist to St Kilda, climbing the steep harbour stairs under the benign eye of the military while provisions were delivered. The blind houses of the empty street were of no interest to him there, but he listened.

He listened to the songs of the seals on the rocks about Shillay and he heard the singing of the sands beneath his feet at Camas Sgiotaig. He heard the cries of the sea-birds on the cliffs of Oigh-sgeir and, travelling the winding waters which hold the islands in their surge and sway, he learned to recognise those cries, to know their nesting places. Far out over the waters he would see the fulmars, and imagined them in their colonies above the natural arch of Griminish Point, where he himself so often stood to gaze across at empty Hirta, watching for the folk.

He watched again from the gannetries on Sula Sgeir, and from the great basalt cliffs of the Shiants among the beady-eyed guillemots and the burrowing puffins. He learned to know the view from clifftop and hill, from Beinn Mhor across the rich grazing lands of North Uist, from the Weaver's Castle across the Sound of Barra. He knew the wide white skies above the open span of bog and moor beyond the Glen Mor Barvas road, and the brilliant flowering of the machair at Traigh Luskentyre, rich with sea pink and red clover, buttercup and yellow pansy.

Watching always westward he saw the march of winter storms, the heavy mass of black cloud rolling toward him with torrents of rain. In the storm-dark, lightning ripped the sky, but its sound was lost in the roar of the waters as wave after wave heaved their weight against the rocky land, spray flying in blizzards before them. In the twilight of a summer midnight he listened to the song of larks above the moor, and heard the soft sighs of the crofters' cattle as they roamed the grass.

One long golden autumn day he stood for hours on the shores of Loch Druidibeg watching the restless wheel and turn of the young greylag geese as they prepared for their journey south. He himself felt no urgency, only a calm fortitude; he would find the folk in the end. Everywhere he went he asked after them, listening and watching. When he wearied and ached with the search he went again to his home where he burrowed among his books once more, working and muttering over the clues and hints he had been given. He had so much to learn.

Among the islanders he became well known, supporting himself among the seaweed gatherers and the lobster boats, or like a travelling tinker with kitchen knives to sell. At every door he longed for news and was treated with courtesy. Whenever a village gathered to ceilidh and he was by, they welcomed him in. He gathered stories of the folk wherever he went: stories he loved to learn, to tell, to store up. Back in his own home the collection grew, the work went on.

Stopping one day for a drink of water at an old black house he was invited in by the crofter's wife for "a cuppie and a ceilidh". The windowless old house with its dripping thatch and drystone, uncemented wall seemed dark indeed, but when he stepped inside he found the calor gas lamp lit and the kettle singing on a trim kitchen range. Drinking his strong sweet tea he told her shyly of his search and she delighted him with a scurrilous tale of a neighbour, long dead and gone, who had, she said, stolen and married one of the Sea Folk. But no good came of it.

"The way of it was this: in my grandmother's time it was and she only a child. But always she knew there was something amiss with the woman in the look of her, or in the way she walked perhaps. But I'm going ahead of myself.

"There was a man who had lost his wife in the sickness and after she died it seemed as if he would lose his mind, not from grief you understand for he was a hard man, but from the work that was left to him. He was one who certainly prayed for the fish to throw themselves on the shore, and the peats to cut themselves, for he was never one to stir unless he had to. But with his woman gone, he had to lift his hands from his knees now. The months passed and he was making a bad job of himself there, and the useless thing that he was, he saw in the end there was nothing for it but to get himself a wife.

"In all this time however the news had gone about and there was not a girl willing to be Black Alec's bride. He was a hard man and big, taller than the door there, and broad, and the black hair on his head was so long the wind could lift it. He had a beard on his face and the hair of it was black too; but it was not for this that he was given his name. The reason for that you will see soon enough.

144

"Now he reasoned to himself that if no girl would have him from the land he must go to the people of the sea. So he went down to the shore to watch and see if he could catch himself a silkie."

"Where did he go to catch her?" asked McBride eagerly.

"Oh, I cannot tell exactly where he went. But it would be out to the low skerries where the seal folk lie to bathe in the sun. For you must know that in the water the silkie is clothed like a seal, but it is on the land that they will walk without their seal skins, like men.

"Now the task before Black Alec was just this: that he must spy out one of the seal women as she left her seal skin and began to walk upon the sand. Then he must take her seal skin, for without it she could never return to her home in the sea and so must stay with him forever. It happened the one evening, as the sun lay on the water and the last green light lay across the sky, that a seal woman came up out of the waves. She was tiny in her limbs, and the hair on her head lay thick all down her spine, and her little body was white and smooth as the inside of a sea shell. She lay her seal skin on a rock and she walked upon the sand. She picked her way carefully as she walked, for her feet were very tender you see, from swimming always in the water.

"Then that Alec got up from behind the rock and took up the seal skin that lay there. As soon as she saw him she knew what he had done and she ran daintily toward him crying to him to give her back her coat. But he would not, and wrapped her instead in his own old coat and carried her up the beach and away to his home. She cried miserably all the way and flung back her arms towards the waves but he would not heed her.

"Well, she wept and she shivered but Alec had set himself to tame her and train her to be a wife. Poor thing, she could only boil water to burn it, she had no notion of cooking. But she was clean in her ways and she would try. And at the end of every day, shivering and trembling, she would turn to Alec in the bed:

"'It is time and past time that I returned to my folk in

145

the sea,' she said.

"'No. It is not yet time,' he would reply.

"She learned to weave and she learned to sew for him and then again she would turn to him in the night:

"'Surely now it is time and past time that I returned to my folk, who miss me sorely,'

"'No. It is not yet time.'

"Then she learned to milk and she learned to bake and again and again she pleaded with him in the bed at night, but always:

"'No. It is not yet time.'

"Well, she wept and she cried and she asked and she pleaded until there came a time when Black Alec could take no more:

"'It is not yet time, seal woman,' he cried, 'for you are too useful here. You cook and you clean, you mend and you milk, you have learned to be a wife any man would envy me for. It will never be time, seal woman, for you are useful to me.'

"Then the poor woman began to think and began to plan, and the next evening the supper was burnt.

"'I am no longer useful, husband. Is it time for me to return?'

"'No, no, woman, this supper is well enough, for I like my supper black.'

"So the woman thought again, and while Alec went to enjoy his spoilt meals she began once more to plan, and dirt piled up in the corners and dust covered the shelves.

"'See husband, I no longer cook and I no longer clean, I am no more use to you for it is time for me to return.'

"'No, no, woman, it is well enough. I like the floor to be black.'

"And Alec swept the dirt from his chair and supped his burnt meal and still he shook his head at her. He would whip her and beat her but it made no difference. She still had her plan.

"She brought milk from the cow and it was full of soot:

"'It is well enough woman. I like my milk black.'

146

"His clothes fell to holes and to ribbons but she did nothing for him any longer, so that he was as he had been before he found her. Then at last Alec knew he was beaten, but still in the black heart of him he would not let her go free, but he took her seal skin from the place where he had it hid away and he sold it, and with the price that he had for it he paid his way to the mainland and was never seen in the islands again."

"And what became of the woman?" asked McBride.

"That I cannot tell you for certain. She remained on the land for only a little while, walking about the village and smiling her sad little smile. But it was no place for her and so she took and drowned herself."

"Do you mean she went back to the sea?"

"Well she did that. But without her seal skin wouldn't she drown?"

"I don't know. I'm not sure that they need the seal skin to swim, any more than they need tails. Did she have any children?"

"No, she did not. And that's a mercy for the poor things would be born with webbed fingers. That I know for I've seen it here in the islands. Webbed fingers and webbed feet have all the children of the silkie."

McBride shook his head at this but the old woman was convinced. To her the stories of the silkie were matters of fact, indisputable as her bible. The tale she had told was part of the past of her own world. McBride had heard the legend told in many ways but each was of interest to him and in the shelter of a hanging bank that night he wrote it down, sighing for the young maids of the folk whose fate at the hands of landsmen was so harsh.

Years before in Benbecula he had heard the true story, reaffirmed again and again in his travels about the island, of the little maid who had been seen in the waters one morning. She seemed no more than a child, not yet five years old, but formed like a woman. She was playing in the waves when she was first seen by a group of men out on the beach to gather tangle-weed for their fields. They stopped their work and stood watching her in wonder as she leapt and played in the sea just as their own children played upon the land. Someone ran to the village and women came down to the beach, pulling their shawls around them and crossing themselves in amazement at the strange sight. Children came too, calling and pointing open-mouthed. Then a boy picked up a stone: she was a fine target out there on the water, better than a floating log. He let fly and others did the same. What a piteous face she must have turned upon them: to be stoned so thoughtlessly when she had been so happy. She held out her arms in appeal to them and the stones hit her, until she sank out of sight.

Within a few days she was found once more; her delicate body was lying in a little hollow on the shore, her face starkly white, and her long dark hair, spreading about her on the sand, moved lazily in the wind. The land agent Duncan Shaw, was called for, and he stood gazing down at her, sad for her lost beauty and freedom. He ordered a coffin made for her but could not find permission to bury her on church lands, so instead she was laid to rest by the chastened villagers on the beach where they had found her.

All of this took place more than a hundred years ago, in 1830, even before Queen Victoria took the throne. Perhaps people were more blind, more evil in those distant days when men had created such divisions between themselves that it was no wonder they felt superior to any other creature on sea or land. What a high pride we men have, thought McBride, that we can set ourselves up as a standard and then, without compunction, torture, vilify and even kill anything which we sense to be other than ourselves.

Yet these people of the islands are good people, warm, honest and open-hearted as any others, brave and defiant beyond the will of many or they would not be able to make their homes on such a slender rim of earth as lay upon these sea-scattered rocks. Everywhere the earth was put to use, even on the smallest elbow of land raising itself above the water. Where no men could live the sheep and cattle were put to graze.

One blustering day in late summer McBride went to help land Alan Finlay's boat load of sheep on a distant island, empty of all but the animals. A couple of tumbed bothies above the south-west beach were all the shelter there was for the men who went there shearing, and at lambing time the ewes were all too wild for any help to be needed.

The heavy boat, clinker-built and wide, was packed with sheep standing tensely side by side. In the bows crouched McBride and the boy, in the stern Alan Finlay stood working his way into the natural harbour with an oar over the transom. The unloading was a tricky business: the boy stood on the rocky skerry above them, Alan held the boat alongside and McBride, taking his time from each passing wave, heaved the animals ashore. Once the first were up, however, the rest became desperate to follow and, climbing on one another, pressed toward the side. Two scrambled ashore for themselves, another made a sudden dash and in that moment the undertow drew the boat back and the sheep was struggling in the water. In the same unreasoning mood which had pulled the boat from the skerry, the sea now flung it back, pressing the sheep down beneath its side. Leaning into the rock Alan slid into the water which was chest deep here and held the boat off his sheep. But the animal was nowhere to be seen, it had passed completely under the keel and was being carried back against the weed-washed rocks beyond. Stumbling on the uneven floor, Alan waded after it. Long minutes passed in which the sea, idly swaying against the land prevented the man from making any headway. His arms clear above the water, he pressed himself bodily through the waves but it seemed the animal was finished. He lugged her back but her head remained sunk in the water; somehow he heaved the dead weight up against the rock, the boy holding her as he climbed out. McBride, while he held the boat, watched the struggle to revive the sheep: it was held up by its hind legs like so much washing as the water ran out of it. Then, lying the animal down, Alan knelt over, her pressing and pulling on her ribs, willing the breath back into her. After ten minutes' relentless pumping she moved, twitched all four legs at once and stood up. Seeing the pride and satisfaction of the man, how was it possible, wondered McBride, that others could have treated the folk as the stories said they did?

"Oh, you and your Sea Folk, you're mad after them," laughed Alan. "The silkies are only seals after all, and the stories only stories."

The fishermen of Mallaig laughed at him too, but they were good enough nevertheless. They carried him often from the islands to the mainland and back as his search dictated. He grew old in his search, a little, grizzled, tramping man, often confused in his mind, liable to see more in front of his eyes than was actually there. If he muttered or even shouted to himself, the people were courteous and did not listen.

"Never mind the old body," the women would say as they watched him stumping off to a village farther down the track. "He's his own master."

But he was no longer the master of his own thoughts which more and more often now masked reality. Although he continued to write busily on scraps of paper, and his horde in the padlocked croft grew and grew, hiding the walls, he no longer remembered all that he had written and often had difficulty in catching the meaning of his own sentences as he wrote so that unexpected words drifted onto his pages, the first snowflakes of his wintering mind.

A blizzard was blowing behind his eyes when he reached Lochmaddy one raw November morning. He saw only smudges of the fishing fleet gathered in the harbour and the voices of the men above the wall buzzed and rang in his head like dry beans inside a blown-up balloon. He shouted and shook his fist, but could not remember exactly the point he was going to make when the faces turned toward him.

"Why here's McBride! He'll believe you!"

"Aye, tell McBride and see what he will do."

"Cruel to be laughing at an old man."

"It's only sport, then."

"No, no. It's no sport for him - he believes all these old tales."

"It's not a tale I'm telling you. I saw them with my own eyes." A square-built stub of a man swung on the laughing crowd, his fists ready. Then the whirling mists fell from McBride's eyes and he saw him. Stumbling through the press of people he clutched the man's heavy jacket.

"You saw them? You really saw them at last?"

The fisherman looked down at the old tramp whose white-rimmed eyes clung to his with a fierce hope.

"Old man I did. I saw the people of the sea."

"You saw mermaids."

"You saw nothing."

"Silkies, McBride! The silkies at last!"

The old man's senses swung headlong in the noise and bustle.

"I cannot hear you. What are you saying? Where are they?"

He clutched and pawed at the stranger, incoherent in his anxiety.

"Come away here and I'll tell you all I know."

But he would not be quieted, would not sit down. The low band of islands the man described were far beyond his usual search, but he knew the place and it was time for him to go.

"See what you've done now. Hold him someone. The old man's not right in his head."

"You shouldn't tell the poor old body such tales. It's only to make fun of him."

Friendly hands and arms bustled about McBride, turning him inland, leading him away.

"They are not tales I'm telling you. I sam him clearly: a man swimming very slowly toward the land. Then when we went about I saw him again. He got up from the water and walked up the beach and three or four more, women they were, without a stitch of clothing to them, came running down the beach and helped him away out of my sight. I was looking through the glasses all the while. I saw them I tell you."

"It's not possible for anyone to live out there."

"Were they shipwrecked perhaps. Did they wave or cry out at all?"

"He was swimming away from us. I told you."

The argument began again. Everyone had his own theory, his own slip of wit. They shouted with loud laughter, and forgot.

"Where's the old man?"

"Dear God, he's taken a boat."

There was a rush to unloose another dinghy but before any definite pursuit could begin a grey curtain of rain swept across the loch and by the time it had cleared the harbour mouth McBride was out of sight among the islands.

He rowed with a steady pace, taking long low strokes, for here in the loch the water was sheltered and only a light choppiness disturbed the surface and was laid flat by every marching squall of rain. When the rain hid him from the land he paused at last and with a practised jerk brought the motor to life. Through the grey gloom he could see the light on Weaver's Point and set his course toward it. Out beyond the point he went, and with Rudha-nam-pleac two miles away over his right shoulder he turned to the north and away into the sound.

Darkness gathered, nudging closer and closer to him, stealing the horizon and hiding the distant shores. The tide took him, helping him as his sight began to fail. He seemed to sleep, his hands clasped on the rocking tiller, and choosing its own course the boat moved on through the night, out toward the sea.

Morning was calm; only a flat breeze from the land lifted a few white puffs of cloud before the rising sun. The sky was a pale washed grey six thousand feet above him. Within the first hours of daylight the motor sputtered and failed: the small supply of fuel was finished. Stubbornly he bent to his oars once more.

All day long he never saw the sun, but by mid-morning there was a different quality about the light. A wind had found its way across the empty wastes of water to the west and began busily piling up the clouds over his head. Weighed down by heavy loads of rain these clouds moved toward him, trailed raindrops in his face and marched on. The sea tossed irritably at his boat, chucking handfuls of water inboard until he had to stop and bale, then butting savagely to make him lose his step. Through the latter half of the day the seas built up and now his strength began to fail completely. On the side of a great wave one oar was torn from him by a curling breaker. His boat was tumbled down into the trough on the far side and he looked up with a calm dread as the next giant leaned over the side. Scrabbling weakly he worked the oar out of the rowlock and swung it over the stern. In this way he kept his boat head-on to the waves but after another hour the worsening weather and his failing body brought him broadside on again.

The sheer weight of the water that hit him took his breath away. When the boat rose out of the ruck there was water about his ankles and the clear fraction of his mind knew with certainty that it was finished. Nevertheless, muttering at the ghosts of reason, he sobbed away his last atom of strength in working the heavy boat round to face the next attack. Like a runner at the tape he cleared the last wind-whipped top and shook the spray from his eyes. Standing in the stern, his weight against the oar, he saw white breakers in the rain-filled dusk, and a thumbprint of land beyond.

The bows fell with a thud into the trough and would not rise, a tumbling wall of foam fell into the boat and swept beneath him. He endeavoured weakly to hold the oar but all was lost. The sky and the dark seemed to be beneath him and he was rising up into the sea. The boat churlishly bumped against his shoulder, pushing him aside, and his arms were pressed under him as he rolled about. A sudden chill of air fingered his face and he took a long calm breath, then reaching out with his arms in freedom he felt the grip of firm hands beneath him.

He knew who they were: in that last brief moment in the boat he had seen them on the rocks, seen their long dark hair blowing, their arms stretched out to him. He had heard their cries of alarm and recognised their welcome melodious voices. He had found them at last.

As the comforting arms touched and held him he looked eagerly round. He saw about him kindness, love, well-remembered comfort. His mother was there, smiling and whispering in the Gaelic tongue. Bridik came near to him, laughing and widening his eyes in happiness. He seemed to speak but water was in his mouth. Tossing and muttering the old man turned from one face to the next, searching for the words to make them understand:

"I am Bridik's brother, I have come home at last."

They held him in their arms and led him gently down, below the storm's roar and fuss. Lightly they lay under the water touching him, smiling through their even white teeth. With unhurried gestures they conferred together. McBride lay still among them, heart and lungs filled to bursting. With a bubbling sigh he turned on the bedded sand, hunching his shoulder as a man might who pulls the covers over him in the night, and sleeps. Among the folk at last McBride slept, peaceful under the sea.

PART III

Chapter Ten
Hancid's Search

Winter shifted its grip. The rain and eroding wind that had swept the old man away died with him, and during the night a faded moon stared down from above the last passing of the clouds to draw away the ebb. The helpless waves slopped and wallowed at the rocky walls of the inlet as they drained away down the glistening sand, but with the dawn even their simple sound was hushed, and into the damp chill of the new day the Day Star drove long shafts of gold. The last meek tendrils of mist melted over the cliff tops.

Among the outer rocks the stern of the broken boat was braced at an awkward angle above the slack weed and men of the folk struggled to free it, to thrust it away beyond their headland into deeps where it could never be seen. The old man would also be soon forgotten, there was no-one among the Sea Folk who might have known him. The daughter Bridik had spoken of so wistfully was not among the maidens who led McBride away. She, if she had seen it, would have known the cairngorm which he still wore chained about his neck; its other half was hers. But the restlessness of her alien heritage had long since separated Giersi from the folk.

She had returned, after the death of her seal companion, but for one year after another had held herself apart, singing alone on the far skerries, her grey eyes watching the west. Only Hancid, with his gift of patience, could come near her. He found her quiet and

155

sad, but finally at peace within herself. He loved her then, and gravely she had lent herself to him and humbly tried to please him. When the time of borning came she delighted him by bearing twin sons, rare among the folk. Uncaring she could not feed them, and when others took them up, in distress she swam away. Or was it the call of the seals as they left for their winter journeys which had caused her to abandon her babes to another?

In the welcome sunshine of the mild day Larra sat and stretched her old limbs gratefully on the warm rock. She found the cold of the winter cave seemed to lie in muscles and joints longer and longer, and she was glad to be here, out of the wind. Lazily she turned her head to watch the little ones left in her care. Oldest of the womenfolk, she now had few duties and this task was one she had always enjoyed. Little Merrin slept like a closed anemone, eyes shut, fist wrapped on fist across her chest; the nails on her little toes were like the inside of a shell. Even in sleep she was peaceful and content, a dear little maiden, a future mother of the folk. Warmth flowed through Larra as she looked at her and love made her reach out to lift the thatch of dark hair back from her granddaughter's forehead.

With a wry sense of guilt she transferred the gesture to the other two babes also, rubbing and firmly patting their restless limbs. Her hands looked stained and old against their firm infant flesh and she drew back. Was it that which irritated her? Their arrogant youth? Possibly. And their restless searching, for they were never still. And their self-sufficiency, which needed no-one when they had each other. Sudden compunction dictated and she leaned forward once more and with a kind of love touched the vulnerable stem of each neck. Poor little pups, of course they relied on one another for they had no-one: mother gone with the seals, by wind and wave, and father following after!

One infant stirred and looked up at her and with a gush of sentiment she snatched him up, the motherless one, and pressed him to her worn breast. His fists kneaded her collar bone and with a surprising strength he held himself away, turning his head this way and that to find his twin. Seeing him, his mirrored self, lying in the sand hollow, he pointed a rounded fist and with a single sound, petulant and terse, demanded to be restored to his brother's side. With a sigh Larra obeyed.

The Two. Poor brats, they were no-one's favourite. As alike as two tellin shells, no-one could separate them. Their mother had given them no name other than Idmazine and Streggid, first and second; and which was which would have been impossible to tell had she not chained her earth-stone round the neck of her first-born as he left the womb. Giersi was gone, and Larra at least knew that she would never come back. The boys' father had followed, haunted with a sense of his own inadequacy, which could only be erased if she would return. They had both forgotten these little folk.

The ebb was over and as the flow began Borry, Merrin's mother, came to feed her child. Placid, warm, well-fleshed, Borry was a perfect mother of the folk. Loved by both Slidorn and Pletrid, she would never be able to tell her daughter where to look for a father, unless her own looks told her. What did it matter? The child would love two fathers and be glad, and so gain a three-fold foundation for her own life. Three-fold? Not so:

"She will be everyone's darling, Borry. She is so lovely."

The babe at the breast opened her eyes, darted one warm look at the old woman, waved an accepting hand, and with weighted lids applied herself once more to the task of growing up.

Each in turn, the young mothers gave breast to the Two. That they should be fed at the identical moment was essential as they would not be parted otherwise and the screams of the waiting brother rent everyone's nerves. There was no precedent for them, no-one could remember infants orphaned so young. The old ones conferred together, perched about the Elder Rock. They scowled at the troublesome babes, twisting about to look down at them in their shelter.

"It was an evil day for the folk when Seiglid brought his land-begotten child among us," an old grandsire hunched his shoulder at the squalling brats. "Nothing good has ever come to us from the land."

"The Donilid grew to be a strong swimmer," one of his former companions defended him.

"And swam away as soon as he had left his daughter among us!"

"Other fathers have been lost to the waves, their sons have not lacked for guidance, as certain of us here must agree."

"That is true. But what has become of Hancid, that he should leave us, all out of season? What is she, this seal woman, that he seeks? What tide is she to draw him so? She who was never truly one of the folk?"

"It is that land-seed in her, from Seiglid's son, to her, and now to these Two."

And the old ones tightened their faces at what they could not understand. For Hancid was now lost to them and they feared for him in the northern waters where his search had taken him.

Winter after winter passed and they had no news of him, although in his summer days his thoughts turned often to them. He lay on placid seas, gazing up into the midnight daylight above him. The skies, clear and blue, shed rays as the clouds shed rain; the air about him rang with the clarity of light as if the Day Star had struck the round blue bowl of the sky and all Creation sang with it. Hancid's entire mind was dazzled, yet disturbed at seeing the Star hang there so hesitantly, swinging above the horizon at a time when, by his own day's rhythm, he should have been sleeping: but in this calm summer solicitude, where air and sea combined to soothe his storm-wrung senses, he lay awake, lapped about by listless tides which gave him no direction. And he was glad to rest in the northern, light-filled peace.

The storm, now passed, had offered a real fear: death

had fingered him, rubbed him between finger and thumb; but finding him, it seemed, too small, had flung him back. Hancid rocked now on the sighing breast of ocean and reckoned his relief. Gale-driven seas had caught him close to shore and he had been scraped too roughly on to weed-bare rocks, his strength ebbing as he struggled free. Barely breathing, in foam-torn wave-tops he had battled to force his way through the towering breakers and reach his down-deep haven under the thundering seas. But wave on wave had battered him back, and the avenging land had reached out for him. Rolled over nether rocks beneath the seas he had lost all sense of uppermost and swam sternly more than once into the sand when he had searched for air and life.

Now, wave-washed, he bathed in light and lost the dread of it all. He knew the wonder of a world won from fear. Life was more real after the draining of all terror and he felt firm in his knowledge that he was of the folk.

It was his pride to wander the water-ways and set himself directly toward the face of his fate. Men of the Sea Folk measure their lives upon waves of destruction: a hero knows the value of being when daily he looks into the eye of his ending. Bathed in the blue of the midsummer night, Hancid now recognised every muscle and limb, knew where the nails lay on fingers or toes, realised in his breathing the rhythm of his heartbeat and knew each of these signs as clues to his existence. All this pattern was filling and pulsing to prove his, his, his only, life span. And softly he joyed in it, stretched on the placid sea.

Lapped in the storm-drained stillness he recognised, far away, a sound rarely heard near their summer feeding grounds: the long wailing song of a bachelor whale searching for company. The mournful, haunting cry wrenched at Hancid's heart and he turned to swim through the wide bays where he knew the great ones would congregate.

Giersi! Giersi! Her name tore at his thoughts, ripped away his peace so that without knowing it he groaned aloud in the water. Among the folk there had never been such love as Hancid knew for long-limbed Giersi. He had watched her as she grew from a chubby little girl-child, rolling and laughing in the shallows, to the tall, grey-eyed woman of the folk.

When she was gone his love for her would not let a day pass but she was at the centre of his thoughts. He needed to know that all was well with her, to see her grave face smile, to hear her sing, to feel she was once more at peace with her chosen world. But time passed and she remained elusive, hidden among her seals. Year after year Hancid searched, swimming to meet the eternal ice, probing far into land-gripped fjords. Forward and back across the clear northern waters he ventured and his song of loneliness was known to all the creatures. He sang nightly to the puzzled seals who humped irritably away over their rocks, slipping down with a scant splash to the bottom sand peace of their sleeping hollows. He called also to the slanting gulls and petrels as they soared the air space an arm's length above the dipping waves, and they screamed abusively back. Hancid's love was not understood by the creatures, or by the folk; and as the years passed he wandered alone more and more.

Fathoms below, the whale, made curious by the sad song at the surface, rose up from the depths and rested alongside Hancid, his head so close that the silkie could see the barnacles which rested still in the folds of flesh at his throat. The warm wet breath of the whale spattered the water all about him, sweet and clean as salt spring rain. Hancid raised himself against a wave to greet the newcomer but as he did so the shy giant curved and sank away out of his sight. Gazing down through the clear water Hancid saw him once more, patrolling ten feet down, his long lean back speckled with dappled light from the bright sun-sparked surface. This was Megapteron, the winged whale, eight times the silkie's length, his great fins crimpled and wrinkled by the parasitic barnacles who gathered there in these chill waters. Hancid ducked down again to be close to the warm sides, to feel the stroke of mammal flesh once more.

Nervous, the whale drew away, circled, closed, and drew away again. Hancid, needing air too soon, rose to the surface and lay there, looking down the blue lines of light to see the submarine sides of the whale glide gracefully by. Again he began to dive, but a sudden flap of the man-wide flukes sent such a rush of water up at him that he bobbed helpless, head in air. Twice more he tried until the great one gave him leave to move close, then a crusted flipper scoured his shoulders and, turning, a benign eye gazed curiously on him. The whale would know him.

Leaning later against the big-winged beast, Hancid careened his flanks, picking away the flaccid parasites, cleaning sea lice from the fleshy grooves around mouth and eye. Contented, his giant companion rested at the surface, blowing gently, sleeping a little, washed by the passing waves. Hancid had never known such sure ease before.

With the strengthening light of day the two grew hungry and Hancid looked about him. The waters, normally thronged with tiny life, seemed barren, and he was far from harbouring rocks. It is customary for the silkies when venturing to forgo food, but a whale cannot do so. The great ones feed in desperate quantity through the summer, laying down a store for the starving time, the breeding time, in southern waters. In the open seas where Hancid and Megapteron lay, there could be no trawling for plenty, so, like a landsman, the whale laid his traps.

While Hancid watched him intently the whale dived down into the dark. Soon a screen of tiny air bubbles began to rise up as the whale, spiralling below, blew them to the surface. The cylinder of bubbles enclosed krill and tiny fish alike, trapping them as the whale, mouth agape, rose up the funnel he had made. At the surface he pressed the water from his catch with his tongue, swallowed and turned again. Tentatively Hancid too reached into the mesh of bubbles and breakfasted with the whale.

But the food so cunningly trapped could not be called a meal and Megapteron turned away. Such a sense of loss for Hancid! Loneliness doubled after the peaceful contact he had known and, yearning, he pressed through the waves, determined to stay with his companion. All day he kept up the pace, swimming in the whale's wake. From time to time the big-winged creature paused at depth and, stirring the water with his great flippers, called in song trying to locate others of his kind. Then the solemn pilgrimage began again.

Days remained unmarked as the two quartered the northern fjords. Man, the enemy, had scoured the gentle whales out of those waters so now only a lonely few remained. But finally, in a quiet, shallow bay surrounded by low green hills a small family of about a dozen humpbacks responded to the searching cry.

Abandoned to desire and delight, Megapteron flung himself into the air, curving sideways to fall back to the surface between walls of spray. Other whales among the group breached in the same way, identifying themselves before the newcomer. Without fear the massive creatures gathered to glide and swim, close and companionable. All knew the empty seas too well and rejoiced that another was come to swell their numbers, to build up their strength and identity once more.

Hancid they ignored; the silkie was smaller than the smallest of their young and neither males nor females noticed him. He swam close with their leave, and rested often by their peaceful flanks. He fed, as they did, from the open water and only occasionally did he search the low cliffs of land for shelter. When the winds came he left the water, for he knew his strength was not sufficient to hold him from the importunate rocks, but in the stormy waters the whales leapt and swam with glee, pitting their giant strength against the storm and joying in the challenge of waves large enough to turn even their massive sides. When midsummer calm softened the waters bachelors sought out females to impress with swimming displays, hanging head down, wide tails thrashing up the surface into a creamy foam.

When paired, the couples swam lazily side by side, every wave a caress against their beloved's body. The great ones love to be stroked, to be gentled, and would often suffer Hancid to groom the folded flesh below their jaws where parasites lodged.

Placidly content, the females fed hugely and nursed their young. Infant whales hung close to their mother's side or, if she was attracted away to swim among the males, an auntie or nan would mind the child, stroking him and even holding him close with her long, fore-arm flippers. The naughty babes caused Hancid to frown as they played restlessly about a quiet mother, sliding over her tail, butting against her blowhole. Yet the patient female suffered it, content, when all was done, merely to hold the boisterous child on her breast at the surface, until he slept.

Now the reluctant Star remained longer and longer below the horizon and Hancid decided to turn south. An unease among his companions told him that the whales too were readying for the journey and he planned to swim with them a while more if he could. Unformed thoughts were driving the quiet family and after false starts, one dawn they moved finally out of the wide bay together. Some were gone quickly, though it was early for their rush south, others hesitated and returned to the haven, but a number remained loosely constrained to travel in contact, calling when out of sight, sometimes breaching to identify their position. Pairs brushed one another as they swam, babies hung close in to their mother's sides; together they moved south to find the warmer seas.

They swam gracefully for all their bulk, wide flukes swaying upward and down, long slim bodies undulating easily through the water. They did not use their power for speed: not until danger threatened. Then the whales were first aware, their hearing so much more acute than Hancid's. Even as he wondered why they were disturbed he too felt, rather than heard, that relentless, rushing sound in the water: a hunting orca pack was moving in unison and at speed. As the sound

163

magnified, it became certain that they were tracking the whales. And they never missed.

It was the worst possible moment: out in the open sea there were no hiding places. At this season no floating mountains of ice offered sanctuary. With young ones to protect, no use to submerge, they could neither dive the dark depths nor remain long below the surface. The whales, silently, drew close in their trouble. They blew softly under water in order to spend as little time as possible in sight at the surface and moved with slow deliberation, giving no clues to their position. Yet it was clear that the orcas drew closer: with relentless intent they rose and fell, curving across the surface together, the clicks of their spying echo-systems peppered the water about the whales. The family was identified, catalogued, condemned.

Frantic in distress, Hancid entreated the circling whales. It was time to make an escape because the killers spelt death for him too. Yet he remained with his ponderous companions as they swirled gently about, making no move to save themselves. At last, nerves at screaming pitch, Hancid swam closer into the circle and sensed as he did so a tremor, a stiffening of mind and muscle all around him. So. A decision had been reached, and marshalling their young the family turned away. Strong tail thrusts sent Hancid headlong, he struggled to rejoin them but in a moment they were gone, with sudden power they had streamed through the waters and were lost to sight. All but one.

Megapteron lay hapless below the surface. His kind eye was turned down and back as if he sought a last glimpse of his loved ones, his great wings drooped uselessly. Then, lifting his head to the surface, he blew, a hollow dejected sound, and began heavily to swim. Into the path of the killer pack.

Alarmed, Hancid slid into his position at the whale's bow wave, and turned his face to signal his distress to his gentle friend. Megapteron's eye darkened and drooped down. Do not ask, he seemed to say, this is ordained. With slow strokes the great one drew away toward his fate.

Daily in the seas violent death lashes the waters, but it is rare the victim goes willingly. The big whale's sacrifice was beyond Hancid's understanding, and he followed humbly. Let all swim to escape and the weakest will be caught! But Megapteron had chosen his own end: this was his love for his own kind.

The killers hurtled through the water, tall dorsal fins clear above the surface now. Without hesitation each member of the pack swung into his predestined place. In the open water they circled their prey as he waited at the surface. Some cut off a possible escape into the depths by taking station below him and with a foaming frenzy the attack began. The shining dapper bodies of the predators seemed to butt at the slender sides of Megapteron, then as they drew away, strips of white blubber were revealed, staring pink as blood seeped through. One of the rear guard attacked his tail, fastening on it with vicious interlocking teeth. As they chewed and tore, the gentle beast lost his strength, lost his grace, yet purposefully he continued to draw the pack away from his escaping kindred.

The attack went on and Hancid, sickened, tried to turn away. As he did so the hooded, melancholy eye sought his and he knew he must wait still for the end.

Abruptly as the massacre began it was over. The pack slowed, the flurry in the water subsided, and they turned away. Having eaten their fill they would leave quiet, faithful Megapteron to his lonely death. His flesh was torn in many places by the rough, ripping action of the orcas. Their teeth had torn away his body's covering and life's blood ran from him out of many wounds. His tail, his flippers, his stubby back fin were all mutilated, useless. He wallowed in the water, forty tons of heaving injured flesh. He knew defeat for himself, but his justification was the safety of his kind.

In the night, rain fell, icy tears on the tilting sea. Megapteron could hold himself afloat no longer it was time for him to go. With a quiet sigh, courteous and sad, he relinquished the world he knew and slipped away from Hancid's touch. The waves closed over him, and the kind sea washed away every trace of his ugly end.

Hancid, following the custom of his folk, had remained silent at the whale's side, offering only the comfort of his presence, for there are no words that can lighten that parting. Throughout the long watch the silkie had silently held station close to his friend. Now in the empty sea he sang the farewell song, then turned away southward. The sky was overcast, suiting his mood. He had no need of stars: his longing and love for his own folk would bring him home.

The search was ended. Giersi, he felt sure, was being hidden from him by the intervening seas. It may be that he would never find her. But among the whales he had learned something which had led beyond his love. He knew now that he could not swim alone — he too was a part of his people, and without him they were lessened. So Hancid returned at last, to play his part in the survival of the folk.

Chapter Eleven
Dolphin Boys

The sultry weight of the summer heat stilled the daytime sounds of the home beach. The maidens and young mothers with infants still at breast lay idly in the shade of the tilted boulder which was the Elder Rock. In the wearied air their talk dropped to a murmur, and their little ones nodded and slept. Two old nans sat quietly plashing in the shallows, smiling together at an old memory of youth and freedom from the chills of age. Among the dozing grandsires old Dandrid started up, but his warning cry rattled away as he recovered from his dream, and snuffing at the hot day he settled back to his nap. The flicker of summer lightning in a moulded cloud bank to the east was too far off to make a sound on the innocent beach.

Only the noisy boys clamoured and yelled in a warm pool among the creviced rocks, climbing for height, then launching themselves to send the spray flying as they smashed the surface again and again. From his warm perch on the cliffside Graymidon watched them, smiling painfully at his mind's eye view of himself as a youngster leaping and splashing so. For many years the least movement had been a torment for him so that now, with all feeling gone from his crippled leg, he felt easier. But summer days of venture were hard for him, trapped and useless on the beach.

When he climbed, by easy gradients, to his grassy nest in the cliff, he caught a memory often of Giersi, long since gone to her seals, who had also climbed here to hide her hurt. Crippled by her strangeness, by her inheritance from the land, she had often been at odds with her kin down there on the sea's rim. It was possible now to believe that she may have suffered.

Graymidon, aged by pain before his time, lifted himself awkwardly to stare down into the circle of cliff, rock and sea that held his world, and frowned about for a sight of lost Giersi's troublesome sons. Ever since their birth they had been a puzzle to the folk, never predictable, sufficient in their ways, and always strange. They had grown, but little flesh was added to their bones. They had become long and thin, their eyes dark and hooded in the bone of their heads. They spoke little and always watched. They showed no affection for any but one another, though Graymidon noticed that they had wept for the first time when old Larra was given back to the sea, in the fading days of last year's autumn.

After her death there was no-one to mind them and now they wandered alone on the beach and seemed to ignore the folk. Their restless spirits had taken them early to the waves. Before they could walk they were found at the beach's end, crowing with delight as the frothing surge of a spent wave surrounded them. They took their first steps with the water's support and laughed as they were lifted from the land. No-one led them, but they had learned as the seals learn, awkward at first, but competent so soon after. Once they had gained the freedom of the sea then no-one could control them. It was at this time that they began to speak together, but what they said no-one knew or understood. Strangest of all, they could speak within the sea. How they did it was hard to comprehend. It seemed they only clicked their tongues, but each understood and no-one else was welcome.

Daily they were in trouble, for their courage was remarkable. Rude and surly when corrected, they did not wait for advice: too soon they left the sheltered cove and, untaught, ignored the safe channels to dive among the outer rocks. There danger found them.

It was a grey day, deceptively peaceful, but a long deep swell was running outside the cove and the lower headland was awash. The waves sucked at the cliff, tearing down pebbles and grit, intruding down narrow cracks to press the rocks apart, little by little, as they had done since the land first pushed up through the water-clad world. Slowly, inconspicuously, the sea was claiming back its own, while pebbles and grit sank below the surface once more.

The Two watched with delight the unaccustomed rise and drop of the water below the high rock on which they sat. Then Idmazine, with a single-syllabled querying sound which dared his brother to follow him, slipped out onto the surface, hoping to enjoy the belly-gripping drop down the rock face with the sinking wave. Instead, with more speed than he could comprehend, he was swept away, up, up toward the land. He was being flung into a narrow defile between glistening walls of black rock at whose farthest point stark, broken boulders were crumbled and jutted like rotten teeth waiting to crush and grind whatever the waves sent them. In moments they could demolish Idmazine, who would be pounded down into the submerged cavities to be broken into food for grappling crabs.

The piercing cry Idmazine gave as he felt himself wrenched away was too high for normal hearing, yet it rang in his twin's head, searing his brain, defying rational thought. Without a sound he dived down into the receding sea and immediately felt the force that he must contend with if he was ever to reach his brother's side, for to his horror he was being dragged in the opposite direction, snatched away from the hideously bared jaws which threatened him.

With elderly calm and slowness Streggid waited, clinging to a handhold on the rock face, his legs streaming powerless in the tide race. He had won a little knowledge of the force he had to fight: he must use the direction of the wave to thrust him on, deny it only when it threatened to take him away from Idmazine.

169

Left for a moment high and dry, he tucked his feet under him and as the swell returned, thrust off from the tiny ledge in a flying dive to travel on ahead of the wave top. Deep in the rolling swell he cried to his brother:

-'Mzine. Hold. I come-

Were they really words that he cried? His own name for his brother seemed no more than a nasal groan, but at such a pitch that it carried far through the turbulent waters. Idmazine, his feet and elbows already grazed and ripped as he was torn along the sheer side of the rock, heard the cry and his despair lightened. Streggid was with him, in this as in everything.

-Hold. I come!-

The meaning of the staccato sounds was clear and with a new determination Idmazine forced his flayed fingers into a crack, kicked his bruised ankles down to find a purchase for his heel. And there, awkwardly, he stayed. As the next rush dragged at him he heard the cheerful grin of Streggid, within his reach, low down the rock face, and felt his brother's triumph and towering hope.

-Together now. Anything is possible.-

Strongly, subliminally, they signalled their optimism and trust to one another.

How was this? They were fruit of the same womb. They had known one another before time, for them, began. So now they were able, as the rough waves buffetted them, to talk, to confide, and to find strength.

- With the next. We go. -

With a confidence that years could not have taught them, but rather would have taken away, they gave themselves to the receding sea and so drew back from those terminal teeth. With each wave they retreated until the open waters received them.

- Strek! We are free. -

Streggid sang:

  "Go with the wanton wave
   Learn in her laughter

Lean on her warm breast,
She is ocean's daughter."

So they were carried far by the wide wave then, slowly swimming, they returned. With a cunning none had taught them they threaded the inner way and merely half a man's height, yet they walked out of the wind-driven waves and trod the shell-sand slope of the home beach once more.

There were beatings and many words. But they bore both with a patience insolent in its weary wisdom. A half-smile flickered between them. But their eyes were friendless.

In the endless round of years that followed they were drawn to no-one: each answered for the other and their joined minds ranged far beyond the restraints of the cove.

They questioned everyone and everything:

"Who lights up the stars at night?"

"They are alight at all times," they were told, "but the blazing Day Star hides them and only when the sky is dark can they be seen."

This answer was unsatisfactory and they stared into the blue skies until their eyes ached, searching for the shy stars.

"Why is the sea green?" they asked, and found it impossible to accept that the sea, being water, had no colour.

"It drinks the colour of the sky and so changes from day to day."

This attempt also displeased them, for green was not the sky's colour, but patiently they let that thought alone.

"Where do the birds go?" they demanded again and again in autumn and in spring as the great migrations thudded overhead, and Graymidon took them aside to point out tern and skua as they headed south.

"They are friends of the Day Star," he explained, "and as our world tips away from summer's light into winter cold so these brave birds fly out over wastes of water to seek the warmth once more in seas beyond the finding of the folk."

"How do you know, then?" said Streggid, rudely.

"They talk to me," replied Graymidon, smiling gently. "Come with me and listen."

Doubtfully the two lay at his side on the grass-tufted cliff top to hear the mutterings of gannets guarding their young, and from the farthest rocks they watched rafts of puffins fishing. They came to know the guillemot's trumpeting call and the cackling chorus of the fulmars on their winter cliffs. But like the young birds they were restless for the sea and would not keep company with Graymidon for any length of time.

"Where do the waves begin?" they asked, "and what makes the tides run?"

But when the old ones pointed to the silver moon or recited the midwinter Mystery they hunched a shoulder in disbelief. They had early learned the force of wave and tide and knew that inexorable power, so merciless in its show, was due to more than the casual incline of the tilted land. But where were the answers to be found?

"Where do the whales come from?" they wanted to know when they heard of the solemn ones in story and fable.

"That you must ask Hancid, for he knew them once."

"Who is Hancid?" They looked about them, interested, but no-one was able to show them their father, missing now for many years. Nor did they recognise their mother's name, though stories of her filled them with a strange longing which could only be eased in mischief and wild noise.

"What does the seals' song mean?" they wondered one misty morning when the mournful cries echoed across the still water from the low skerry where the grey seals lay.

"Giersi knew," said Borry, her new baby on her hip. "She sings with them still I do believe, far away from here." And her gaze was lost in the shifting fogs.

"Where did she go?" they asked wistfully. "Could we go there too?"

"That you could not!" snapped Borry sharply. "Your time of venture is not come yet."

Then they teased her and tried to trip her, threw sand in her eyes and made her baby cry, until a leather-handed grandsire came down the beach and they had to swim off out of sight in the silent mists.

Drops of moisture formed on their curly hair as they squatted together on the dark rocks below the southern cliff. They had mocked the seals awhile, echoing their resonant cry, popped bladder weed under their feet and irritated anemones with bits of grit. Then, tiring of their games, spoke silently together.

-She?-

-Giersi.-

Her name trickled through their thoughts.

-Far from here.-

The wonder of far away filled them. Could they find answers there? See where the Day Star went? Follow the fish into the deeps? The home beach was for them only a diving ledge, a place to start from. The beyond beckoned them through the mists. It was time to be gone.

Months later, the two hauled out on rocks far to the south. It was full summer now and they lay quiet, enjoying the heat. In the distance they could hear the shrill sounds of landsmen at play, but their resting place was guarded by severe headlands washed by deep waters and they felt secure. They had learned the ways of landsmen on their journey, watching secretly within anchorages and estuaries, and no longer laughed but kept their distance. It had been a joke at first, seeing their absurd swimming, and racing their small boats. Then they had passed great cities whose glow lit up the night sky, and had given their stinking waters a wide berth. A huge ferry had ground past them, its engines' vibrations battering their sensitive ears and, deep as they had dived, they were unable to escape the intrusive noise. They realised then that the landsmen could reach out far over the water with their noise and smell and both were obnoxious to the silkies.

But there was a fascination still and they crept often into coves and bays which their senses told them were backed only by grass and brambles, where birds sang and fish were plentiful. It was on one of these excursions that they met Emmeline.

The little girl had been left by her brothers, afloat in a little black and yellow air-filled dinghy. She lay with her head pillowed on her arms, gazing down into the water just below her, when to her amazement she saw the face of Streggid only a foot or so away, staring up. Too young to be alarmed, or to realise the impossibility of what her eyes reported, she laughed and reached out a chubby hand.

Streggid took it and promptly pulled her in.

What ruffling and thrashing about! She was like a bird taking a bath in a puddle! The Two watched wide-eyed and a little afraid. And what a shrieking from the shore! They grabbed her and popped her back up into her black and yellow air bed with all speed. By the time she had dried her eyes they were gone. They felt a little guilty about that episode but could not understand why.

When they found the divers, also black and yellow, and bubbling merrily, they made sure to stay out of sight, whipping past and back at speed on the very edge of visibility. The divers' log made little of them: "Seals?"

They visited wrecks but found their skin crawling with dread at the ancient death tremors and would not stay long. They liked to bob about among fishing fleets in the dark before dawn, but fled when the nets rattled out. They startled two drunken fishermen whiling away a hot afternoon on their little cabin cruiser by sinking their floats again and again; then sniffed suspiciously at their trail of beer cans. One squally morning they observed a sailing race, and tumbled with delight around a capsized catamaran while the crew struggled to right her.

174

In all their adventures they had not forgotten Giersi, or the grey seals, but their new haven was far from those haunts and other quests led them on.

They were exploring, early one morning, a holiday harbour where pleasure craft bobbed at anchor or nodded alongside their mooring buoys. On one yacht they could hear landsmen asleep and kept well away, hidden by the soft vapours which still hung twisting and swaying on the surface, catching and reflecting the pearly cloud-light of the dawn. The water was bright clear but on the bottom a cobwebby ooze hung about the litter of jagged tins and smeared bottles. A flounder fed on undentifiable scraps, stirring up flurries of mud with its jutting lower jaw. To the surface clung an oily film which slithered undeeded from propellor shafts and outboard motors, from dirty rags and discarded cans.

The Two stayed below, underneath the keels, listening and looking, ready to dash back under the jetty if anyone moved. It was a heart-stopping form of hide-and-seek they had invented, exciting enough to be worth the disgusting taint of the fouled water.

An alarm cry rivetted their ear drums, eyes swivelled in terror, searching for reassurance in each other's face.

-Strek!?-

-I'm well. What?-

The cry came again, insistent, but pitched, they now realised, far higher than their own frequency. Yet its meaning was plain.

-I am in distress. In need.-

It came from the harbour mouth, a sound not unlike their own, more compelling than the alien shrieks of Emmeline's half-forgotten family. In silent understanding the Two parted, swimming in opposite directions; after a few strokes they would each turn and make their way individually toward the signal. They would meet as they homed on the caller, pinpointing his position: they had tracked in this way many times, pursuing fish or locating lobster pots. Now the hunt was more urgent.

A little short of their quarry Idmazine surfaced. Yes,

175

he had remembered correctly: just ahead a lighted bell buoy swayed, guiding boats in to safety. It was from that point that the signal came. He swam cautiously forward. The water, more active near the open sea, was churned and murky; he could just catch a glimpse of Streggid away to his right. They were closing on the caller now, but in the shadows under the buoy it was difficult to make out who was there.

A dark shape lunged awkwardly, a shining dorsal fin caught the light and was gone. Idmazine flung himself backward, kicked out with his feet and shot away, face up, to the surface. That tough triangular shape had filled him with an unreasoned fear. He drew breath, then paddled about below the surface peering anxiously down, trying to see his brother. Streggid exploded into the air above him, lungs bursting, and immediately dived again.

-Come!- he commanded.

From below the buoy the signal came once more. There could be no refusing the desperation.

-Help me!-

Idmazine swam down. He could make out Streggid pulling wildly at a handful of something. Weed? No, rope. No, it was net. A fragment of net was twisted about the dark creature who lay calmly alongside Strek's waist while he tugged and pulled, trying to set it free. Through the water Idmazine could feel the effort to remain relaxed and what it was costing the trapped creature. The tension was unbearable. He thrust Streggid aside.

-No I shall.-

With his hands feeling the way, for light was scarce here, blocked off by their bodies as well as the wide buoy above them, he reached along the net to where it was caught in the chains below the buoy. His fingers were not clever but with a thrust of his feet against the chain he caused a momentary slackness in the twisted cables. All but a few strands of the net were released. Now it should be possible:

-Pull!- he grunted.

There was a surge of gathering muscle at his shoulder, then a stroke against the water which drove him tumbling down the chain. As he rolled upright once more he heard Streggid's triumphant cry.

-'*Mzine, all's well!*-

The strange creature lay on the surface, its fear ebbing away. One wise eye rolled toward them both. It breathed suddenly, with a slight sucking noise, and they saw the blowhole on the crown of its head. A dolphin!

Idmazine lay his hand on its side, just above the flipper, below the tangled muddle of net which was still wrapped about its body.

"We are not safe here," he explained carefully. "Come with us and we will help to rid you of this net."

The eye focused alertly, trying to understand. They all three submerged.

-*Come!*- Idmazine used the sign known to all the folk, placing a finger behind the creature's flipper and pressing him to come along. The dolphin rattled a weary response, trying for a lower frequency. They could not understand but gently led him back to their hidden bay.

His fear had exhausted him and he spent the morning resting, just below the surface. One eye slept, but the other stayed on watch, and regularly he rose to emit a sighing breath then sank back again. The Two left him alone, recognising his need, until the midday heat forced them, splashing and playing, into the water. The dolphin, immediately alert, dived for the bottom where they followed him and crooning comfort persuaded him to let them tackle the tightly wrapped net.

The fingers of the folk are not nimble and fishermen's nets have always been a danger. Old Graymidon on the home beach had suffered with that knotted strand about his thigh as long as the two could remember, the twine cutting deep into his withered muscle. But the dolphin lay still as they wrestled to untie him and slowly, as the afternoon wore away, the task became easier. Long evening shadows lay across the bay when the last mesh was untwisted and the dolphin was free.

177

With a crackling call he swung away from them, his dark body shimmered below the surface, and he was gone. They saw him again briefly in a silvered curving roll out beyond the headland. Then the adventure was over.

"What did he say?" asked Idmazine as they sat, tired out, on their rock once more.

-*Mm?*- Streggid was enjoying the dying warmth of the flat surface.

"As he left, Strek. I thought he - well, I thought he spoke."

"Said goodbye, I suppose."

"No. I think he said 'Hungry'."

"So am I. Let's eat."

Again before he slept, high on the rock in a warm smooth hollow, Idmazine thought over the strange encounter. How had they understood the dolphin? Was it in fact using their private, underwater talk?

Next morning there was a chill in the air and the two were glad to tumble into the water. Briefly gleaning the rocks near their sleeping place they breakfasted, then threw themselves into an energetic game, chasing, trapping and submerging one another.

Full of excitement Streggid clambered out onto a low ledge of rock, a massive stone hugged to his chest. Soon 'Mzine must circle below him, searching; then he was in for a surprise! Streggid smashed into the water above his brother, caught him with his legs while clinging wildly to his anchoring stone, and fell to the bottom. A peaceful cloud of young fish darted away from the explosion of air bubbles and two hermit crabs, shocked by the quake of their grounding, squatted back into their borrowed homes.

Idmazine struggled to get free.

-*Submit! Submit!*- With a fresh supply of air in his lungs Streggid continued to tighten his grip, to wind his legs more firmly about his brother's body.

-*I surrender.*- Released at last, Idmazine drifted to the surface, shook diamond drops of water into the clear air and laughed as he drew breath.

"How did you do it?" he cried as Streggid surfaced at his side. "I couldn't lift or shift you!"

"Come, I'll show you."

They swam down side by side and there, nosing at the discarded stone, was the dolphin. An inexplicable joy filled them, all three, and they swooped through the water together for a moment. Then the creature curved away.

-Stay!-

It turned at their despairing cry and circled them, just at the limit of visibility. They saw the smoothly muscled body, broad flat tail flukes and the sturdy dorsal fin which had so strangely disturbed Idmazine at first. As it swung up above them they realised how light in colour were its underparts, then it turned and stood on its head, twisting and turning to catch sight of them with each eye. They felt its excitement and delight, akin to their own, and waited tensely.

-Yes?- The dolphin spoke.

It was too wonderful, they rushed for the surface and hung there gasping for joy as their friend dived on into the air above, then with perfect control curved gracefully back into the sea once more. They swam together, learning confidence, learning limitations. The dolphin came close, rubbing himself against the young folk, who shyly stroked his smooth sides, then he would rush away, his great flukes driving him faster than they could follow.

"He's magic."

"He's the most wonderful creature I've ever seen."

Streggid's restless excitement drew him away, searching for the dolphin. Idmazine followed thoughtfully: there was so much at stake, could they truly communicate with another of the sea peoples? If so, there were questions he longed to ask. Would they be able to understand the answers?

There were problems at first: it was easy to go too fast or to lose the correct wavelength, but practice eased their difficulties. All too often the two were aware that it was their own ignorance which made the dolphin's

179

meaning unclear to them: they had no points of reference, so little experience on which to build, while he knew so much. It was as if, having learned to sing in tune, they found that they could not follow the words. Dimly, they groped for understanding while he patiently repeated, restated, rearranged what he wanted to tell them.

Like all chance-met travellers they spoke of their journeys:

-You are from?-

-My people. The Blue Wave.-

-Your people?-

-Far from here. I swam for many days. I swam one-owe-owe, one-owe-one.-

They did not understand his counting, they knew only one, two, one more and many; yet he could

-Many days- he repeated.

ated.

-One moon gone and the present lunation not yet full.-

He had been travelling for over a month, that much was clear.

-Do you travel alone?-

-Is this your time of venture?-

-Alone, yes. I do not understand 'venture'.-

They tried to explain, and Streggid rushed up into the air in order to fill his lungs and roar out the old ballad of Khermara. The dolphin watched him eagerly, enjoying the tonal cadences, but understood nothing. While the two hung in the water above him, chattering excitedly, he observed them closely. Small in size, he guessed they were an immature form of their species. They performed well in water, but were not pelagic, wholly given to it as his own people were.

He beamed his echo-location signal at them and rapidly computed the input he received: hard-boned with complex jointing in four limbs, warm-blooded, air-breathing mammals, only one stomach therefore probably carnivorous, male sex organs external, large brain size. He analysed the impressions he had received, the vibrations he had felt, as he swam with them: they loved and protected one another, they felt protective toward himself, though also in awe of him. Perhaps because of their immaturity, they had little or no fear and were full of a joy in life which he had experienced only among his own people. And they were free. He swam close once more, enjoying the contact after being so long alone, liking the feel of their hands stroking him. He could detect not a single sensation of antagonism or aggression within them, though he had been perturbed by the violent game they played. What was the reason for their uncontrolled splashing and jumping, he wondered? What was the meaning of their fascinating musical sounds? They were worth investigating, he decided.

He raised himself upright on his tail, his quizzical face appearing between the two.

-I am Simo- he announced. *-Who are you? So. Come Strek and 'Mzine, let us enjoy the water.-*

It was a favourite phrase; in the days that followed the Two came to know it well. At dawn they were wakened by Simo's smiling face looking out of the waves at them. *-Come, enjoy the water!-* he greeted them. And at evening, as he swam away to feed among the creatures rising on the swell after the fading light, *-Enjoy the water!-* he would call in farewell. And enjoy it they did. In Simo's company they were extending their awareness of everything around them, delighting in every new experience he offered them. The dolphin was stretching them as nothing and no-one had ever done before: they swam daily more strongly as they forced their muscles on, training alongside his perfection, preparing for the open sea. He opened their minds too, showing them the simple laws which governed their environment, leading them to question him ever more deeply in order to arrive at an understanding of the cause and effect which channelled their lives.

He told them about the laws of gravity:

-Everything that has weight must drop down to the

rock which is the earth's centre.-

-It is only being alive which keeps you afloat. When you die you too will drop down.-

-Because it is above the water everything which is dropped on the land must finally fall into the seas.-

-When a landsman has no use for a thing he lets it drop and the waters bring it here. Everything is discarded here, the sea is the landsman's cess pool.-

-Why do they act that way?-

-The people of the land live above the water and cannot see into it, just as we of the water cannot see into the rock below.-

-Observation. Only by seeing can you learn.-

-Deduction can only be achieved on a basis of observation, of experience.-

He taught them to observe, to watch the lives of other creatures around them, to discover their habits.

-In knowing others we come to know ourselves, to know what part we play in the complicated pattern of life in the water.-

He took them out beyond the headland at dusk when they would normally have been settling into their sleeping places. There he showed them the stirring of life which changed the water world at night. Bottom-dwelling fish were moving about, deserting their camouflaged beds of sand and grit; lobsters and crayfish who had slept all day scuttled out of their holes, long feelers trembling about for food. Simo led the two farther and farther from the land, where crowds of fish swept by, hunting swarms of tiny, almost invisible plankton.

-The plankton feed on diatoms. Their food comes from that centre of good things: the ocean floor.-

-Then fish feed on the plankton and we eat the fish.-

-When we die our goodness goes to the bottom, to the centre, where all begins again.-

The Two listened and looked about them, amazed at this teeming world of which, dwelling always between the tidal zones, they had been unaware. The tiny plankton winked and glittered with light of their own

182

and, stretching up out of the water, Streggid was delighted to see his wet arm glowing with their clustered shapes. He dived, and cutting through the dark water trailed a comet tail of brilliants. His brother also swam jewelled with wonder.

-*What?*- Streggid drew back in disgust, grabbing at the unseen thing which clasped his wrist. His flurried movements made Idmazine anxious and he swam curving about him, hindered by the dark. Coming close he felt the whip of a fleshy tentacle about his fingers and twisting away snatched at his brother's arm, hauling him upward.

Swaying from trough to wavetop on the purple-dark sea the Two fumbled with the repulsive softness of the snakelike feelers which tugged and pulled at their skin. Simo swept past them, his open mouth grinning, his rows of even teeth gleaming. With a twist of his jaw he grabbed the thing away and, tossing his head, swallowed it. Streggid lay back laughing against the waves, bubbles of foam sliding cream down the surface beside him. 'Mzine hung at his side puzzled.

"The sea serpent!" gasped Streggid. "Vilidorn's serpent."

Idmazine tried to shrug aside the idea, the Lay of Vilidorn was only a story; but the dolphin when he returned was more serious.

-*A headfoot creature. Nothing more. But they can be dangerous, the big ones. Tell me your story.*-

He loved to hear the legends and fables of the folk, though they lost when translated to his utilitarian language. His own people had no history: their present and past were one in a world which, ever changing, had remained their same safe habitat through all time.

-*Yes. A headfoot.*- he repeated with satisfaction. -*They are creatures with a well-developed head surrounded by their foot which bears long prehensile tentacles. They escape by giving out a cloud of ink in which they disappear. The giants from the wild deep ...*-
He tried to explain the measurements of the giant squids but they could not understand him and when he said

183

that the length of all three of them together was not sufficient to display the size they could not believe.

-Go.- he was gentle with them. -Sleep, little ones. In daylight we will enjoy the water once more!-

Slowly the Two trudged back, thinking of all they had seen. This time they kept to the surface, afraid of losing their way. In the morning Simo was thoughtful.

-Time passes. You understand now the phases of the moon? So. Soon winter will be here. What will you do?-

Shrugging, they shook their heads. It was not in the nature of the Two to look beyond the next sunrise. When the time came they might go or stay. Any new course could bend and sway them.

-Come. I will go south. Come with me: the Blue Wave, the Favourable Islands.-

They shouted with pleasure and dived about him. Of course it was just what they wanted. Yet when they first left sight of land the Two were apprehensive.

It was a grey day whose chilling wind seeped into their wet flesh and they were glad to dive down and cruise with the waves' turbulence far overhead. Simo swam thoughtfully, saving their strength, but it was not until they were feeling the strong swell of the wide ocean about them that he paused to rest at the surface. Now land was nowhere in sight. From wave to distant wave the Two gazed about them, and a helplessness untied their courage: the open sea was infinite and above and beyond it lay only the white sky.

Then the dolphin's cheerful head appeared alongside them.

-Feel the depth! Now at last you have something to hold you up.-

His delight was tangible and they forgot their distress to rush on at his side, leaping in the long waves. He was full of the future:

-I will show you more of the little headfoots, so good to eat. In the Blue Waters you will see creatures you never dreamed of. The pretty little fish! The tasty big ones! Be careful of the jellies, they can sting you I *believe. I will show you such sights! Did you ever swim a ship's bow wave? Such excitement.-*

He tried to explain the dynamics of the trick, the position of the tail, the placing necessary, but once again the minds of the young folk were not prepared for such calculations and his meaning was lost: he was wearying them too soon.

At night they slept at his side, soft on the rocking wave, worn out by their journey. With the dawn it was time to move on and, refreshed, they swept along with the dolphin who was eager now for the warmer water and hurried on the future.

They were swimming lightly twenty feet down, taking their time from one another in order to rise together to the crumpled ceiling of silvered air swaying above them. Then a change in the light made them look up. As if storm clouds had edged across the sky, the light of the Day Star was diminished and angled awkwardly down on them. The way ahead was darkly overcast. In a panic swirl of bubbles Simo turned away, diving up toward the light. Surfacing at his side the Two gasped at the acrid smell which lifted into their nostrils from the sullen waters.

-Oil.-

Simo lay inert and panted steadily.

-Fill lungs. Dive. Now!-

They tried to follow but he was using all his power to escape the suffocating peril which coated the sea far ahead. They could not understand his fear and after long moments of terrified swimming they lost all trace of him in the shadowed water. Unused to his hyperbreathing they had too small an air supply and could not keep up the pressure. Unprepared for what they would find there they rose toward the dark, forbidding surface.

Streggid rose first, arm outstretched to ward off the seemingly solid intervention of the oil. But he was through before he knew it — before he had time to close his lids protectively and save his eyes. In pain he opened nose and mouth, then flung himself down once

185

more, gagging and spitting. Idmazine held him firmly, pressing one hand across his brother's mouth and nose, protecting his own face with the other. Kicking sturdily he held them both upright above the sluggish wallow of the heavy waves, then at last refreshed himself as best he could with that sickening pollution of air. Streggid gasped and retched, his mouth and nostrils on fire, eyes useless.

-Breathe Strek. Breathe. Gently. Fill your lungs.-

Down at last, through the thick slime once more, and on. Idmazine led the way through waters lifeless and unlit. They crossed paths of doomed fish who sped first one way and then back, completely disorientated in the gloom. A few had already ventured too near the surface and were suffocating, their gills ruined by a sludge of oil. They floated helpless, drooping on their sides, and Idmazine brushed them irritably aside. They themselves had to breathe only once more before the deadly cloud was passed. Then they lay on the clean waves and their courage ebbed away into the depth beneath them. Streggid was unable to see, blinded by the oil which clung beneath his eyelids in a piercing agony. Both felt their tongues and lips raw from the taint of the oil, their noses abraded by the smell of it. Of the dolphin there was no sign at all. If he had come safe through they would never know now, and he must have despaired of them.

"Take me to the shore, 'Mzine, I'm useless here. Take me and beach me." Streggid's bitterness was shocking to hear.

Idmazine turned away from the depths, away from the paths they had travelled so happily with their friend, and strained his senses to find shallower water. He listened, and tested the water about him; the dolphin's lessons had been well taught and before the day's end he was leading his brother through the backwash of waves on to a stretch of sand which banked and duned far into the land. No lights pricked out in the dusk and as far as his ears could hear there was no sound other than the roll of the surf. Awkwardly they staggered over the smooth beach, their feet dragging in the ankle-deep dust of the sand, and together fell onto the lap of the dry dunes. There thay huddled down among the stiff marram grasses to await the return of light.

The dawn's haze greeted them in a whisper of sibilance as the spiked grasses rustled at their sides and the limitless waves rushed and fell on to the shifting beach. There was no horizon anywhere, only mounds and gulleys of sand and the trembling tops of the majestic waves which marched up to them from the open sea. They stood helpless, bathed in the mysteriously diffuse light: no angled rocks beckoned with a promise of food or shelter. They were alone in a bare bowl of spray and sand.

Idmazine walked the hard ridges of the still wet sand searching for worm signs. He dug wildly, but as a boy he had scorned to glean and gather and had no skill. He set Streggid, sightless as he was, to scrabble and dig, finding the casts with his fingers. They caught a few little morsels and their hunger was roused. Dolefully they squatted back on their heels; this beach was no home to them.

"Wait, Strek. At least we are burying the oil as we dig. My hands are almost clean."

"It's the sand." Streggid rubbed handfuls fiercely on his arms and neck. "'Yes, I can feel it going!"

"And my skin with it." Yet Idmazine too was glad to rid himself of the cloying slime which shamed him.

They scrubbed and rinsed, scratching deep into their hair to remove every last trace. Lifting himself out of the water, clean at last, Idmazine was halted by the sight of his brother crouched on the sand, fistfuls of wet sand pressed against his smarting eyelids.

"No!" He rushed forward, pulled the tensed fists aside. "No, no," he crooned more gently and his arms went about Strek's shuddering body and he waited while a storm of tears swept over him. "That is not the way Strek. It will take time. Time and the ocean. The seas will wash it all away, be sure of that." He murmured and comforted as day faded and evening chill ruffled their flesh.

"What will happen to all the oil 'Mzine?" Streggid asked out of the darkness as they waited for sleep to hide their hunger.

"It is thick and will grow heavier. In the end it will drop down, as Simo taught us."

"Down to the centre of good things?"

"Yes. To the source of all our lives."

"And then?"

"I do not know Strek. I do not know."

With daylight Idmazine's bewilderment grew. He was not used to being a leader; although he was first, until this time they had always thought together, but now Streggid seemed withdrawn in his own dark world. It was clear that they could not stay on the wide and open sands, without food or hiding place, any longer. But he was unable to decide where to go. After a helpless search in the rippled sand under the spent waves he had found a couple of colourless tiny shrimps and a fingernail-sized crab. Without a word he took Strek's hand and they went with the wave. The chain he wore about his neck since birth had never weighed so heavily.

In the water, Streggid's other senses revived. He could feel the ripple of the water as it passed over his brother's body, and keeping this against his cheek he was able to follow him without seeing him. Attuned to the motion of the water it was he who again felt the pull to the south.

-Shall we go?- Idmazine asked.

-Where?-

-South. As Simo said. The Blue Wave. The Islands.-

-The Favourable Islands. Yes. I like that.-

So they turned sadly to complete the journey the dolphin had planned, following the currents as thay had been taught, searching the sky for signs. The waters grew warmer, food was abundant, and the ocean path drew them on, but alone now they found it hard to enjoy the water and as the moon grew then declined, so they

188

began to lose heart, unable to find faith in the islands Simo had been so eager to show them. Their pace slowed and for the first time they began to know despair, alone in the wild ocean. Streggid, whose eyes were only slowly recovering, sank deeper and deeper.

"Why do we go on?" he cried. "What is our purpose?"

Idmazine, resting beside him on the sliding waves could only shake his head.

Then, through the water around them, they felt, rather than heard, a rushing approach, distant yet clear. Lifting himself on the smooth swell Idmazine looked out over the wide wastes of ocean. He could see nothing, yet he sensed within himself a tremor of expectation, a lifting of the weight which lonely responsibility had pressed on him for so long.

"Strek! What is it?"

Streggid turned his head about on the water, listening.

"They're coming!" he shouted. And did not know who, or why.

Then, quite close, the first row of gleaming, curving bodies passed them. Dolphins! Row upon row, beyond counting. They called to one another as they rushed by, in high staccato cries, too quick in pattern for comprehension.

"Simo!" shouted Idmazine aloud. "Simo!" He could not stop himself, was not aware of the tears on his cheeks.

-Stay. Wait for us!- Streggid's desperate cry darted into the water, pitched as high and rapid as he was able.

Rank after rank the dolphins passed. It was impossible to reach them, yet suddenly they were there. The Two were surrounded by grinning, curious faces. Wise eyes narrowed, observing them; signals beamed about them identifying, cataloguing. While the school passed in its hundreds one small company had turned aside, testing them.

-Who?- asked one, distoring sound to such a low frequency that before they knew Simo they could never

189

have understood.

Excited laughter trembled into life but Idmazine answered gravely, telling of their journey, their destination.

-Favourable Isles.- The dolphins' pronunciation was different. They hurled advice, directions.

-Follow us.-

Before they could re-form and dash away, Streggid's cry detained them.

-Wait! Do you know Simo?-

-Simo?- The dolphins hurtled about, amused and delighted.

-We are Simo. All are Simo.-

They turned away, preparing to leave.

-You will find us again at the islands.- One gentle female hovered near for a long moment. *-We will be there before nightfall.-* She was gone.

-Perhaps your friend will be there, too.- Her voice signalled back. Already the dolphins were far away.

Streggid began to sing, the pleasure of that meeting had washed away despair. Together they pressed through the long waves looking for the setting of the Star. Soon, soon they would find island beaches once more. Their venture was about to begin again.

Far away to the north, in the seas beyond Sgeir, a single dolphin searched. From the waters of the cove he watched the home beach of the silkies, but the Two were far away and no others could understand his call. Sadly Simo turned away to rejoin his own people. But he would be back in another season, hoping always to meet his friends once more.

Chapter Twelve
The End

The Day Star crept up into the sky so laden with mist
and rain that its face was hidden and only a sodden light
filtered into the cove to rouse the sleeping folk. Old
grandsires sat up scratching, peered out under cragged
brows to check the tide which measured out their lives,
then resettled their stiff joints muttering and coughing.
Little babes nuzzled at their sleeping mothers and were
folded into a feeding comfort. Maids and useless boys
alike squirmed and fidgeted together trying to recapture
sleep, reluctant to move out into dullness and damp.
Only the nans hobbled outside onto the shrouded
beach: it was the ebb and each clasped her gleaning
bowl to fill with good things for the families. As they
gathered, little ones, shouting, scuttled about them or
splashed in the shallows, warmer in the water than in
the soaking air which glistened in the nans' silvered
hair like a frost. Limpets and winkles they took;
mussels and whelks were easy to find, even the little
shanny fish were scooped up in their practised fingers.
But no-one took more than was needed, each pool and
gully of water still held a tiny population after the old
women were gone: the balance must remain.

The families were wakening when they returned.
Young men strolled among the rocks to relieve
themselves, others squatted among the pebbles and grit
under the overhanging cliffs. Shivering and wincing,
young mothers went daintily down the beach to wash
their babies in the waves before they hurried back to eat

their own meal. Chattering angrily the old folk brushed away the importunate boys who sidled in and out searching for extra titbits. A chubby little maid, leaning safe at her grandsire's side, giggled and rolled mischievous eyes at their antics while the old one smashed shells apart for her with his hand stone and anvil, popping the shattered morsels into her open mouth. His stubby fingers, shiny with age, scrabbled the broken shards together, piling them with the rest to be scattered later by the cleansing tides.

The steady drag of the raining mist across the sea had worn away the waves and every droplet fell into its own widening circle on the smooth water. The hungry boys rushed yelling through the shallows to dive and disappear. They were off to chase and fish. Maidens chattered idly as they worked with stone and sand rubbing hollows into stubborn drifted wood to make the bowls which would mark their status as mothers of the folk. Quietly they sang the old songs together as they waited for the time of borning.

The dull day whispered by until, with the flowing of another tide, the clouds parted and a watery golden light slanted down across the cove. Expectantly, the folk waited below and about the Elder Rock, and the hoped-for time of story-telling drew them all together once more. Old Dandrid who had drowsed the day away waiting for this hour hunkered into his appointed place.

"I will tell you Hancid's Story," he began, raising his hands for silence. "How he found the whales and learned that they will give their lives for one another."

"Will we ever have to do that?" asked a solemn-eyed youngster when the recital was ended.

"It cannot be," replied the old one weightily. "We have no enemies here on the home beach."

"When we venture far across the foam we know danger."

A strong man, Slidorn, rose up, his barrel chest scarred by some near disaster. "Then we face it alone, knowing that the outcome rests on our own skill, our

192

knowledge. There is no enemy that the folk should fear, none that can force such a sacrifice from us."

"Not even Men?" It was a bitter cry; but though everyone looked about no-one could tell who had spoken.

The stooped man stood motionless, watching. The very air seemed still around him, poised, waiting. He had been there for nearly an hour, intent, gazing through the thick glass into the misty water of the tank.

Inside the tank a young dolphin slept, his body arched just below the surface. The water about him was silken smooth and he tested it whenever he woke; sensing its bland, lifeless texture, recognising and rejecting the stale scent of his own weary body, feeling slightly disturbed by the presence of the chlorine. He discharged a faint echo-location signal but the responses were as negative as ever: there was no other living creature in this cell; it was calm, drab, and utterly without any kind of stimulation. There were no haphazard sounds, no unexpected movements. Nothing. How could he keep his mind active? How could he preserve that sense of identity which for all the years of his life his people had impressed upon him? He was Simo, Dolphin, heir to the freedom of all the waters of the world, yet a captive.

With a despairing thrash of his tail he swung away: down to the far end of the pool, turn, back to the shadowed end, turn; far end, turn. He counted the number of strokes each length took, computing the fresh total with each stroke. He checked the position of the risen sun and tried again to calculate where he was, but it was impossible. He did not know for how many day since his capture he had been unable, in his shock and distress, to remember anything.

He had been scampering along before a ship's bow wave, happily maintaining his position in the rapid slide of the moving water. Then the experts who held the prime positions close under the bows had dropped back, giving him his chance. He had moved in confidently, held his place thrilled by the rush and the spray, and then he was no longer swimming at all. He was out of the water. Vapid, useless air lay along his flanks, unresisting as he braced himself, making movement impossible. He lay still, helpless, only partially conscious. He knew nothing. Then he was in this pool, this cell.

His eye rested on the solid blue wall close to his side. Its texture was smooth, it curved to meet the blue floor. Through the water he could dimly see the other blue wall. It curved up from the floor. Their was hardly a distinguishing feature anywhere. He had found one blistered crack whose interest had soon faded, a grill where the water went and a pipe where it came. The massy glass window at the shadowed end of the pool meant nothing to him, its texture was smooth, bland as the wall; its other side was dark, revealing nothing of the watcher who stood silent for so long. But Simo had seen the men who captured him, had worried at their image in his mind many times.

There was no resemblance, he concluded sadly. These were nothing like the Sea Folk he had met, those delightful young companions could never come to this. He dreamed of them often, missing them as he missed the soothing sensation of another mammal body brushing against his own, as he missed the interest of another mind to explore, explain, predict. Bored and lonely, the dolphin moved petulantly about the tank.

To Meredith, the watcher behind the glass, the dolphin's tension and distress were painful. In the same way he had himself paced out the hours of failure and frustration in his life. Even now, so near completion, he would not allow himself to relax, but his doubts were stilled. The dolphin had made a good recovery and would be fit for the experiment where so many others had failed him. And the new tracker device implanted in its tail, that too showed no sign of weakness. The signal it emitted should make it possible to trace the creature anywhere in coastal waters, now that it could be picked up from the land. And he tried to project to the dolphin his dream of success. This time! he thought, this time I shall make a contribution!

But his hope, his expectation, could not reach the dolphin within the tank, measuring, computing, never at peace, reckoning out the days until its release again into the stimulation, the movement, of the living sea.

The sea murmured and flowed, soft among the outer rocks. The night was calm and mild: the moon, a fingernail of pale light low on the horizon, was reflected across the gentle swell in a shimmered line which lay straight into the cove. A glissading breeze lifted from the wave slides to whisper among the dried weeds and water-softened wood on the high drift bank left by winter's storms. Among the grey and dusty pebbles a mass of dried whelk's eggs shifted and pittered on the slope.

Awake in the cave, Merrin heard the slight sound and tensed. She was reacting too acutely, she knew, but she felt vulnerable, like an egg whose soft shell was only a single tight layer of skin. She was not strong enough, impervious enough, to protect the life within. The baby moved inside her and she grunted at the discomfort, moving heavily to find relief from its weight. Her time was very near and, over- reacting again, tears fell, although she would have called herself happy. She had waited so long for this and now was apprehensive: nothing must fail. Her fears, unusual among the maidens of the folk, disturbed her mother and Borry came to her, furtive in the slanting shadows, to give her the charm.

Fat Borry, folds of flesh at wrist and elbow, squatted at her daughter's side breathing noisily.

"Take it, take it," she panted. "Keep hold of that, for it won't be long now, and you'll be sure to come through as clean as that shell. I've put the words in it. There's nothing to worry you, my pretty. Nothing to worry." She stroked Merrin's cheek, smoothed her hair, fondling its curls. Then, pressing palms into her chubby knees, levered herself upright. "Won't be long now." She smiled bravely and waddled away. Her visit had frightened Merrin more than ever.

She looked slyly at the monster shell in her fist, smoothed and clean, the opening pink and full-fleshed. Like lips. She covered it quickly with her hand, ashamed of her thoughts. Like the other maidens she had laughed and joked recently, pulling winkles from their dark shells intact. Every whole creature promised a successful birth they said. She wished her fingers had proved nimbler.

She shifted again in her sleeping hollow, trying to ease the ache in her back, but it gripped suddenly tighter, groping deep into her groin. Her heart jumped and flexed as if it would swim up, out of her ribs: was this what she had been waiting for so long?

The young moon had set into the west when she gave her first, joyful cry. It was certain: her babe was ready in its time of borning. Mothers and nans hurried round her, wide-eyed little maids watched, fingers to their mouths.

"Outside! Outside!" Everyone was calling and laughing, helping her to her feet, supporting her in the ritual. Out of the cave, out of the womb into the world, the world of water and of air.

She had prepared the place days before in the shelter of a leaning rock just above the tide line. The flood was running now, close on the other side of the rock. Soon all would be complete. She stumbled as she walked but loving hands reached out, arms held her, and she lay back at last catching the rhythm of it as the sea lapped closer, calling the babe.

It seemed as if, one after another, master waves drummed on her body and their undertow tugged deep within her. She breathed, shallow gasping breaths, whenever she was able. She could see nothing, hear nothing but the sea roar in her ears. She remembered the shell and thought she was listening to its convoluted call, deep down. Deep. Down. With one wilful effort she arched her body, reaching for the surface once more, and it was done. Eased into the world on a sigh, her babe was born.

Borry and an old nan took it up, lifted it away into the quiet waves for washing. Maids of her own borning helped Merrin to her feet. Weary but triumphant she slid into the smooth sea and waited to be clean. Then proudly carrying her little daughter she led them all back up toward the slumbering cave.

Out on the skerries the seals called, watching suspiciously the activity on the pre-dawn beach. The womenfolk turned and looked back. Colour was drifting into the sky once more, another day waiting to be born.

"What is coming for you?" Merrin whispered to the infant in her arms, gazing into the folded face and rubbing dry the downy fur on shoulders and arms. "What lifetime of new days here among your folk, measured out by the rise and fall of the sea, your home?" It was not thinkable that a girl-child would ever leave the home beach.

A quiet beach off the lonely west coast of Scotland: that was where the dolphin had gone. Meredith tested his readings, checked the computations. They had lost contact, but it was only temporary, he told himself. Nevertheless the old fears were there, the tensions. As he paced and calculated his positions he felt, uncannily shifting beneath the skin, that he, like the dolphin, was measuring out a circumscribed future of loss and failure.

He must not fail. The yacht, electronically equipped, beat back and forth about the islands, and a desperation beat behind his eyelids. He made notes, took bearings, pushed himself and the crew beyond weariness, yet slowly, insidiously, the langour of the islands prevailed. His course seemed directed through cloud; mists of melancholy loss drifted across his way. He willed himself on, and his goal was only dimly seen. He had loosed himself from the groping obstructions of the land. The answer, surely, was in these seas? Distances were finite even here, time was exact. His wayward mind ran back and forth over the figures, proving the closing contours of the hunt. Though still the signal did not come.

He felt his senses losing their edge as he dully patrolled the water. Mild day followed misty dawn and he paused in his marking of time to stand at gaze against the starboard rail. The broken seas creamed back from the slicing bow, falling away behind in confusion. It is my life, he thought, this ocean, and meaningless. Stupidly he watched the waves' day-long march to the edge of the world and felt no wonder at the eyes that watched him there. Two sleek wet heads appeared briefly on the wave's side. Even white teeth grinned at him, and were gone. He rushed, despair forgotten, to the tiny viewing window below the waterline. What had he seen? Urgent orders brought the yacht head-on to the wind and they lost way. He peered into the green peace below the tip of the waves, longing for another glimpse of them, watching as they passed below his keel. Not dolphin, not seals. A flicker of grey limbs, furry; pale disc of a laughing face. Then they were gone: Streggid and Idmazine, still tempted to the craft of men even as they returned down the stream of years to their home beach once more.

Merrin rarely thought of the Two. They had been her born companions, but always held themselves apart. When they left she had shed a few tears, for she sensed how alone they were. Now, with her babe on her hip, she realised the closeness they had shared, one with the other. She found herself completely engrossed with her child, needing no other company from one tide to the next.

She sat in the shallows, the afternoon heat warm on her shoulders, drying her hair, and idly watched the play and run of little pebbles in the sand. Every so often she would reach out to catch any whiter than the rest, but it was a half-hearted collection: when her hand was full she dropped them all back again. Out among the rocks beyond the cove she heard the cries and calls of laughing boys, diving and splashing together. So they learned and grew and went their way, but her little one would surely be with her always. The babe slept in the crook of her arm, toes dabbled in the water, making from time to time little smacking sounds with her lips. When she woke they would go up the beach; it would be time to feed.

Young Jarny came to sit beside her, wanting to hold the babe, but Merrin distracted her with a handful of tiny white pebbles.

"Oh Merrin! Find some more and we will make flowers!"

She laughed at that: she had never grown out of the old custom, so dear to little maids, of making patterns of intricate colour and texture in the firm sand high up the beach. They called them 'flowers', and like their counterparts up on the cliffs, with the autumn gales they were swept away.

Thong weed marked out the five segments, a starfish design. Along the slender lines a mosaic grew, white quartz and agate, blood dark jasper and misty chalcedony. The pattern was filled and repeated on every side, the tiny jewel stones bedded in whorls of darker sand or emphasised alongside the black reflection of basalt. Pieces of shell, scattered like a lacy fringe, linked the delicate lines; Jarny was absorbed, intent on her own creation.

Merrin watched the satisfying repetitions take shape, even scraping out a comfortable hollow for her babe to lie in while she helped to search for shapes and shades. The long summer twilight muted the colours until at last they left their labours, stiff from crouching and bending, and lay awhile in the waves.

Cruising in the mouth of the cove, Simo, the dolphin, caught their movement and signalled to them. He expected no reply; he no longer believed that he could meet again those two with whom, so many months ago, he had enjoyed the water.

Through the waves he examined the silkies, learning

199

their sex, sensing their quiet content. Throughout the day he had observed them in the water, keeping out of sight. Now, in the dying light of the westering Day Star he watched them leave the ebbing ripples and move awkwardly up the beach.

-Id Mzine!- he called, -Strek Id!-

He would not forget them, and returned again and again. But he was too soon to witness their return. It was not yet the time of homecoming. Unaware of the ranging signal, of which he was the centre, ignorant of the transmitter which he carried, the dolphin left the intervening safety of the cove and sought again the wide swell of the seas. As he swam he emitted, from time to time, his own forlorn cry.

After sighting the two silkies, Meredith, disturbed, returned to land. In the fishing harbours, the ferry ports of the islands, he made new enquiries.

"Divers working off the coast? No. What would they be doing out there? No, there's never a one."

"Seals you have seen, I'm thinking. It is the seal folk, nothing more."

He set aside their superstition, hardening his mind against such dreams. But the pale face of Streggid, smiling at him through the water, lay just at the surface of his mind.

He was directed to a derelict cottage, once the home of some fey and dreaming wanderer. There, he was told, he would find papers, translated words to confirm his search.

"This is the home of McBride," the old man's lilting Highland voice explained quietly, while the others, knotted in their scarves against the wind, stood whispering in the heather their Gaelic tongue.

"But the door's locked." He fingered the heavy padlock, rattled its chain.

"Yes. That is right. He wasn't knowing he would never come back."

Meredith stepped away, looked up to the roof at the

smoke-black chimney, eyed the lookers-on. Did they expect him to break down the door? They muttered again in their own tongue and he was exasperated, embarrassed all at once, unclear about their expectations.

He stood back, raised his foot and stamped at the weather-whitened planks. The old door shuddered and clanked on its chain. The men muttered again. Did they disapprove? Meredith would not look back now, but stamped and thrust against the barrier. Suddenly the bolts were unseated. Gripping only dusty shards of broken wood, the screws leapt free and the bar swung aside. In the silence the padlock rattled over the chain. The men eased forward.

The door had settled on its hinges and scraped on the lintel as he heaved it inward. On the house step where once the silkie had entered to Mary McBride, they paused and peered about in the dusk of the shuttered room. Piles of paper were drifted up every wall. On shelves, in boxes, in old plastic bags stood all the remnants of McBride's scattered mind. The crofters shook their heads and stepped back. It was true then: the old body had been altogether crazy.

Meredith moved closer: in the bags packed with damp, the papers, splotched and spoiled by mildew, had to be prised apart.

"The sealskin," he read, "seal of anonymity. Rumpelstiltskin. Guess my name. Kiss my arse. O the pride of them! They know all the answers, but never... (What was this?)...to be seen. Not by me..." The words were blurred, deranged. There was nothing here.

Mice had nested in the cardboard boxes, making confetti of the notebooks stacked there. Woodlice hastened away as he pulled the cartons irritably aside, and long-legged spiders scurried for cover.

"Shore sightings: nineteenth century." "Sea sightings: North-West." He read the faded titles. "Capture of maidens". He turned the pages back and they crackled and stuck. Rusting staples fell aside.

"...carried her up the beach and away to his home.

201

She cried miserably all the way and flung back her arms toward the waves but he would not heed her." The old madman had some erotic fancies then!

Meredith let the book fall and turned to the shelves. Hakluyt's *Voyages, Henry Hudson the Navigator*, maps and charts, scientific papers; all bore testimony to the ragbag of the old man's mind. He drew down one printed monograph and recognised with surprise a familiar paper: Diatomic Production Rates by D.R.McBride. Was this the same man? He ran his eye again over crumpled papers. Theory of the Existence of Marine Hominids. Henry Hudson's name again: what had the old man found? Mermaids? Excitement shimmered and sickened him: was he going mad himself? Disenchanted he turned and walked away, there was nothing rational here. Yet the paper remained, it was stuffed into his jacket pocket, a possible way forward.

He wished bitterly as he tramped back across the moor, the sibilating crowd at his heels, that he had never allowed himself his moment of belief. The decay of the old tramping man should be a warning. Apathetic, bitter now that he had lost the dolphin, he had let himself be forced into an anomalous situation.

The dolphin swept, desperate, across his mind once more and he turned to look back at the slim white arm of the shell sand beach below him, the foaming breakers chasing one another to the land, and the wide dark ocean paths beyond.

"The dolphin," he spoke aloud. "Could a dolphin harbour out there?"

Pitying, they reassured him. One or more were seen from time to time. Far from this coast they swam the foam around a rocky outcrop beyond Sgeir.

"They watch the selchies on their rock."

Meredith did not understand the fishermen's mutter, but took directions and bearings for the empty island they described. He had found, possibly, the shelter within which the signal had been lost. An unmapped outcrop, it could perhaps be the explanation. And if there existed, out there, free in the seas, the people of his vision, he would gain perhaps a sight of them, see again that haunting, water-whipped smile. He could not deny his search.

The maidens scanned the waters eagerly as they sat chattering and laughing on the outer rocks. The time of Equinox was near and soon the young heroes would be returning, longing to rest a while cuddled close in soft arms, pillowed in comfort. Their ease would only be short, too short. After winter's storms withdrew, they would be restless once more, watching the horizon, roaring the old songs of venture and bravery. They would tell their stories, wrestle, play, and be gone. But when the fresh chill of autumn misted the air once more, creeping damp about the cliff roots as the Star slid down into dusk, so the menfolk would return, and on golden afternoons maidens swam to the limits of the cove, watching to welcome them.

They combed out their long hair, with fingers and with fish-spine combs, lay knotted wrack about their necks or ribboned themselves with slippery kelp. Merrin, watching them from her rock within the arms of the cove, smiled and remembered how she and her companions once had the habit of placing pretty shells in their ears, thinking to attract the bold looks of a returning hero. Were all maids so light-hearted? She hitched her little babe into her lap and laughed at the solemn wrinkling of her eyes in the sunlight.

"Will you have a father then, I wonder? Will the man return and share our sleeping?"

Her thoughts wandered idly across the image of a man of the folk, tall and spare, his grizzled hair sparse about his chest and forehead. Old enough to be her own father, that she knew, and yet he had been the force, after so many failures, to bring this little one to life within her. She could not tell how she knew it; nor could she fathom her own feelings if he should return. She would hold his sad head against her breast perhaps, to give him comfort, no more. He was a stranger to her, still.

Out on the rocks the maids were singing. They had seen a boat! It was a song of the deep they chanted, their voices blending in mocking harmony as they waved their arms above their heads in sinuous copy of the tall weed deep dowm. Oh wicked! Merrin gave a gasp of silent laughter, even as she crouched down out of sight: now the boat was turning from its course, and in a blink the maids were gone. As he approached, the searcher would see only the seals, flinging their echoing songs at the intruders and slipping, disgruntled, into the tilting waves.

What an adventure! Laughing and squealing, the maids ran about the beach, whispered their daring in dull old ears, and longed for heroes to giggle and dally with. Their half-stifled whispers went on into the night until stilled by an old nan's angry hiss.

As the days and nights rode by, like waves and troughs in a slow-running tide, so the home beach filled once more. Erstwhile boys came home men, tall and assured. Their stories resounded, as many had before, with tales of bear and walrus, floes of ice and laughing lights.

"When the sky itself fills with such colour that the air seems drenched in beams of light, what can we do but ever train our search northward?" One hollow-eyed youth shook his head over hands clasped slack between his knees, "I will find it, one time there, my destiny. The light will call me again and I will go."

His nan stroked his hair, fed him juicy morsels from her bowl, and in secret wept stray tears for his youth and certainty. So it would always be.

Ignoring the seals on the sea-washed skerry, Meredith had irritably put about once more. Faintly his receivers were at last picking up the signal again: the dolphin was close. But the distant stations on the mainland were unable to help him, the range was too great. His brain was made sluggish by the weight of former failures. Once again he was being forced to remain in obscurity. It had been a madness, the grey folk he had seen. They could not exist. In all this wild waste of ocean he was fated to achieve nothing, there was no place for him here.

The returning Two, swimming westward through velvet dark of night-hushed seas, passed close under his boat, but he had ceased to watch. They knew nothing of his intricate perceptions as they moved on across empty seas toward their birthplace. They had lingered often on their long return, hesitating to put behind them the freedom of their venture. Questing among remote settlements of men, searching among the seals, they were learning daily their heritage in these chill waters, and memories of southern warmth were slipping away. Their strong rhythmic strokes drove them steadily through the waves, they had no need to speak, each balanced in thought.

-*Id Mzine! Strek Id!*-

In a flurry they turned, their driving progress halted, searching, listening. There was the cry again, they had never forgotten it.

-*Simo!*-

They tumbled joyfully into the new course, separating according to their custom and closing onto the dolphin's call. Was it possible that Simo was here? That he still lived? There was so much to exchange since the oil slick, would he find them different? Would he too have grown wiser? Could he still teach them?

Their greeting was as exuberant as ever. The dolphin arched into the air above them, his sides flickering with tiny plankton lights while they flung back their heads to roar a song of welcome. But the dolphin butted them sharply from below, the slap of his tail was a warning to silence them.

-*A boat*,- he told them, -*near. Too near. And, yes I feel it following me.*-

-*Following!*-

-*How?*-

-That I cannot know. I have turned aside, but the boat shifts and is again taking my course. I weary of it.-

-But where are you going?-

-Why so far north at this season of the year?-

-I search. For the Two!-

-For us!-

-Swim with us, Simo. We go to our home beach. Come! Enjoy the water!-

But the dolphin hung back. For all his delight, the presence of that pursuing boat disturbed him. Around it he sensed disillusionment and loss. And something more: a centred pain of self-hatred which drove this man to his own destruction, and every being about him was at risk. The dolphin could not discern ambition, it was a greed he could never know, a hurt which never struck a people so entirely at one. But he sensed the harsh intent of this man who sailed in mists of his own making, troubled and without course.

The gentle creature had slid away from the threat into the deep safety of the shadowed waves: the human condition remained a mystery to his kind. But now, with an urgency that caught at them, snagging up their own fears, he tried to make clear to the two Sea Folk what he had felt.

-Go to your beach! Warn your people! That sombre boat turns there again and again, and the haggard man means you harm. I can bring you no comfort.-

They had no need to speak. All that the dolphin had shown them filled them with dread. Silently they accepted the duty and, laying their hands on his side in thanks and farewell, they turned away to close up the last dark interval.

The Equinox was more than two nights past, and the season so unusually mild, that many folk, old and young alike, crouched among the rocks and watched the moonlit ebb. Ardent nans dabbled in glim pools, but, for the rest, all were at ease. Later there were those who said they waited. Was it so?

206

They came, the Two, all so quiet that they trod the shell sand floor of the cove before they were discerned in the silver light. They walked easily up the beach, and only stopped, turned, when they had topped the storm bank. Aware of the stir of apprehension all about them, they paused and silently looked back down the moon-bright bay. A crabbed old grandsire sidled up, grimaced at them under his bushing brows and shook his head.

"You never came to anything. I knew it would be so."

Others crept forward, eyed the sun-brown limbs and searched about for faces to explain. Who were the handsome strangers? Maidens whispered among their friends and tossed their hair. Smiling softly, her baby on her hip, Merrin stepped up.

"First and second sons of Giersi, how good to see you home!" She laid a hand briefly against each face. "Had you success in your venture?" The formal words held a new meaning, as she remembered that, as boys, they had gone, so all supposed, to seek their mother out, wherever she might be, among the seals. "Venture has laid age upon us woman, and we are tired." Idmazine matched her formal ways.

"Tired and hungry!" Streggid watched the good bowls filled by thrifty Nans.

"Eat then, graceless one", cried Borry, "but never dare to sleep until I know; have you found your mother? Does Giersi still live between wind and wave?"

In the gathered crowd a tall figure moved, straining to hear.

"We have no news of her," came Idmazine's reply.

"She is known everywhere", said Streggid, "but none will point her out since she pleaded for privacy."

"The seals know! But I cannot hear what they say!" The tall one threw back his head and cried, tears gleaming on his cheeks.

Merrin turned to look gravely upon her child's father. When had he returned? What caused his anguished cry? She stood beside him, her fingers on his arm quieted him and the folk nearby gracefully gave him peace.

But Streggid could not halt the words that tumbled on his tongue:

"You sir, you searched for her too? In a hard world you cared for Giersi? Why was that?"

He squinted painfully about, his weak eyes unable to discover among the shapes and shadows the man he sought. Setting aside Merrin's anxious fingers Hancid stepped out:

"I knew her as wife, and greet you as sons. Sons from seas I never knew." Troubled he shook his head, greying hair restless about his face. "Why have you returned after so long? What welcome do you expect?"

It was a harsh, unlooked for cry and the Two drew closer together to strengthen their purpose in face of such rejection.

"We are come", said Idmazine, his voice deep, sonorous, reaching even to the inquisitive faces of sleepers peering from the cave, "We are come from favourable islands, across lengthy ocean streams, returning to our home beach at last. But we bring warning of danger to the folk, now, and very near. Even today we have seen, turning at the entrance to this cove, a slim boat, sailed by a man who will bring our end. An evil purpose is in his heart, and trouble lies about him in a fog. We must speak on Elder Rock, for what we have to say concerns all here. It may be that it is time to leave the home beach, for now you are known: this man will betray you."

Consternation greeted his words. Whispering and shaking their heads old folk turned to one another, young men braced themselves for action and maidens hurried to press dear ones to their sides.

One old nan brandished her bowl above her head.

"I am ready", she cried. "My life has been all and only for the folk. If I must sacrifice it at last in the open sea, isn't that where all must finish? I am ready!"

But others shouted her down and the crowd moved, angrily, to the Elder Rock to hear what the messengers had to say. For generations the folk had known only this rock as home; it was hard to prepare for paths of

208

ocean in a moment's thought.

"I will not listen further!" cried Graymidon when night was dying in the eastern sky, and the talk was come full circle with nothing clear. "My way was planned for me many years ago." He indicated his withered leg. "I cannot leave. But you, all of you, are the folk and must survive. Go now with these lads who offer salvation, go with the seas which have been our home since Parscid Time, when he, Protector, led us from under the hand of Man, gave us our freedom: to be one of the people of the sea. Go now, and leave me."

"There is truth in your words, Graymidon, my friend. But no need for bitterness, you will not be alone." Smiling his sad smile Hancid stepped forward. "Go, all of you, for you have no choice. Find warmer waters, stronger light. But my heart's life is here and I must stay to seek her out. I will never leave these nothern wastes of ocean, where light lies gentle on the restless waves and the seals move in their migrations. This, why, it is my life stream. I cannot leave!"

Turning he helped Graymidon to rise and stood tall at his side. "We shall not remain here, to become the slaves of men but will take the westward track of the moon's setting. It may be we shall remain unseen, but our progress will be slow, while the men can move with speed. I do not know what the outcome will be, but I see that the time of parting has indeed come."

Then slowly, with quiet pride, the two made their way out from the land. And all the folk stood silent to let them pass, accepting their sacrifice.

Meredith watched angrily as the crew hauled once again on wet lines, trying in vain to set the flagging sail to catch the vagrant breeze which backed and eddied above the rocking waves. Whoever would have predicted weather so unseasonably calm? This whole attempt had been a history of chances missed and wrong decisions taken. He should have abandoned the dolphin, taken more interest in the hints and dreams of

209

the broken notebooks, the rotting files of the old man's mind. Somewhere there lay the way to track down the silkies. He knew now where he had been at fault: that little rock outcrop he had approached on the afternoon tide must have been their home, where what he thought were seals had mocked him with arms streatched out, combing long dark hair. But he, failing to seize the moment, had lacked faith in his own vision, had turned away to follow the hesitant signal which for days had haunted him. Now contact was lost again, the mainland station useless, and he was still uncertain, trying to turn back.

He could imagine the world's reaction if that was all he found. A sailor's dream of mermaids, nothing more. But he needed to test the vision, and in the bone deep chill of dawn he wrestled alongside the crew, searching for a puff of wind to take him back there. Gulls cried to him, but he could not hear what they said. His mind was turned to grit, to dust. His theories, his manuscripts, the learned papers he'd prepared were all a rustle of paper lies. He would give the lonely skerries one last chance. Then he was finished, it was the end.

His boots pressed patterns on the grey beach sand. Sea-birds high on the cliff fell silent as he scuffled across young Jarny's flowered setts.

In the echoing cave he gazed for long moments at the hollowed sleeping places, briefly held a golden cowrie shell in his cupped hand, then let it fall. *They had been here.* He knew it as he sifted through a pile of shattered shells, lay his hand on the smooth prominence of a commanding rock. These were no proof, however. The wind lifted and blew through his hollow mind. There was no more substance here than in the shifting mists, the trickling sands. Rumours, remarks and haunting melodies were all he had. And yet he knew: the silkies are a reality and must be found one day.

He walked slowly down the slope of the pebbled beach, across the white sand to where his helpless boat bobbed beside the outer rocks. As he waded through the broken waves and the tide wreck a hollowed form of curved wood rolled against his ankle, but he did not turn his head. As he traced a long reach out of the little bay, waves lifted the forgotten bowl and tumbled it among the scrabbling stones.

The majestic clouds that had swept across the sky all day were hurrying toward the edge of the world, and with misty fingers outstretched were catching the last of the Day Star's light in wild hues of red and orange. The sea was gilded and the low streaming light made of every wave a sea in miniature, its stately sides faceted by the ripple and flow of etched wavelets shining and alive. Between the glittering tops the dents and vales were dark, all colour gone, lightless as the deep trenches of the sea bottom. Resting on the sliding wave sides the we head and gleaming eyes of a lone swimmer watched the boat tack away. Idmazine dived to swim strongly on, watching for the last of the folk in their great migration lest any should be left behind. He was seen only by the sea-birds as they flew upward, calling their last sad farewells.

APPENDIX

On the Theory of the Existence
of Marine Hominids (*Homo Aquatilis*).
by D.R. McBride PhD

Since Classical times there has existed a belief that for every form of life observed on land there must be a marine equivalent. This unfounded and spurious belief was encouraged by the existence of such creatures as the marine turtle, the marine lizard or the marine snake. Since such lower orders were represented it was not difficult for credulous peoples to accept that there lived under the sea an example of what they took to be Nature's highest achievement: Man himself. Thus Greek and Latin literature abounds in encounters with sea-nymphs, the nereids or daughters of Nereus, the sea god. It has long been thought that it was from these mythical tales that the romance of the mermaid sprang. In the light of recent research, however, it may be necessary to review historical claims that a relative of the human race has indeed been sighted in an entirely marine habitat.

The earliest such sighting was reported by the chronicler Ralph of Coggeshall in his *Chronicon Anglicanum* of 1207. He tells how fishermen caught a wild man in their nets off the coast of Suffolk, and showed him to their lord, Sir Bartholomew de Glanville, Constable of the castle of Orford during the reign of Henry II:

"He was naked and was like a man in all his members. He was covered in hair and had a long shaggy beard. The knight kept him in custody many days and nights, lest he should return to the sea. He eagerly ate whatever was brought to him, whether raw or cooked, but the raw he pressed between his hands until all the juice was expelled. Whether he would not or could not, he did not talk, although oft-times hung up by his feet and harshly tortured. Brought into the church, he showed no signs of reverence or belief ... He sought his bed at sunset and always remained there until sunrise.

"It happened that once they brought him to the harbour and suffered him to go into the sea, strongly guarding him with three lines of nets; but he dived under the nets out into the deep sea, and came up again and again as if in derision of the spectators on the shore. After thus playing about for a long while, he came back of his own free will. But later on, being negligently guarded, he secretly fled back to the sea and was never afterward seen."

213

During the explorations and discoveries of the sixteenth century many tales of mermaids were brought back from the sea, along with exaggerated accounts of sea monsters and other wonders. However in 1608 Henry Hudson, sailing on his second voyage in search of a Northeast Passage to China, recorded a sighting of a mermaid in the Barents Sea. According to the two seamen, Thomas Hilles and Robert Raynar, who saw her:

> "Her back and breasts were like a woman's and her skin very white; and long hair hanging down behinde, of colour blacke; in her going down they saw her tayle, which was like the tayle of a porpoise, and speckled like a macrell."

During this same year another mermaid was sighted, also in the North Atlantic, off Newfoundland.

Again in North Atlantic waters some two hundred years later Captain Asa Swift, the master of the *Leonidas,* out from New York, records, in the *American Journal of Science* of 1820, a "strange fish" which was seen to follow the ship:

> "The second mate ... told me the face was nearly white, and exactly like that of a human person; that its arms were about half as long as his, with hands resembling his own; that it stood erect out of the water about two feet, looking at the ship and sails with great earnestness. It would remain in this attitude, close alongside, ten or fifteen minutes at a time, and then dive and appear on the other side ... Mr Stevens also stated that its hair was black on the head and exactly resembled a man's; that below the arms, it was a perfect fish in form, and that the whole length from the head to the tail was about five feet."

In 1809 *The Times* had printed a report by a Scottish schoolmaster named William Munro describing his encounter, on the beach near Thurso, with:

> " a figure resembling an un-clothed human female, sitting upon a rock extending into the sea, and apparently in the action of combing its hair, which flowed around its shoulders, and was of a light brown colour ... the forehead round, the face plump, the cheeks ruddy, the eyes blue, the mouth and lips of a natural form ... It remained on the rock three or four minutes after I observed it, and was exercised during that period in combing its hair, which was long and thick, and of which it appeared proud, and then dropped into the sea."

Other local people also admitted to having seen similar creatures, their descriptions compatible with those of the schoolmaster. From these and other recorded experiences it seems possible that a species of aquatic hominid did exist in the waters of the North Atlantic over a period of many centuries. Such a species has in fact been postulated as an evolutionary link between the anthropoid apes of the Miocene Age and the earliest of human remains, *Australopithicus Africanus.*

The theory of an aquatic evolutionary stage during the Pliocene Age was first put forward by Professor Sir Alister Hardy in his article "Was man more aquatic in the past?" (*New Scientist* 7, 1960, pp 642-5), which explains many conditions found in modern man but unknown among primates.

For instance, the vertical posture of man, recognised even in the earliest skeleton remains by the extension of the knee joint, would be facilitated by a ten million year evolutionary period spent supported in water. It is not suggested that this primitive hominid escaped into the deeps at this time: it is probable that he was an inter-tidal dweller, feeding on crustaceans known to have been in existence at that time, and on other abundant forms of marine life. Searching and groping for these foodstuffs under water would have made an evolutionary necessity of the sensitive and agile human hand. It is also suggested that on a beach, surrounded by pebbles on all sides, man first made use of this primitive tool to break open the shells of the creatures on which he lived.

Other physiological evidence in support of this aquatic theory is to be found in the streamlining of the hair tracts on the human body, seen most clearly on the human foetus while still immersed in the womb. These follow exactly the lines which would be produced by water flowing over the body. Furthermore, as a result of this ten-million year immersion, it is possible to understand the layer of subcutaneous fat which is a feature of man's ability to retain body heat, but which is found in none of the primates from which he evolved.

The recorded descriptions quoted above all seem to suggest just such a creature as the aquatic phase in man's evolution would have given rise to in historical times. The unfortunate fact remains, however, that no direct evidence has been found to substantiate this theory from the Pliocene Age, possibly due to the fact that the remains of such creatures would have been washed away and devoured at sea; which would also have been true of any more recent inter-tidal marine hominid remains.

The discovery and rescue of a full grown male of this species in the waters off Cape Cod in the northern United States offers proof not only of the aquatic theory in man's evolution, but also that *Homo Aquatilis* is not yet extinct.

This specimen, as previous accounts have suggested, was human in form and appearance, although almost entirely covered in thick body hair, brown in colour but with lighter tints. Only the face and the inner surface of arms and legs were entirely free of hair.

Although of less than medium height, 5ft 2ins, he was thickset, weighing 133 lbs, with well-formed muscles of hip and thigh. The whole body showed evidence of a covering of subcutaneous fat, which may be active in the same way as blubber in the whale and walrus.

Facial characteristics were entirely human, though the features were flattened after the manner of mongoloid peoples. The nose however was firm and of a muscular tissue which could be opened or closed at will. The hands were broad, with short fingers; the feet wide with bones spread but with a webbing of skin between each toe. While the legs were long in proportion to the body they were rotated slightly outward and the feet were splayed apart. This made movement on land appear awkward but was a great asset when swimming: the motion being similar to that of butterfly stroke. Since in the water this meant both legs were kept close together it is easy to see why earlier observers often believed that they had seen a creature with a tail, similar to that of a fish or seal.

Like other aquatic mammals the subject must have been capable of diving to considerable depths since the rib cage, though strong, had an elasticity which would be capable of protecting the lungs under heavy pressure. He was also able to adjust his metabolism in order to survive submerged for long periods of time: the physiological mechanism of bradycardia, the slowing of the heartbeat, was noted when diving, and to a much more marked extent than is evident in land-dwelling man.

As this species spends long periods of time immersed in the sea there is little need for perspiration as a method of cooling, so fluid intake need be only a fraction of that of land mammals. When on land, however, the subject found hot weather particularly uncomfortable and needed frequent dousing with water in order to maintain body temperature adequately. Fluid requirements were for the most part met by moisture in food, although it is interesting to note that, like the merman of Orford, he was careful to wipe away any trace of salt water from fish. There would appear to be adaptations to the function of the kidney which reduce the filtration rate to very low levels when necessary.

Diet was entirely carnivorous, marine life only being preferred. While in captivity the subject was never known to accept red meat in any form, nor any vegetable foods. He was uninterested in cooked foods, though obviously able to distinguish what they were. Teeth were small and flat, best used in chewing and grinding, with no pointed canines for tearing food, so that it was reasonable to assume that this species subsists entirely on small animal prey. The sense of smell was well developed, though not as acute as that of a dog; vision was adequate, though less that accurate at distance (Sph -075, Cyl -025, Axis 90, both R & L). Such hearing tests as were carried out by a method of limits showed an extremely sensitive auditory system, which may in fact exceed that of *Homo Sapiens.*

With only a single subject for study it was not possible to make any observation of social habits, though the general impression was of a gentle and entirely non-aggressive individual. This was also borne out by the lack of any of the attributes of the hunter, such as canine teeth, acute sense of smell, longsightedness etc. The species is evidently not nocturnal; like the Orford merman the subject slept by night and was only active by day.

Possibly as a result of captivity this specimen was very subdued in his behaviour patterns, though obviously stimulated by a return to the sea. He wept easily, uttering sad sounds which may have followed definite patterns. This aspect of the research is still under way.

Although eager to learn, nevertheless the specimen under observation seemed unfamiliar with any kind of artifact, though he readily understood the use of a pan or bowl for carrying or storing. If, as is postulated, this was a direct descendant of the marine phase in man's evolution, his development has been non-aggressive, and he has adapted most successfully to his environment, in the manner of the Eskimo, the Australian Aborigine or the Bushman. Such a species has little need of technical progress since he has accepted the limitations of his natural habitat and has grown within those limitations to the fullest extent of his powers.

If it were possible to observe such a species in large numbers it might then be conceivable for land-dwelling man also to learn this all-important technique; for in the twentieth century it is becoming increasingly evident that the progress path we have chosen is more destructive of our environment than we were able to foresee.